CAPTAINS STUPENDOUS
OR:
THE FANTASTICAL
FAMILY FARAWAY

Rhys Hughes

Published in the United Kingdom by Telos Moonrise:
Steampunk Visions
(An imprint of Telos Publishing Ltd)
5A Church Road, Shortlands, Bromley BR2 0HP, UK

Cover Design: David J Howe
Cover Art: Martin Baines

First Edition

ISBN: 978-1-84583-886-7

British Library Cataloguing in Publication Data. A catalogue
record for this book is available from the British Library.

Dedicated to:
Safaa Dib

Praise for Rhys Hughes

'Rhys Hughes seems almost the sum of our planet's literature ... As well as being drunk on language and wild imagery, he is also sober on the essentials of thought. He has something of Mervyn Peake's glorious invention, something of John Cowper Powys's contemplative, almost disdainful existentialism, a sensuality, a relish, an addiction to the delicious. He's as tricky as his own characters ... He toys with convention. He makes the metaphysical political, the personal incredible and the comic hints at subtle pain. Few living fictioneers approach this chef's sardonic confections, certainly not in English.' *Michael Moorcock*

'Quirky and fantastic and sometimes quite twisted, Rhys Hughes is a treat for those in the mood for something utterly different.' *Ellen Datlow*

'Rhys Hughes is an accomplished player with words, plots, effects, relationships, sensibilities; you name it, Hughes tries to stand it on its head. More often than seems attributable to mere chance, he succeeds.' *Ed Bryant, Locus*

'I wore throughout the undisplaceable, unsequelchable rictus of a grin of both delight and amazement.' *Michael Bishop*

'Hughes' world is a magical one, and his language is the most magical thing of all.' *T E D Klein*

'There are no easy phrases to describe Hughes' fiction; it's so exotic. His writing is incredibly precise and at the same time his imagination is so unfettered.' *Jeffrey Ford*

'Hughes' similarity to Spike Milligan runs deeper than the occasional shared lurch of phrase, for he writes as though he'd been bloodied in the same wars Milligan fought for eight decades: the same up-yours melancholia about the malice of the absurd – about the absurdness of the world defined not only as an inherent lack of species-friendly grammar in the convulsion of the real, but also a sense that anyone who acts as though he believes what he is told by our Masters will almost necessarily inflict pain on others.' *John Clute*

'It's a crime that Rhys Hughes is not as widely known as Italo Calvino and other writers of that stature. Brilliantly written and conceived, Hughes' fiction has few parallels anywhere in the world. In some alternate universe with a better sense of justice, his work triumphantly parades across all bestseller lists. ' *Jeff Vandermeer*

'A dazzling disintegration of the reality principle. A rite of passage to the greater world beyond common sense. Raises the bar on profundity and sets a comic standard for the tragic limits of our human experience. Like Beckett on nitrous oxide. Like Kafka with a brighter sense of humor.'
A A Attanasio

'Dazzling prose. Put your feet up and dip in. Life will never seem quite the same again.' *The Third Alternative*

'The incredible richness of language, the inexhaustible array of puns, double entendres, weird metaphors, non-lexical use of words, and original turns of phrase ... Rhys Hughes is essentially an absurdist humorist, though often of a peculiarly black, tricky and sometimes bloody sort. Much of his work is travesty, drawing for substance on other works, which he uses as a basis for destructive humour, for reinterpretation in a different mode, or as a starting point for his own work. This statement is not meant in disparagement, for Hughes's new versions are highly original in conception and often brilliant.'
Supernatural Fiction Writers (Scribners)

'Rhys Hughes is one of the most wildly inventive talents we are graced with today.' *All Hallows*

'What do I like about Rhys Hughes's work? Fun. Hughes sees and precipitates in words the latent humour in almost anything. Ranging from what our culture considers pleasing and smilingly ridiculous to horrors that have to be laughed at if they are faceable at all, Hughes is a laughing observer, both inside and outside. With Hughes you get humour that is white, various shades of grey, black – and I don't know why humour cannot be characterised by other colours. I am also enormously impressed by Hughes's stylistic brilliance. The richness of language, the occasional Cambrianisms, the inexhaustible array of puns, weird metaphors that form the point of a story. And I envy him his netted imagination. As a man who sees connections where others do not, he offers enough ideas, if parcelled out, to fill a catalogue of fantasy for a generation of writers.' *E F Bleiler*

'Every Hughes story implies much, served with wit and whimsy and word-relish, high spirits and bittersweet twists.' *Ian Watson*

'So you want to know about the Faraway Brothers, do you? Born somewhere in Gascony, they were, in the 1880s, all three of them birthed at the same time from the same womb of the same mother. Grew up in the same household, they did too, eating the same food, reading the same books, counting the legs on the same spider because the family couldn't afford a real clock; but later on they went their separate ways. Scipio took to the sea, to ships, islands and women; Distanto took to the air, to balloons, islands and women; Neary, unluckiest of the triplets, remained on land, taking only to locomotives and stations and chastity. Many adventures they all had and often their paths crossed and sometimes they clashed, and I happen to know a song about it that goes something like this... Hey, where are you going? Come back!'

The Ballad of the Fantastical Faraways

Contents

PART ONE: SCIPIO

THE COANDĂ EFFECT

The Iceberg

Atlantic Ocean, 15 April 1912.

The iceberg that struck and sank *RMS Titanic* the previous night now proceeded on its way south, borne by strange currents; and a Czech sailor by the name of Stepan Rehorek managed to take a photograph of it as his own ship passed, but he wasn't fully aware of its historical significance. The floating mountain of murderous ice was already melting rapidly and soon would be gone completely.

Or so he assumed; but he was wrong …

A melting iceberg will fizz as trapped air bubbles thousands of years old are steadily released into the atmosphere of the modern world; and because the mass shrinks far more quickly at the base than the summit, it becomes unbalanced and abruptly rolls over to achieve a new stability. This periodic turning is a dramatic and sometimes catastrophic spectacle to behold, according to witnesses.

Rehorek's photograph shows the *Titanic* iceberg to be of the 'drydock' type. There are three main categories of drifting iceberg: tabular, pinnacle and the irregular drydock. Ultimately all have their protuberances, peaks and edges dissolved away and become relatively smooth spheres of ice in the final stages of their dissolution. Finally the last ice crystal deliquesces and vanishes and becomes part of the ocean once more, endlessly diluting itself in the unfathomable depths.

On this occasion, that didn't quite happen.

There was another ship in the vicinity; posterity never

mentions it, for it was on a secret mission, and the captain responsible for controlling the shady sailors that crewed it was a tight-lipped character who never spoke of his work to anyone and even kept his men in ignorance of destinations, commissions and legality. Marlow Nullity was his name: pirate, smuggler and blockade-runner. A scoundrel.

He had accepted an assignment from a certain Mr Hugo Bloat, richest dweller of the town of Porthcawl, in the country of Wales, and a collector of morbid curios. Bloat lived in a house full of objects that normal people would deem unwholesome or malign: skeletons of criminals, tombstones, voodoo masks, a library of occult books bound in lizard skin, charms and fetishes from numerous exotic cultures, a golden knife said to be from the lost city of Ubar in the Rub' al Khālī.

Bloat was cruel but not dull and he kept himself alert to potentialities in his particular sphere of interest. He read a dozen or more newspapers every day and possessed a private radio transceiver more powerful than anything owned by many European governments at that time. Prolonged study of weather reports for the Atlantic had convinced him that a disaster involving an iceberg was very likely, and he decided that an opportunity for an extremely unusual addition to his collection of bizarre artefacts had presented itself. He chuckled horribly.

He sent a message to Captain Marlow Nullity and ordered him to sail his ship into the designated danger zone and wait for further instructions. Thus when Hugo Bloat picked up the distress call of RMS Titanic on his radio, he was able to relay the message to Captain Nullity and guide him to the scene of the grim accident more rapidly than any rescue vessel; but picking up survivors formed no part of Mr Bloat's plan. His interest in the sunken liner's passengers was minimal.

It was the iceberg that compelled his attention.

Captain Nullity intercepted the mountain of ice shortly before Rehorek passed it, but his nameless ship was on the far side of the frozen mass and doesn't appear in the photograph.

Neither crew was aware of each other, a stroke of luck for Nullity and his decadent employer. Bloat wanted him to keep the iceberg always in sight, to follow it until it shrank to manageable size, however long that might take. And so Captain Nullity trailed it south for weeks, watching it roll and dissolve.

At last it reached the specified dimensions. He steered alongside it and ordered a sailor on deck to fish the thing out with a net attached to a long pole. The infamous iceberg that had claimed so many lives by sending an unsinkable liner to the seabed was now no larger than the fist of a child. It took the sailor several attempts to catch it. He drew it up and passed it to Captain Nullity, who carried it to his cabin, nodding stoically as it rapidly numbed all feeling out of his fingers.

In one corner of his cabin was a metal box, some sort of refrigeration device, festooned with pipes that gurgled; and into this apparatus Captain Nullity lowered the chunk of ice. Then he sealed it tight and adjusted the thermostat downwards, grinning to himself. Mission accomplished! Time to sail for Porthcawl and claim his reward from Hugo Bloat. Within a few weeks he would be fairly rich again.

His nameless rusty ship with its peculiar cargo steamed northeast and took care to avoid the conventional shipping routes. Once past Cornwall it would be a simple matter to enter the Bristol Channel and arrive at the harbour of Porthcawl in the dead of night. Mr Bloat had bribed the local coastguard; no problems from the authorities were anticipated. This was the easiest part of the entire adventure.

But events didn't go quite to plan. There was a storm and freak waves smashed a hole in Captain Nullity's hull. He gave orders to abandon ship and he took to the lifeboats with his crew. That was at 45°N, 15°W. The refrigerator containing the shrunken iceberg floated free of the wreck and was carried by currents parallel to the coastline of Portugal, all the way to the mouth of the Mediterranean Sea.

The refrigerator contained its own power source,

powerful batteries in waterproof casings. Sealed in its special tomb, the ice didn't melt. Slowly the box drifted through the Pillars of Hercules. Unseen, it continued on its way eastwards, past Italy and Greece.

It took months for the box to float the length of the Mediterranean. By chance it passed through the Dardanelles and the Bosporus into the Black Sea. After drifting randomly for another month it was eventually washed up on the beach of Costineşti, a fishing village close to Romania's border with Bulgaria. The peasant who found it was collecting seaweed; with the aid of a rope he dragged it to his hut.

An engineer by the name of Dumitru Banuş was staying in Costineşti at the time, recovering from injuries he had sustained in an accident in his workplace. The peasant attempted to sell the mysterious piece of flotsam to Banuş; and after a quick scrutiny of the object in the gloom of the hut, a price was agreed. Banuş's curiosity had been whetted by the dullness of life in the village and thus he welcomed any distraction. Opening the box, he was bewildered by what lay within.

But he shut the door of the refrigerator and decided that his colleagues at the university should be given an opportunity to examine it. There was no telephone line between Costineşti and Bucharest; he had to hire a boat to take him to the spa at Eforie Nord, a dozen kilometres up the coast. He called Professor Bogdan Velicu from the hospital there. Velicu listened to his friend in respectful silence, then promised to set off personally for the fishing village the following morning.

Banuş returned in the boat to Costineşti; and when Velicu arrived in a motorcar the next day, he opened the box to show the scientist the frosted sphere inside. Velicu inserted a hand into the vaporous space, touched the surface of the gleaming sphere and licked his finger. Then he gasped and for a few moments shivered uncontrollably. With Banuş's help he carried the refrigerator to his motorcar. They lowered it gently onto the back seat. With a sombre expression, Velicu said:

'I think it's better if proper tests are conducted at the university. I don't know why, but I feel there's something peculiar about this block of ice. It might be argued that scientists shouldn't act on a hunch, but it would be a shame if we missed a spectacular discovery because of restraint! I'll write and keep you aware of developments.'

Banuş nodded and waved farewell to Velicu. The professor began the drive back to Bucharest with his prize. A few days later the sphere of ice was housed in his low-temperature laboratory while a methodical battery of tests was applied to its shining form. Velicu subjected it to many kinds of radiation; to amplified sound and radio waves; electromagnetic fields; he refracted and reflected light with it; inspected it through microscopes; weighed, prodded and photographed it.

At last he believed he had some sort of answer.

By this time, Captain Nullity had been given enough money by Hugo Bloat to buy a new ship, and he was busy with the futile task of searching the high seas for the lost refrigeration machine. He never expected to find it, and he never did, but he enjoyed the work nonetheless. The sea was his soul, the sting of salt spray on his skin made him feel more alive than any breeze on land, however sweet or soft.

Captain Nullity makes no further appearance in my tale, but a different sailor of similar type does. I learned later that the oceans are the stage for unexpected deeds of all kinds, good and bad; and that such men as Nullity play a crucial part in the fate of the waves, symbolically speaking, though they are a dying breed. The name of that other sailor is Scipio Faraway and it may even be a familiar one to you.

The Airshow

I had the privilege of meeting Scipio Faraway some years earlier, at the Brescia airshow in 1909. I was attending in my professional capacity as a journalist and I was somewhat disappointed by the event; the endless wait while mechanics repaired the primitive flying machines was tedious. I was an ambitious soul back then. Years later I learned that a clerk by the name of Franz Kafka was also present; he would turn himself into one of the finest and most disturbing writers of the century. I believe he wrote a short text about the airshow itself.

It was when Bleriot was throwing an understandable tantrum over yet another delay to the fixing of his engine that I turned to leave and walked into a man standing directly behind. The blow stunned me and I couldn't repress a curse.

'*Cachu planciau!*'

Almost immediately, the stranger recited a short verse I hadn't heard since my childhood. I was amazed.

'You understand Welsh!' I cried in disbelief.

'Yes: the language of Merlin.'

I was amused by the eccentricity of this comment and offered him my apologies for the impact, though it had damaged my senses more than his, and in fact he seemed completely untroubled. I explained that I was in a permanent rush due to the incessant demands of my editor and that work pressure had made me clumsy; it was a feeble excuse for barging straight into a person and I blushed when I had finished giving it. But he betrayed no flicker of impatience or scorn.

In fact he shook my hand. 'Lloyd Griffiths,' I said.

He smiled and winked at me.

'Rarely are journalists to be trusted, but I do like the look of you. You work for a London newspaper?'

I laughed. 'Nothing so fancy. *The Western Mail*. It's Welsh and based in Cardiff; my destiny and desire is to write for people who have little or no respect for the King of England.'

He bowed slightly and grinned broadly.

'My father was originally from Wales,' he said, 'and went across the sea to Gascony to work and marry. He was responsible enough, but in his heart he was a wanderer, and that's where I get my own wanderlust. I'm here in Brescia only briefly.'

'What do you think of the airshow?' I asked.

Scipio Faraway adjusted his cap thoughtfully and gazed across the field at the spectators and the flying contraptions near the sheds. I followed his eyes and saw the American pilot Glenn Curtiss, feet propped on an empty gasoline tin, reading a newspaper, while his mechanics fuelled his craft, a display of incredible nonchalance.

'I like it. There's much potential here. But the man I came to see didn't turn up, as it happens. It's a pity.'

'You have a favourite aviator?' I pressed.

He answered quietly, 'Yes, there's one inventor I'm keen to observe, a maverick. It seems he's developing an entirely new method of propulsion and was supposed to make his debut today, but clearly his system isn't yet ready; maybe at the next airshow?'

'You came to Brescia especially for that?'

He shook his head. 'I was passing through Italy anyway. I'll stay until the judges choose between Curtiss, Bleriot or Rougier for the awarding of the Grand Prix. Then I'll move on.'

'And where will your next destination be?'

A distant look came over him and he shrugged slightly. 'I don't know. France, Tunisia, the Antilles, China, India … I'll go wherever the currents of life take me; those can't be resisted.'

I wondered how many other currents he *had* successfully resisted, how many storms and whirlpools and waterspouts he had beaten and escaped, how many undersea volcanoes, tidal waves, thunderbolts he had cheated. Suddenly I was seized by a powerful envy; this enigmatic sailor, with his black pea coat, unshaven chin and hypnotic eyes, had made me oddly and profoundly dissatisfied with my own present condition. I told myself that a romantic lifestyle of endless wandering wasn't, in reality, so fine a thing, but nonetheless I was deeply affected.

'Maybe I ought to interview you one day?' I suggested. 'I'm sure you have many incredible stories to tell?'

He bowed politely and smiled, but without a great deal of enthusiasm, and I understood that unlike so many similar characters I had met during my career, he wasn't obsessed with fame. Whatever it was that burned so fiercely inside him, that kept him moving from place to place, it wasn't a desire to be recognised or acclaimed.

'If our paths ever cross again,' he conceded.

'That's at the discretion of fate,' I said with a cough of embarrassment and a small blush, for I generally prefer to avoid invoking supernatural or poetic forces; but he smiled again, more broadly this time, idly scratched the palm of one hand with the fingers of the other and looked up at a blue sky unsullied by buzzing aircraft.

'Fate or the man who makes his own.'

I considered these words and found them unanswerable. 'Good luck to you, sir,' was my response, 'but if you'll excuse me, I must telephone my editor to file my latest report, though in truth nothing much has happened in the past few hours. I managed to get a glimpse of Puccini, but I fear my readers won't care much about that.'

'The Welsh are a musical nation, though,' he said.

'Indeed. Goodbye, *Monsieur!*'

'Farewell, Mr Griffiths. It was a pleasure.'

I shook his hand and was again impressed with the strength of his grip, but when he lowered it I noticed a deep scar on his palm. He had inflicted this on himself while still a boy, with a pair of scissors, after being told by a fortune-teller that he had no fate line; I learned all this much later. That's the sort of person he was. Even then he had judged it appropriate to gouge his own destiny into his own flesh.

The Bicycle

The years passed and I thrived as a reasonably successful journalist. After the Brescia Airshow most of my assignments were on my home soil, but I sometimes visited other countries to report on various events or disasters my editor believed might interest our readership. Few of those occasions had glamour or excitement, but the circulation of *The Western Mail* kept increasing, so clearly my editor was no fool. In 1910 I voyaged to Greece and Denmark; in 1911 I was nearly sent to Albania to cover the rebellion against the Ottomans but fell sick before departure. I had picked up a rare fungal infection. The journalist who went in my place ended up with his head hung on the wall of a minor warlord.

War correspondence wasn't my usual duty; I interviewed eccentric or visionary personalities in an ongoing series of character studies. The fact is that my newspaper was becoming more sensational in tone; there was some foolish notion by the owners of imitating the *New York Herald* and creating news for its own sake, however irresponsible the result: most of the lunatics I interviewed were harmless enough and those who weren't generally lacked the means to cause harm in the world. Curiously one of them turned out to be a man who believed he had developed a propulsion system that could vastly improve the performance of aeroplanes. In truth he was a fraud, but a rather amusing one.

His propulsion system involved a pilot dropping grenades into a chute that would roll them into a combustion chamber at the rear of his aircraft. The detonations would push the vehicle forward with jerks of increasing force. The inventor's name was Rolfe and I believed he was related to an author of the same name. After listening to his explanations for hours and finally asking to inspect the models he claimed he had successfully flown, he finally admitted his work was theory alone. I turned to leave in disgust but he tried to recapture my attention with an improvised demonstration. I was astonished when he began rummaging in a crate for a grenade. Then he urged me to step out into his garden.

He had a bicycle there and he rigged up a combustion chamber from a length of drainpipe that he shortened with a hacksaw and tied to the frame with cable. Before I was able to protest at his lunacy, he had mounted the bicycle and inserted the grenade in the pipe. The blast erupted with equal pressure from both ends and he moved neither forward nor backward, but the rusty bicycle shivered to bits. He collapsed in the middle of a pile of metal debris, cogs rolling around him, while I shook with silent laughter. Yet he wasn't dismayed by this failure. He insisted the principle was good and that the application alone was at fault.

'After all,' he pointed out, 'the pulse system worked well for Wiberg.'

I frowned. Since my chance meeting with Scipio Faraway I'd forgotten that he had gone to Brescia for the sake of meeting a maverick inventor. I wondered if this 'Wiberg' was the same one. It wasn't, for he was already dead, of course, and in fact had expired in 1905; but that was something I only learned much later. Even journalists can be guilty of failing to put all the right questions at the right time.

'Who is Wiberg?' I asked Rolfe, as he stood and brushed himself with his fingers, his trousers glittering with splinters of iron from the shattered bicycle. He licked his lips and said:

'Martin Wiberg. Swedish inventor. The few people who have heard of him conclude that his greatest contribution to civilisation is a device that can print logarithmic tables; but in my opinion he should be better known for the pulsejet engine. It's a vessel with a valved intake and open outlet; air flows through the intake and is mixed with fuel, then the valve is shut and the mixture ignited. The explosion pushes the gas through the exhaust pipe, moving the engine forward.'

'Then the valve opens again to allow more air in?'

'Exactly! The thrust is pulsed.'

'I imagine the system makes a great deal of noise?'

'Unfortunately that is so.'

'And he fitted one to an aeroplane, did he?'

Rolfe shook his head emphatically. 'Such an engine would be far too bulky and heavy for any existing airframe to support. An aircraft powered by a pulsejet would never leave the ground. That's the entire point of my own simplified system, which in essence is a recoilless gun that utilises a regular input of self-contained energy packets, thus avoiding the need for an automatic fuel injection mechanism. Odd how making a system *easier* can prove to be such a headache!'

I grinned with sympathy at the irony of that.

'Will you ever find an aviator brave enough to risk flying an aeroplane with a pocket of grenades?' I wondered, but I already knew there would be no shortage of volunteers. We live in an age of wonders and dangers, a time of new myths and challenges.

He didn't need to answer. And although I had decided to write a comic piece about Mr Jason Rolfe and his bicycle experiment, I had no intention of mocking him; the humour would be compassionate, for though I didn't share his specific vision I admired his spirit. His dream never bore fruit in subsequent years, but at the very least he had fuelled my own dreams and nightmares with engines that pushed gleaming aircraft through clear skies at rates of speed almost unimaginable!

A week or so later, an iceberg struck the White Star liner *RMS Titanic* with the loss of 1513 lives. I was as appalled as everyone else, but I never guessed my destiny was intimately linked to it, nor that the paths of Scipio Faraway and I would cross again in the wake of a maritime disaster more incredible in form if not in scale.

The Sailor On Land

As for Scipio, he had left Brescia on foot, walking over the Alps with that long, easy stride of his, his head held high and his eyes fixed on whatever star burned most brightly above the jagged peaks. Where there was no path, he made his own, resting from storms in the abandoned huts of shepherds, dreaming of past exploits and adventures to come while the wind swirled the snowflakes outside. On full moon nights he climbed in the silvery glimmer until dawn and greeted the sunrise by doffing his cap and bowing with old-fashioned grace.

How many lonely suns had risen and set in those enigmatic eyes? For a man who never stopped wandering, collecting new horizons with every day that passed, the crisp heights of the mountains were no less familiar than the broad blue deeps; and the mists that shrouded the summits, quite as breathable as the vapours of the steaming jungles, held no terrors. The oceans of snow and ice might be sailed and explored to their limits. From the crests of the huddle of brooding stone giants he gazed down at France, where the scent of blooms awaited him.

Within a month he could have been in Paris, but he lingered awhile in the forests of the Bourgogne, at the insistence of a girl he met there. Scipio never gave away his heart on a whim, nor did he ever exploit the feelings of others, but he *was* a man who loved women, and they loved him. Even an individual who carves his own fate must acknowledge a higher power at irregular times of life. At last he left for the capital and briefly took up residence there, among the bohemians. Down grey rivers that were streets he strolled, his coat billowing like a sail.

It is difficult for me not to daydream of this abstruse figure ascending the fabled steps of Montmartre, sipping absinthe in a tiny café or tapping a foot to the wild melodies of itinerant musicians. But did he ever think of the humble journalist he met once in a field in Italy? I doubt it.

In Paris he found what he sought; then he left for more exotic climes, for the tangled forests of West Africa, and because he was a man who hated injustice he ended up in a rebel village in Sierra Leone, the home of fugitive workers who had been treated worse than slaves.

He helped to ambush the trackers that had been hired to slaughter the fugitives, and the grateful villagers gave him a diamond for his trouble, but such objects meant little to him. Then he walked due north out of the forest, and between the brooding ruins of the ancient Songhai kingdoms, and over the dunes, and across the pastures of the Tuareg nomads where wine is drunk only in secret and belief in genies is considered good sense; and in the shade of an oasis he failed yet again to read his favourite book, Voltaire's *Candide*, right to the end.

The Collector

My editor said to me one morning, 'Today I want you to pay a visit to a certain Hugo Bloat of Porthcawl. He's one of the richest men in Wales, a rather mysterious individual who —'

I lifted a hand to cut short the description. Ben Gordon, my editor, had a tendency to speak for hours without pause. 'I know who he is and what he does, at least some of it; but he's notoriously protective of his privacy and doesn't deal with journalists.'

'That's why it's your lucky day, Lloyd. He has agreed to give his first ever interview to us, to *The Western Mail*. It seems he wants a chance to protest against, and possibly refute, certain slanders that are in circulation about his tastes and inclinations. Some ignorant peasants insist he dabbles in black magic; others in smuggling.'

'And what's your opinion of him?' I asked.

Gordon smirked. 'I suspect he does both. Yes, Hugo Bloat, wickedest man in the country, an obscene experimenter with dark voodoo magic and a consumer of contraband goods. He sent me a cask of strong Haitian rum to win my affection, and it worked.'

'You want him to appear in a positive light?'

'Come now, Lloyd, I won't go that far. You are free to pursue the truth to the best of your ability. All I'm saying is that you must embark on your interview without any preconceived ideas about this reclusive man. So it will serve everyone best, including the reading public, if you adopt an air of extreme neutrality in his presence.'

'That's one of the most cynical things I've heard.'

He grinned. 'Hasn't your fungal infection cleared up yet? There's still a rather strange odour about you.'

'My condition is incurable; but it doesn't hinder my work.'

'Wonderful. Off you go, then!'

I smarted. Lloyd Griffiths, journalist without integrity … That was the person I saw when I stared into the mirror. But I did my duty and felt the thrill of anticipation as I did so, for any opportunity to get closer to Hugo Bloat had to be exploited to full advantage.

My editor had provided me with a motorcar and I drove through the mist to the isolated mansion of Mr Bloat, overlooking the sand dunes to the east of Porthcawl, a journey that took several hours down the unsurfaced roads. I assumed the owner was expecting me, but I rang his front doorbell without result. Didn't he keep any servants on the premises?

At last I was forced to skirt the house and seek an alternative entry. I was surprised by the odour of decay that seeped from the building. Some of the cracks and fissures in the outer walls were wide enough for me to peer inside rooms; they were invariably stuffed with mouldy furniture or decaying books. At last I found an open door at the rear and stepped into a narrow hallway floored with boards that creaked horribly. A thin voice from somewhere above floated down:

'Is that you, Tom? Come upstairs at once!'

I frowned and called back, 'No, this is Mr Griffiths from *The Western Mail*. I'm here to interview Mr Bloat.'

'Ah yes! How unfortunate! I had forgotten!'

I proceeded further down the hallway and emerged at the bottom of a rickety staircase. At the top stood a gnarled man with eyes that twinkled noticeably even at that distance, like new stars in a dying constellation. I blinked up at him and he waved a bony hand in a gesture clearly intended to put me at ease. But it didn't work.

'Is Mr Hugo Bloat at home?' I asked pointlessly.

He stiffened slightly. 'I am he, of course. I never dwell on the ground floor now, because of the damp. It's bad for my health. The fight between that which exists and that which exists not is eternal: in my case, decay of my surroundings sharpens my mind.'

'And yet you forgot about my arrival,' I said.

He smiled thinly, perhaps with resentment, as I mounted the staircase. When I reached the top step, he moved back a few paces. Then he turned and guided me into a sumptuous chamber that was the very antithesis of the abandoned rooms downstairs. I noticed the masks on the walls, all the crystal ornaments, the shrunken skulls.

'It's like a bizarre museum or exotic bazaar!'

He nodded and indicated a chair. I sat down. He offered me a glass of cognac and I didn't refuse. Then he said, 'I spoke to your editor and asked him to arrange an interview, but I didn't anticipate it to be so soon. I have made prior arrangements for today.'

'So you are expecting another visitor?'

He nodded, unable to see that I had already started the interview. It's a trick journalists use when their subjects try to wriggle out of our snares. I had no intention of leaving without a good story. In one corner a peculiar clock ticked ominously; it was carved in the image of the Grim Reaper, a cunningly-wrought mechanism with a moving scythe blade that indicated the hour. Hugo Bloat glanced at it unhappily as he sipped his own brandy and then rubbed his forehead with his free hand, for the first time raising his arm high enough for me to note a cobweb in his armpit. This was very strange indeed. He answered slowly:

'Yes. It's a business matter. I have work for him.'

'What are you hiring him for?'

'Well... He's a sea captain with his own vessel. He has a schooner and it is docked in Bristol. Some of my property ...

Something I want ... In the sea, in the middle of the Atlantic ...'

'You want him to recover it for you?'

Hugo Bloat suddenly narrowed his eyes and clenched his fists. 'This is a private matter! Why should I tell you anything about it at all? How dare you enter my residence and then—'

I decided to alter my approach. 'Why don't you have any servants, Mr Bloat? The expense is certainly no problem for you. Are you forced to do domestic chores without assistance?'

'That's none of your ... Get out! Get out now!'

The interview was at an end. I sighed and stood up and left the room. I don't think he followed me onto the landing; I didn't bother looking back to check. But as I descended the staircase I passed a man coming up. His face was sunburned and scarred; the knuckles of his hands were callused and his beard bristled. He was a fighter, but he nodded amicably enough and smiled at me. Then he reached the top step and entered the chamber I had just vacated, for I heard Bloat say:

'Tom! At last! Come inside and sit down quickly!'

I shrugged. It was none of my concern who the eccentric collector and madman invited to his house or what errands he sent sea captains on. Yet I was intrigued against my will. I left the house and reached my motorcar but I didn't enter and drive away. It occurred to me that I might intercept the newcomer after his business with Hugo Bloat was concluded and find him to be more willing to talk than his employer. I hadn't yet given up on securing a story for my editor, though it probably wouldn't be the sort he was hoping for. On the contrary, I had a hunch that Bloat's reputation was likely to sink *lower* as a consequence.

For half an hour I sat in my vehicle. Then I heard the creak of boards and saw the grizzled fellow emerge.

'Tom!' I called out, and he squinted at me.

'Do I know you?' he rasped.

I recognised his accent. He was a Belgian. He undid the

buttons of his coat and let it fall open; I saw a holstered pistol beneath. He continued to squint as he walked toward me, gravel crunching beneath his boots. I saw no trace of friendliness in his expression. Was this already the end of my career as a journalist? I trembled.

The Modern Pirate

I swallowed my fear and grinned. 'Mr Bloat asked me to give you a lift in my car. He's an old friend of mine.'

Tom fingered the flap of his holster. 'That withered monkey has never had a single friend in his entire life!'

'I meant the word ironically, of course.'

The fellow seemed to accept this and his manner softened, though his squint remained. At my further invitation he entered the passenger side of my vehicle and settled himself on the fake leather. I took up my position in the driving seat and started the engine by pressing a button; these latest models don't need to be cranked by hand. Then I released the handbrake, pressed the accelerator pedal and steered down the rutted road between a towering dune on one side and an impenetrable forest on the other. Tom said nothing as I drove; he was the quiet type and it was up to me to ease him out of his shell with small talk.

'Twenty knots in second gear. Not bad, eh?'

'Aye, she's a sporty crate.'

'How did you get here?' I asked him.

'I walked from the train station at Bridgend,' he said.

'That's seven miles. I'll drive you back now, but what time does your train depart? You mustn't be late!'

He shook his head and suddenly became more voluble, clearly having decided he could trust me fully. 'No rush. Any express from Bridgend to Bristol will do. My ship is waiting for me in the docks there.' He jerked a thumb back over his shoulder, in the direction of Bloat's mansion. 'That wealthy old scarecrow has engaged my services for a most unusual job. I think he's wasting his money, though.'

'Is it a smuggling caper?' I ventured timidly.

He smiled. 'I wish it was! Now *that* is something I could get my teeth into! No, he wants me to sail in circles looking for a piece of flotsam that he insists is still drifting on the currents. Some sort of refrigeration device apparently! Have you ever heard anything so absurd? He had one captain looking for it recently, a certain Marlow Nullity, but the fellow turned up nothing, so Mr Bloat dismissed him.'

'You are a more reliable mariner, no doubt?'

'Not so. I know Captain Nullity and he's no amateur. If he didn't find the object, I doubt I will. But I can't turn the job down. It would be stupid not to take Mr Bloat's money. Plus this mission gives me a chance to do a bit of my own business on the side.'

'And what kind of business would that be?'

Without hesitation, he laughed and cried, 'Piracy! Yes, I'm a corsair, a freebooter, a sea rover! I suppose you thought the age of pirates was long gone? A common misconception!'

He went on to give me an outline of his life. While still a young man, fresh from college, he had travelled to Africa, where administrators were in short supply. The personal fiefdom of Leopold II, the Congo Free State turned out to be a hellhole that corrupted everyone who entered it. Tom was no exception. He became a cruel overseer on a rubber plantation and the experience toughened him up considerably but conditions eventually became too dreadful even for him. After three years of lashing famished slaves to death with hippopotamus-hide whips, violating native women and watching his colleagues die of horrid tropical diseases, just to enrich King Leo, he stole a ship and fled.

'And you've been a pirate ever since?'

He nodded. 'A proud one. Captain Tom 'Red' Alaerts, the terror of the high seas. I have competition out there, of course, but … Well, I'm good at what I do. You would see that if – '

He fell silent and muttered into his beard.

'If what, Mr Alaerts?' I pressed.

'I'm short of a crewman. I don't suppose you care to sign up? It's hard but rewarding work. On the sails.'

I was about to protest that I had no maritime experience, but suddenly I was overwhelmed with the excitement of the prospect of going to sea as the deckhand on a pirate ship. It occurred to me that my remark about the speed of the motorcar had fooled him into thinking I was a seadog. For a joke I had said 'knots' instead of 'miles per hour'. It was my duty to press home this advantage. 'Why not?'

He offered his hand and I shook it awkwardly.

I was about to ask him if he knew a man named Scipio Faraway, but he spoke over me, 'Why not drive all the way to Bristol? Better than taking the train! Do you have enough fuel?'

I checked the gauge and nodded. 'Yes.'

My editor would be furious with me. I could imagine the crimson face of Ben Gordon swelling when he learned of what I intended to do. In fact it was such an unappealing vision to hold in my mind's eye that I quickly dissolved it and decided not to tell him until I came back. The moment he heard my story he would forgive my rashness and impudence. It was still a gamble, of course, but worthwhile.

We reached Bristol four hours later. On the way to the docks we drove through an industrial zone, skirting the hangars of the Bristol Aeroplane Company. One of the hangars was open and a team of technicians was assembling a large monoplane with very slim wings inside. A dignified man stood and watched them and called out instructions. He glanced up at me as my car clattered past and our eyes locked for a moment. If only I had realised at the time who he was!

The Oasis

Scipio Faraway looked up as the rider dismounted. Then he stood and with a smile raised his hand to his heart. 'Salaam!' The rider made an identical gesture and uttered the same greeting, his large eyes twinkling; then both men sat together in the shade of a palm tree and Scipio poured mint tea for his guest. 'What news, Rais Uli?'

'Everything has been done as you asked.'

Scipio nodded. 'Thank you.'

'I rode on ahead to tell you this. Soon the caravan will arrive and then I will watch you do the impossible.'

'*Bismillah.*' Scipio smiled.

Mulai Ahmed el Rais Uli nodded. 'The blacksmiths of Chefchaouen laboured for many months to create the object you specified. They had no idea what it was for, but I know.'

'You are a shrewd man, my friend.'

'Tell me, *Monsieur* Faraway, do you really think it is wise to carry out your plan? Won't you lose yourself in the bowels of the earth? This oasis is said to be haunted by demons.'

'Do you really believe that, Rais Uli?'

'No, but it's prudent never to *disbelieve* anything. For many centuries it has been considered better to avoid the oasis of Ras el Aïn and even the thirstiest of travellers always prefer to push on to Aït Benimathar. There's surely substance to the legends?'

Scipio sipped his tea, considered the point. His golden

earring glittered in the light that filtered through the fronds of the palms; his red waistcoat was unbuttoned and his coat spread under him. 'That's true, and yet there are times when men must persist with a chosen course of action, not only in spite of danger but because of it.'

Rais Uli laughed. He accepted that the remark applied to both of them, for he himself had embarked on a hazardous path that required courage of unusual proportions, namely open warfare against the French and Spanish colonial masters and the establishment of a Republic of the Tribes of the Rif, the *Tagduda n Arif*, an independent Berber federation that was free to govern its citizens as it chose. There was a price on Rais Uli's head and it seemed likely that someone might try to collect it sooner or later. Pulling his beard, he frowned at his friend.

'What gave you the idea for this venture?'

Scipio Faraway leaned forward.

'On my last trip to Morocco, I found an old map in a book in Ketama. It seemed to show a subterranean river that flowed all the way from this oasis to the ocean. You have told me yourself that sometimes the broken oars of ships surface here, salt-water creatures too. I believe it and see no good reason why the map should lie.'

'But what if the river proves to be unnavigable? What if you get stuck in that iron coffin of yours with its little round windows? Who will come to rescue you then, my brother?'

Scipio shrugged. 'No-one. That's the risk.'

Rais Uli said, 'We have different dreams, you and I, but at least we *do* dream and struggle to turn those dreams real. I want a sovereign state for my people and a place for us on the world stage, but who in Europe will take us seriously? Our blacksmiths give you this gift, but I fear it's a poor exchange for what you have given us. With that knowledge we may even shock the world into respecting us.'

'Every new country must make its mark.'

Rais Uli finished his tea. 'This is a time of new countries; they hatch like the eggs of a cockatrice. In Europe they swell and jostle, twisting the old borders: why should we not have our own state too? Are we not men? The Republic of the Rif will improve living standards for the poor, uproot and destroy the *kif* fields that rot our minds and replace that devilish weed with healthier crops, provide clean fresh water to every farmer, medicines to every child that needs them. Long ago we were admired; soon we will hold up our heads again with pride.'

'It is a worthy project, Rais Uli.'

'Thank you, *Monsieur* Faraway, but the European powers won't like it. We must match them in every aspect and aspiration. That northern nation that won its independence recently—'

'Norway,' answered Scipio.

Rais Uli nodded vigorously. 'Yes, that's the name. How did it manage to gain the respect of the world? It sent a man to plant a flag at the South Pole! After that, the sneers vanished. We must do something equally wild and heroic. You have helped us.'

Scipio rubbed his stubbled chin. 'Take care not to celebrate victory too soon, my friend. What you propose is extremely difficult. To fly over the tallest mountains on the planet!'

Rais Uli sighed; his eyes glittered.

'No aeroplane in existence can fly so high, but with the design of this new engine in our possession I believe that might soon change. We have superb craftsmen and don't lack spirit. Ever since I heard about them, I have dreamed of soaring above the Himalayas! Is it strange that a son of the desert should dream of ice?'

Scipio shook his head. 'No, it is right.'

Into The Atlantic

On the stroke of midnight, Captain Tom Alaerts gave the order to set sail from Bristol harbour into the broad channel that separates England from Wales. I wasn't sure what I was supposed to do, so I copied the actions of my shipmates and evidently I aroused no suspicions. I have always been a good actor, very fast at learning new tricks. An able seaman by the name of Mads Pedersen befriended me and we worked together. The schooner made good speed on the calm waters.

'Have you been with this vessel long?' I asked.

Pedersen nodded. 'More than ten years. I escaped from prison and was on the run and was very eager to get out of Denmark. When Captain Tom turned up in a tavern in Copenhagen looking for men, I signed up at once! "Red" Alaerts asks few questions…'

'But you were in jail unjustly, no doubt?'

Pedersen grinned. 'I was a bank robber and deserved to be locked up, but I don't like that sort of hospitality, so I thought it best to strangle my guard, dress in his uniform and stroll casually out of there with my hands in pockets, a tune on my lips. It takes nerve, that kind of deception, but I'm good at it. Mads "Sanity" Pedersen is how I'm known, for my serenity under pressure! What about you?'

'No nickname. I'm plain Lloyd Griffiths.'

He stroked his chin. 'We'll soon change that. Everyone who sails with Captain Tom needs a special name. You smell strongly of fungus; maybe I should call you "Mushroom Pong"...'

Under the tutelage of this fellow, who had learned his own shipboard skills on the job after his prison escape, I soon was able to climb rigging with a sure foot, reef a sail in an efficient and orderly manner, tie a wide selection of knots, splice rope and accomplish the other tasks that enable the smooth running of a sailing ship.

'To be honest, though,' admitted Pedersen as he marked my progress with a critical eye, 'the schooner is an easy vessel to work on; the larger windjammers are an entirely different proposition. Some of the masts on those behemoths are so high that a monkey or vulture would get dizzy. It wouldn't be so much fun on those!'

'Then let's be grateful Captain Alaerts prefers a schooner,' I said, but Pedersen shook his head solemnly.

'This crate is falling apart at the seams, rending like an old boot, and I suspect that Tom is planning to exchange her for something bigger, better and cosier if he gets the chance ...'

He refused to say more on the topic, but it wasn't difficult to work out his meaning. Pirates frequently keep the vessels of their victims. It makes good sense to use the best available.

As for the commission of Hugo Bloat, we covered enormous tracts of empty ocean searching for his precious flotsam. The quest was as futile as Tom had predicted it would be. My contempt for Mr Bloat intensified as the weeks wore on. His wealth had damaged his sense of realism, but that is a common enough danger for the very rich. It's no less a hazard for the poor! When I thought of Bloat, I still pictured the cobweb in his armpit; I wondered if he had another to match it on the other side? So engaged was I in these thoughts that suddenly —

I lost my grip on the rigging and fell.

My foot caught in the ropes lower down and stopped my plummet. But now I hung uselessly, head down. Pedersen warned me not to struggle to pull myself up; it would be fatal.

'*Haliad hallt!*' I croaked.

He was amused. 'What language is that?'

'Welsh,' I gasped. 'I always curse in Welsh, though I hardly speak the language in my everyday life.'

'Don't move; I'll come and get you.'

'Hurry up. I'm slipping!'

Captain Alaerts appeared on deck from his cabin. 'Well, my friends, I think we might be in luck today. I've just spied a sail on the horizon. Tea clipper from the Orient. Get ready!'

He glanced up at me and nodded, as if it was perfectly acceptable for one of his sailors to be hanging upside down by his left foot. I hissed to Pedersen, 'What does he mean?'

My shipmate reached my side and restored me to a more dignified and secure position. 'The howitzer!'

I frowned. 'He expects us to be gunners?'

'Of course. I'll show you.'

Captain Alaerts disappeared back into his cabin and when he emerged next I was amazed; he had shaved off his beard and wore a pair of round spectacles. Now I understood why he often squinted; it had nothing to do with the salt spray or wind. Between his teeth he clenched a cigar. A pair of revolvers dangled from his hands.

Pedersen said, 'Tom always changes his appearance before a battle. It must be for luck, though I suppose if he loses he can always deny his own identity! It's worth a try at least!'

I shrugged. The odder and more eccentric the players in the unfolding drama, the better my eventual story would be. *The Western Mail* was sure to have a scoop that no other newspaper in my country could hope for in the wildest dreams of the most insane editor! When I closed my eyes, the possible headlines scrolled on the inside of my lids. Pedersen nudged me and roared, 'Daydreaming again.'

I snapped my eyes open. 'Yes. A bad habit.'

'It'll get you killed unless ...'

'Unless what?' I cried.

He laughed. 'You die in the battle first!'

Meanwhile In Romania

After Professor Bogdan Velicu had finished experimenting with the globe of ice, it lay forgotten in its refrigerator in a corner of his laboratory. The year 1913 brought more trouble to Romania in the form of a new Balkan war. The previous autumn, approximately six months after the sinking of *RMS Titanic*, tensions that had been building for centuries erupted with a murderous aftershock. Montenegro declared war on the Ottomans. A week later, as arranged by a network of secret treaties, Serbia, Greece, Bulgaria and Romania entered the fray. The war lasted six weeks and the Turks at last were pushed out of the Balkans.

After the armistice was signed, thousands of men, women and children lay dead and the Ottoman Empire had virtually no territory left in Europe at all. Although Bulgaria had benefited the most from the Turks' loss and had expanded its borders the furthest, its economy was weak and its army demoralised by the brutality of the recent campaigns. Serbia and Greece began to gaze enviously at its acquisitions in Macedonia and Thrace; and Romania also had designs on the southern Dobrudja region, ostensibly to ensure a stable balance of regional power. The First Balkan War might be over but a second seemed inevitable!

And so it happened. Serbia began preparing to attack the Bulgarians; a maverick Bulgarian commander, General Savov, launched a pre-emptive strike against Serbia. This was a strategic error. Bulgaria appeared as the aggressor; and the other Balkan nations joined the Serbs against Bulgaria. This new war was welcomed and encouraged by the Turks, who hoped to sow discord and disaster among the alliance that had recently humiliated them. The government of Romania wasted little time mobilising its forces and marching south to fight a traditional war, but it also spared no effort in seeking less orthodox advantages.

A government agent with the authority to requisition the equipment of his laboratory visited Professor Velicu. More than that, the newcomer had an interest in Velicu himself; it appeared that the most skilled physicists, chemists, biologists and engineers at the university were now obliged to contribute to the war effort. Normal duties were suspended, all peacetime research projects were put on hold: the development of weapons became the solitary function of every specialist. During the First Balkan War, few innovations had been used by Romania: the regime hadn't even owned an effective air force. That had to change!

Surprisingly, the government agent who met Velicu wasn't Romanian himself but a foreign advisor hired because of his reputation as a genius of unconventional warfare. His name was Jukka-Petteri Halme, a Finnish mercenary with cold eyes that belied his jovial smile. A former associate of the notorious arms-dealer Basil Zaharoff, he was wanted as a criminal in a dozen countries. He slapped the professor on the back and laughed in a theatrical manner that was more frightful to the nervous academic than any explicit threat. Jukka paced about the laboratory, picking up items of apparatus and putting them down again.

'You understand your responsibilities, don't you? All the force of your great mind must henceforth be harnessed to the single aim of victory. The drama that is unfolding has the potential to be magnificent! Despite what pacifists say, war is the only proper pastime of mankind, both a cleansing ritual and a work of art. Do you agree?'

'I've never thought of it in that way before—'

Jukka curled his lips in a sly grin. 'Ah! But you *will* come to share my view, I'm sure. You are a researcher with expertise in the chemical bonds of matter? Primarily an analyst, no?'

'That's correct,' said Velicu, 'but I don't—'

'I imagine there is enormous potential in your chosen field. Have you ever experimented with poison gas?'

'Chemical warfare!' stammered Velicu.

Jukka made a casual gesture with one hand; with the other he casually swung an expensive microscope. 'That was just a suggestion. It seems to me that the development of toxic gas bombs might be a profitable avenue of study for a man in your position.'

The professor turned pale and rasped, 'I'm not sure I have ideas along those lines. The rules of war insist—'

'Those rules have been rewritten.' Jukka picked up a flask, swirled it for a moment, raised it to his nostrils and sniffed gingerly. With a flick of his wrist, he splashed the professor's face with the contents. 'And what is this substance exactly? Is it an acid?'

Velicu recoiled and spluttered; then he shook his dripping head, wiped his eyes with a cloth. 'No, just a mild disinfectant. I've been working with grafting tissue cultures onto crystals.'

'That sounds rather promising! Tell me more.'

'The project was concerned with amplifying the efficiency and range of radio transmission, but it failed.'

'Too bad.' Jukka stifled a yawn.

Velicu began trembling. 'What am I supposed to do? I know nothing about making weapons! I'm just a—'

'Come now,' softy chided Jukka. 'I'm willing to help you in any way I can. All you need to do is give me the notes of all the projects you have ever worked on. I'll read them in my spare time and make a list of various possibilities we can explore together. It's my job to collect notes and read them; already I have sifted through thousands of papers belonging to the School of Artillery, Military and Naval Engineering. Now it's the turn of your university and this department.'

Velicu cast a sidelong glance at the refrigeration unit in the corner and said, 'Many of my notes are private —'

Jukka blinked once. Then he covered the distance between himself and the professor with a jump. One hand gripped Velicu around the throat; the other produced a thin serrated knife from a hidden pocket. It all happened so rapidly that the professor saw only a blur. He twisted but the fingers of his attacker tightened like iron talons.

The smile of Jukka was precise and inhuman.

'Where I come from, a man learns to use a blade when he's a child. It's a harsh life and land. I remember breaking an icicle off my roof, long and thick as a lance it was, and going out to hunt wolves. I had to find and kill them before the icicle melted. Big brutes, never afraid of man. One winter it was so cold they came into the centre of Helsinki and ambushed people on the streets. But I *flourished* there!'

Professor Velicu was turning blue. His eyes bulged.

Abruptly the pressure eased. As the professor sagged to his knees, the Finn cleaned his fingernails with the point of the knife, his expression and posture blasé. 'The most crucial lesson to learn is that disobedience is the devourer of life; that and hesitation.'

'I'll do anything you say!' croaked Velicu.

Jukka nodded. 'I feel confident you will. Yes, my friend, you'll never want to cause trouble for me. We have an understanding. Be sure to give me your notes now, every last scrap.'

Blood And Fog

Thick mist rose up from the sea and the distant sail of the clipper was lost to sight, but Captain Tom welcomed it. He preferred to prove his nautical skills by fighting in poor weather, he said, but I also suspected he needed the cover to fully exploit the element of surprise. The fog rolled so solidly over the deck that I felt the world had dissolved, become nebulous but too opaque to admit the passage of light and air. A cloying cloud, the cosmos now, and I was lost inside nothingness.

Did Scipio Faraway experience the same sense of dislocation in the fogs he must have encountered in his own life? I found myself comparing my reactions with his at the slightest opportunity; yet this was ludicrous, for I couldn't possibly know how he dealt with such situations. Clearly he had a strong symbolic value for me: in the brief time I had spoken to him the invisible power of his presence, his aura, had seeped into the fibres of my flesh, into the workings of my soul.

I wanted to be like him, but I didn't know how!

A command interrupted my reverie. 'Wake up, Mr Griffiths, or you'll miss the show!' This was Captain Tom's voice. I shook my head clear of futile yearnings and jumped into action.

Pedersen and the other sailors were dragging the

howitzer up from the hold and positioning it at the railings. Captain Tom's normal tactic was to shoot a stream of tracer shells in the general direction of the target ship as a warning. Each charge had been adulterated with strontium nitrate that would colour the fog and smoke crimson; and, because thermite still burns underwater, the boiling of the sea in the vicinity as the flares snaked to the seabed would provide another shock.

'Psychology! That's the best way!' he added.

'But we can't see what we're aiming at. What if the howitzers score a direct hit on the clipper?' I asked him.

He shrugged and bit his cigar. 'It sometimes happens. In that case we just wait for the next to come along!'

This seemed an irresponsible way to conduct an act of piracy, but for him it worked; he was successful. So I decided to suppress my objections and concentrate on the task in hand.

We fired three shells in the general direction of the other vessel, each one at a slightly different elevation. I strained my ears to catch the boom, but then recalled that these shells were incendiaries and any impact, even if it were against the hull of the clipper, would be too muffled to hear. For a few minutes we stood motionless.

Captain Tom nodded, removed his round spectacles, wiped them clear of mist and remarked, 'They must have received that message. Now let's move in and claim our rightful prize.'

We nosed cautiously through the fog. At last the clipper loomed out of the creamy murk; but there was something odd about it, as if the hull had melted from a direct hit, yet on closer inspection the vessel turned out to be completely undamaged by our assault. It was simply a peculiar design, unlike any other clipper. A long section of the deck extended over the sea and appeared to act as a ramp, but for what purpose none could guess. To my relief, the crew had already escaped in lifeboats, abandoning the ship without a fight. Unlike all the other pirates, I hadn't looked forward to the consequences of a robust resistance.

Captain Tom was dismayed. 'I was hoping for action, but the thermite shells certainly do frighten the majority of sailors. No matter! The clipper is ours now. Let's grapple her closer.'

Mads Pedersen pointed upwards. Through a rent in the fog, an obscure flag fluttered. 'I don't recognise it...'

'Those are the colours of Bessarabia! I didn't know Bessarabia was a seafaring state! How extraordinary!'

'I didn't even realise it was a nation,' I said.

Captain Tom smirked. 'Aye, we live in confusing times, sure enough, and borders are more flexible than they've ever been. All sorts of places are declaring independence and forming federations that last a few weeks or merging with other countries. I daresay that some rebels in Bessarabia decided to call themselves free, bought this clipper, converted it until the shape was the way they liked best.'

Grappling irons had been thrown across and the clipper was hauled to the decayed side of our own vessel.

The men started jumping over. Once all were aboard, the lines would be cut and the old schooner allowed to drift as a derelict while the pirates enjoyed to the full their new, improved home. I watched as the men leaped with remarkable agility, then I realised I ought to follow quickly. But fog had slicked the deck and I slipped.

I struck my head on a protruding nail...

Blood filled my mouth and an involuntary sleep pressed its thumbs on my eyeballs. I sank into oblivion.

It sounds like a cliché but it wasn't. I blacked out.

When I awoke, I was alone. I called out but there was no reply. With a pounding skull I lurched to my feet and reached the rail. The clipper had left without me! I had been accidentally marooned on the rotten schooner and I knew my erstwhile comrades wouldn't come back to save me when they realised I was missing. Pirates do have a code of honour, but in such circumstances it's every man for himself. I doubted I could steer this ship to any port, even without thick fog.

'*Spwng dorth!*' I cried; another Welsh curse.

I knew I was one hundred leagues east of the Azores, but

that was the limit of my navigational insight! I was doomed. A slow death by thirst, starvation and madness awaited me; better to search the hold for a blade with which to end my miserable life.

But I was never given the chance to do this. A shrill whistling assailed my ears, forcing me to cover them with my hands, and there was a purple flash; then a gaping hole appeared in the middle of the deck. I teetered on the edge and peered over. For an instant I saw right through the schooner to the foaming sea beneath! Then the water filled the crater and the vessel went down with astounding rapidity.

I was sucked behind its spiralling descent. I thrashed my arms, kicked my feet, and suddenly broke the surface. A few shattered planks drifted in my vicinity and I clutched one for support. It was obvious that a meteorite had struck the schooner; and the unlikelihood of the event struck me as an excellent joke. I laughed jubilantly, insanely. Nothing could ever match it for originality and unexpectedness!

Or could it? Something bubbled near me.

I continued laughing. I believe I was genuinely mad at that moment. A sea serpent? Was it coming to devour me? Why not! Anything may occur in this life of ours! The black bulk rose malignantly out of the deeps; then I noticed something bizarre about it.

The body of this aquatic monster was riveted!

A hatch opened with a clang.

A man's head emerged.

Scipio Faraway!

The Iron Coffin

Without even calling out, I flung myself in the sea and swam to him, and he reached down and pulled me up. Then he pushed me through the hatch and I fumbled with the rungs of a ladder into the belly of the beast. Sitting in the middle of the iron floor, I shivered, while Scipio shut and locked the hatch and joined me in the dimness.

'There's no electric lighting, I'm afraid,' he said.

'Where did you get this— this—'

'Submarine. Would you believe me if I told you it had been forged by the blacksmiths of a forgotten Jewish town in a part of Morocco that still uses 16th Century Castilian as its primary language? That it was given to me by the last of the Barbary Corsairs, a man who plans to liberate the Rif from foreign control? And that I steered it along an underground river in pitch darkness from a cursed oasis?'

'Yes! Yes!' I almost shouted.

He opened a bottle of brandy and offered it to me. 'Drink it slowly if you don't want to make yourself worse. You have been adrift for several days, by the look of you, and so...'

I shook my head. 'Only a few minutes!'

'Really! From your ragged appearance I imagined it was much longer, but perhaps you were already ill?'

'*Monsieur* Faraway,' I pleaded, 'I'm not an adventurer by profession and I suspect that my constitution is weaker than that of most men who survive the wreck of a pirate vessel; I am a journalist, and I doubt you have known a journalist as tough as a sailor.'

Scipio laughed. 'Well, there was Jack London.'

I gasped, 'You met him?'

'Yes, certainly. A personal friend. I told you once that I had distrust for most journalists, and the reason I made that remark is that no-one can ever match Jack for integrity and force of character. Other journalists will always be in his shade. No offence!'

Suddenly my heart felt light, for here was evidence that Scipio Faraway *did* remember me and that I was more than a lost soul at sea picked up for simple reasons of common humanity.

'None taken!' I blurted. 'None taken at all!'

'Do you require food, Mr Griffiths? I have some bread, olives, honey, but very little else. There's a fishing rod over there if you care to test your skills, but nothing to cook with.'

'No, my stomach is too queasy to accept nourishment. Where are you heading now? To what horizon?'

Scipio tapped a dial with his finger. 'The power has almost gone. Time to head back to shore. Portugal is the nearest mainland coast; I have many friends there and it will be good to see them again. Have you ever visited the city of Oporto, Mr Griffiths?'

'No. Is it worth seeing,' I asked him.

'Certainly. A most picturesque place indeed, but I won't alarm the port authorities by sailing there directly. It's better if we dock at some obscure fishing village and make our way overland. I recall a pretty village not far south of Oporto called Buarcos.'

I voiced no opposition to this suggestion. He adjusted controls, pulled levers and opened valves. 'What is the motive power of this submarine?' I asked. 'I don't hear the noise of an engine!'

He glanced at me. 'Steam, Mr Griffiths, but applied ingeniously. Fires in a sealed vessel under the sea are impractical, so the steam was created *before* the submarine dived into the oasis, and stored in a series of special insulated containers; giant vacuum flasks that stopped it from condensing too rapidly. By carefully releasing the pressure over a period of time it is possible to harness it for several days. But once the pressure drops beyond a certain point, the vehicle is dead.'

'An innovative system,' I agreed, 'but perilous.'

'Nonetheless it served well.'

'Tell me about your life!' I begged.

He helped himself to a swig from the brandy bottle. 'There's too much for a short voyage, but I can briefly reveal that although I was born in Gascony, which officially makes me a French subject, I'm singularly immune to that delusion called patriotism. I'm a citizen of the world. I grew up in a tiny village but travelled to China on a ship when I was very young; I took an active part in the Russo-Japanese war in the summer of 1904, and that's where I met Jack London. Some of my later colleagues were less savoury than he was; for example, I teamed up with a deserter from the Tsarist army and we went to Ethiopia together as prospectors; shortly after that, I travelled to Patagonia, where there's an archaic settlement of Welshmen.'

I nodded vigorously. 'The only colony my country ever tried to set up! One day I must visit it for myself.'

'It's worth the effort, I assure you. Subsequent seasons took me up the coast of South America to Uruguay, Brazil, Suriname; then I returned to Europe and found myself in Italy.'

'What happened to you after Brescia?'

The submarine had dived below the surface of the waves, where faster progress was possible, but Scipio kept it at a depth that didn't preclude an easy exit in an emergency. Clearly the reserves of steam were low indeed. He used a periscope to judge our position.

'Well,' he said slowly, 'I learned that the inventor who didn't turn up intended to appear at the Paris Airshow instead, a year later. So I walked to France and made sure I was present when he revealed his prototype. It was even better than I had expected.'

I recalled what he had already told me. 'The new propulsion system? Oddly enough, I interviewed another eccentric with similar ideas, Rolfe his name was; a pulsejet engine —'

'Clumsy and noisy, Mr Griffiths,' said Scipio, and I was amazed again to discover that I could teach him nothing. He already knew about Martin Wiberg's design: although impressive, it wasn't comparable to the system created by the inventor in Paris. 'It's true that pulsejet engines might have a future in the aviation industry, but Coandă's motorjet variation is more reliable and more efficient.'

I narrowed my eyes. 'Coandă? I don't —'

'Romanian. Born in Bucharest. A very interesting man, Henri Coandă, a graduate of the School of Artillery, Military and Naval Engineering. He also studied in Berlin at the Technische Hochschule. Later he befriended the ambitious aircraft designer Gianni Caproni, but wanderlust overcame him and he embarked on an automobile trip through Persia, Afghanistan and Tibet; when he returned he was a changed man, inspired to devise an experiment with reactive forces that no-one had tried before. He built the aeroplane and flew it; I was there.'

'That was three years ago, in 1910?' I said.

Scipio nodded. 'The following year he went to England to work as the technical director of the Bristol Aeroplane Company. I think he has been concentrating on disc-shaped craft.'

I gasped at this news, for it connected neatly with my own experience. The figure in the hangar I had passed in my vehicle while driving Captain Tom to the Bristol docks! That had been Henri Coandă! Truly this world of ours is full of odd coincidences.

'What happened to the motorjet?' I asked.

Scipio licked his lips. 'His aircraft crashed on its maiden flight, but not because the basic principle was faulty; on the contrary, the accident was a result of his *success*. The engine's exhaust ignited the flimsy fuselage and the fierce blaze spread to the wings. He was lucky to land before they fell off! He was thrown from the plane and injured, but not badly. The engine worked perfectly well, but an unforeseen physical phenomenon had ended the flight. The study of this phenomenon became his new obsession. Soon he had established a new principle.'

'Will you explain it to me?'

Scipio said, 'During his brief flight, he observed that the burning gases expelled from his engine closely hugged the contours of the aircraft. The surface of the fuselage seemed to attract the exhaust flow. He spent many months subjecting models to various kinds of vaporous discharge in wind tunnels and finally gathered enough data to formulate a dynamic theory to account for the effect. When his results were published, it became known by his name: the Coandă Effect.'

I was fascinated to hear this and roared, 'Now that the reasons for the failure of his motorjet plane are known, surely it's possible to construct an improved version with exhaust positioned *behind* the fuselage? Any craft that utilises his engine to its maximum potential will be far in advance of all modern conventional designs!'

Scipio held the brandy bottle up to the watery light that issued through the porthole. He watched the contents swirl, and for a moment I imagined he was dreaming of other seas and other conversations with other men. I felt suddenly unworthy of his company, but he simply said, 'You speak no lie. It could change everything.'

'Why not sell the secret to the European powers?'

Scipio laughed softly at this.

'I gave it to a fellow by the name of Rais Uli. I didn't ask for payment, but in return he arranged for this submarine to be built for me. He's a man of honour, if somewhat too impulsive. Yet I would prefer for all secrets of such importance to be kept out of the hands of the European meddlers. Rais Uli is an old-fashioned man.'

'The Barbary corsair you mentioned earlier!'

'Yes. I don't intend to overlook his defects. We all have them. He likes to boil the eyes of traitors and other enemies with heated coins. I regard the symbolism of the act as primitive and messy. Is there a problem? You look pale. More brandy, Mr Griffiths?'

The Converter

Professor Bogdan Velicu hovered nervously as Jukka Halme crouched to peer into the refrigerator. The Finnish mercenary reached in his hand and stroked the irregular pearly sphere.

'Very curious. It vibrates with energy! Yet it is ordinary ice! What can be causing this bizarre effect?'

'It will melt if you don't close the door!'

Jukka looked up. 'Pardon?'

'The block of ice! It's melting already and —'

Jukka smiled, his expression became very soft. Velicu relaxed. Like a trap powered by a spring of immense power, Jukka pounced on him and knocked him to the floor. The professor groaned. Then Jukka leaped back and prowled around his supine body, his nostrils flared. He was like some forest predator, a wolverine or bear.

Having conducted this atavistic ritual to his satisfaction, he dropped to one knee next to Velicu. 'Manners, my dear professor, are always crucial to proper communication, wouldn't you say? You've seen my knife, and I surely don't need to remind you that the serrated blade has 13 teeth; a conscientious researcher would have counted them instinctively the first time he saw them. Listen carefully.'

Velicu whimpered as Jukka drew the knife from his pocket and held it to the light. 'In Finland the winters are harsh. We learn from an early age that survival depends on ruthlessness and cunning! I recall the time when the lake of Inarijärvi was frozen solid and I decided to ride right across it on a reindeer. "Don't be foolish," my friends shouted after me! But already I was gone, the maddened beast barely under my control, hooves clattering on the ice, the wind whipping my face with snowflakes as big as buttons! The joy of madness filled my soul!'

Velicu groaned and rolled his bulging eyes.

Jukka stroked the professor's forehead tenderly with his free hand, and though it felt as rough as a wolf's tongue the professor managed to refrain from amplifying his hoarse groans.

Jukka sighed nostalgically. 'Yes, a dark joy filled my soul, and hunger of monstrous ferocity seized my body! I yearned for the taste of flesh! So I cut a living bloody steak out of the reindeer I sat astride and crammed it into my maw, the gore oozing between the gaps in my teeth onto my new shirt! How my wife would complain when she saw it! Then I remembered that the poor girl had tumbled into a deep well the previous month. I was free to gorge myself until I was full.'

He chuckled horribly and salivated at the memory.

'But there's a twist,' he added.

Professor Velicu was too scared to reply.

Jukka regarded him tolerantly. 'The twist is that I never seemed to get full no matter how much I ate! I hacked slabs of quivering flesh from the back of the beast, which screamed as I did so; and have you ever heard a reindeer scream, professor? But it kept running and couldn't shake me off and I kept cutting and devouring!'

'Please— Please—' stammered Velicu.

'All the way across Inarijärvi, right to the opposite shore, I sliced and chewed; and when I finally reached the other side, my mount was almost a skeleton, but still alive! Ah, that was how I learned to carve without the risk of a quick death. And if you ever oppose me, professor, by objecting to anything I say or do … How much of your heart do you think I will be able to remove before you expire?'

'All of it! Every last morsel! Forgive me!'

Jukka closed his eyes in ecstasy and appeared to drink Velicu's terror, as if he was an emotional vampire.

'Tell me everything about that block of ice!'

Velicu twisted his head to gaze at the refrigerator. The remnant of the iceberg really was melting: already it had lost a quarter of its mass and a trickle of water was crossing the laboratory floor. He said, 'I'm convinced it's a focal point for vast energy.'

'Yes, yes! But what *kind* of energy?'

Velicu swallowed with difficultly. 'I think— I think—'

'Don't be *heartless*, my friend.'

'Spiritual energy!' blurted the professor.

Jukka opened his eyes.

'Did you say what I thought you did?'

'Yes,' croaked Velicu, fully expecting the knife to penetrate his chest and remove a corner of his heart.

But Jukka seemed to have forgotten his threat. The light of fanaticism in his eyes went out like two stars behind a cloud. With a fluid gesture he replaced the serrated blade in his pocket, then he offered Velicu his hand and pulled the trembling academic to his feet. The Finn blinked once and rubbed his chin and sat on a corner of a workbench, inviting Velicu to sit opposite him on another bench.

'Tell me honestly, do you believe that such energy might be *liberated* in our own lifetimes? Do your dreams encompass such a scenario? It has always seemed to me that much energy is wasted in this world of ours! In the far, cold north we are more sensitive to such matters. The alchemy that transforms a burning log into warmth for the lonely hunter is our national magic, so to speak; our windows use four panes of glass. It's a question in which I have both a professional and a personal, instinctual interest. Does it seem feasible to *exploit* spirits?'

Velicu answered uneasily, 'I have been considering something along those lines, a device that can convert spiritual energy into physical force. The utter annihilation of matter produces amazing amounts of energy: the work of Einstein,

Planck and Rutherford has already established this fact. As for the annihilation of spirit…'

'The output would be greater or smaller?'

Velicu sighed and closed his eyes tight. 'It would be immense, beyond all human understanding! But the spiritual substance would cease to exist once it had radiated all its energy.'

Jukka smiled. 'What of that? Is it a problem?'

Velicu licked his moist lips; he was sweating profusely under the cold stare of the Finn. 'If there is an active consciousness in the substance … If the substance in question is partly or wholly composed of the souls of the dead, as I'm certain it is … Then it will be the most despicable sacrilege to destroy it, to obliterate consciousness that is supposed to have eternal life.

'A blasphemy against the very cosmos!'

Jukka absorbed this in silence. Then he jumped lightly to his feet and approached the professor. 'We need to construct a converter. Can you do that, do you think? This Second Balkan War of yours might turn out to be even more dramatic than anticipated!'

Velicu began to shake his head. Then he felt something in his side, an irritation like an insect bite. He looked down and with horror saw that the blade of Jukka Halme had penetrated his body as far as the hilt. The Finn worked the knife with precision, crooning as he did so, 'I'm just taking a corner of your liver, professor. There!'

He withdrew the blade and held up the sliver of organic matter for the professor to see; then he opened his mouth, placed it on his thick tongue and swallowed. 'So thin!' he cried. 'It dissolved like one of the wafers of the Catholic communion! And now—'

Velicu gasped and clamped his open palm to the wound, but there was almost no blood; Jukka had operated with the precision of a surgeon. He spluttered, 'I'll do whatever you want!'

Jukka nodded. 'A converter, if you please.'

'But how will the released energy be contained? I'm sure you're aware that when nitroglycerine was discovered by Sobrero in 1847 it had almost no utility because it proved impossible to harness the release of energy. If I manage to do what you ask, how …'

Jukka looked out of the window at the sky.

'I have the blueprints for an interesting propulsion system. I took them from the School of Artillery, Military and Naval Engineering; an engineer by the name of Henri Coandă drew them. I'm wondering if modifications might be possible so that it expels the exhaust of combusted spirits rather than the vapours of orthodox fuels.'

Velicu glanced again at the refrigerator.

'The question remains *why* that block of ice should be charged with so much spiritual energy?' he muttered.

Jukka shrugged. 'It's enough to know that it is.'

He strode to the refrigerator and slammed the door. The fist of ice was now the size of a small fruit, a berry.

The Coloured Glass

Night had fallen but there was a bright moon and Scipio was able to steer the submarine by the shafts of pale light that speared through the tranquil water. He peered through the periscope and said, 'Here's something that should interest you, Mr Griffiths.'

He encouraged me to clamp my eyes to the lenses. I did so and saw a ship less than half a league distant. For a moment I didn't recognise it, for I was still a landlubber at heart, slow at such things. Then I realised I was staring directly at Captain Tom's new ship, the stolen clipper! A wave of bitter revulsion rose up inside me.

'The scoundrels that abandoned me to my fate!'

Scipio shrugged. 'Our submarine isn't fitted with torpedoes, so there's nothing I can do to avenge your honour. You'll have to swallow your rage on this occasion, I'm sorry to say.'

I frowned. 'Wait a moment! Perhaps I will get my revenge after all, but indirectly. There seems to be a disturbance on the deck. Can you steer a little closer to it, *Monsieur* Faraway?'

He could and he did. Soon enough I was able to clearly discern figures engaged in a fierce duel, two of them; clearly a pair of quarrelling pirates had decided to settle their dispute in the most anachronistic fashion. Most countries and cultures had forsaken formal duelling in the past century or two, although I knew the custom still existed in Corsica, Abkhazia, Cuba, Uruguay and a handful of other more 'romantic' nations. Even Wales had recently abandoned the tradition …

'I bet they are fighting over something as petty as one doubloon or the best space to hang a hammock!'

But I was wrong about this, and as Scipio edged the submarine a dozen yards closer I saw that the combatants were Captain Tom himself and the Danish bank robber, Mads Pedersen! So this was a more serious fight and probably was connected with overall command of the crew. Mads was an aspiring usurper who had seen a chance to overthrow the Belgian and rule in his place. A fine example of natural law among lawless men at sea! My teeth gritted together as I watched.

Tom Alaerts carried a sabre in one hand and a poniard in the other and in his belt was wedged a revolver. Mads 'Sanity' Pedersen was armed with not only a cutlass but also a mace; he too had a revolver in his belt. The fighters lashed out, parried, weaved and counter-attacked. Suddenly Mads struck a blow at Tom that severed the Captain's right arm: it plopped onto the deck still clutching the sabre.

'*Pen pidlan gawsog!*' I breathed softly.

Blood spurted. But Tom didn't retreat; he jabbed with his poniard, and the point of the weapon went through the left eye of Mads and penetrated his brain, snapping off inside with a muffled, squelchy note. Mads swung another blow, even harder this time, amputating Tom's left leg below the knee. At the same time, Captain Alaerts drew his revolver and fired twice into the Dane's chest. Both men crumpled to the deck and lay there, while the other pirates swarmed around.

'Well, that's finally settled,' I said grimly.

I turned away from the periscope and sat in the corner. I had started to wonder if a life of adventure was really for me. Wouldn't I be happier in the comfortable and safe offices of *The Western Mail*, writing my trivial stories about famous people? As if reading my dismal thoughts and eager to dissipate my despair, Scipio said, 'In Buarcos I know a delightful café where the wine is excellent; and there's an inn with soft beds. The walk to Oporto is along a very fine beach.'

'Thank you for your consideration, *Monsieur*!'

'We might be there in an hour.'

'Will you be able to land in the darkness?'

He made a dismissive gesture. 'The moonlight is adequate. Plus I will recognise the lights of the village. I know the order they are arranged, and that will guide me to the harbour.'

'You are an immensely resourceful man.'

He accepted the compliment with good grace. I seemed to derive hope and strength from his presence, as if his aura was a field of force radiating these qualities to everyone else in his vicinity. I don't wish to give a false impression: he wasn't a supernatural being! But certainly he was touched with a special magic that most men never possess. I wondered if he might be the prototype of a new kind of human being, the first modern hero, and if this evolved breed was destined to stride effortlessly through the decades of the 20th Century like demigods. Probably I had read too much Nietzsche in my youth. The way things turned out, of course, was against the utopian needs of every dreamer.

Our century became the bloodiest in history.

But back then, in 1913, I was still naïve enough to hope for perfection, for paradise on Earth. With your privileged perspective, you wonder how so many millions of courageous men could sacrifice their lives so readily to foolish causes, how intelligent people swallowed and digested lies that left the cities of Europe in ruins. At the time, we hadn't grown our cynical shells tough enough to withstand the perverted wishes of the monsters we had among us: we even lacked the perception to penetrate their disguises. I now believe that Scipio Faraway was a throwback to an earlier age, to the heroes of the Trojan Wars and beyond.

While I was lost in my rambling thoughts, we had been approaching the shoreline of Portugal. 'Here we are!'

Scipio had used the last wisps of stored steam to float the submarine to the surface. We bobbed on the moonlit water and peered through grimy porthole glass at the breakers. Beyond them were the lights of a village. I marvelled at the colours: topaz, emerald, red; the lamps of homes, taverns and inns. I rejoiced. 'Land again!'

Scipio Faraway frowned and adjusted his cap. 'The layout is exactly the same as I remember it, and yet—'

'There's nothing wrong, surely?' I gasped.

He climbed the iron ladder to the hatch, hurled it open, stood exposed in the cool night air and squinted at the shore. 'Everything looks right. It's Buarcos, I'm sure it is. But the—'

Suddenly the hull of the submarine groaned.

'A sandbank!' I wailed.

Scipio replied, 'There shouldn't be one at this spot. The village harbour is free of obstructions. We have beached ourselves! But how? Come here quickly, Mr Griffiths, if you value your existence! Our vessel is about to roll over. You'll be trapped inside!'

I scrambled up the ladder and joined him.

'Into the waves!' he cried.

Not for the first time in my life I splashed and thrashed in brine. But it was only a few feet deep. I staggered to the beach, coughed water out of my aching lungs, collapsed to my blistered knees, crawled the remainder of the distance like a bewildered turtle. I was only dimly aware that Scipio was behind me. Pushed by the waves that were breaking on its spherical hull, the submarine rotated with a mighty splash, so that the hatch was at the bottom. An iron coffin indeed!

I now saw that the lights of the village weren't really lamps at all; and in fact there weren't any houses. Small driftwood fires burned on the sand and panes of coloured glass stood in front of them to give the illusion of the windows of Buarcos. The whole thing was a villainous trick. We had been dazzled and caught by wreckers!

As a Welshman I should have been less gullible in this respect, for the coasts of Wales, as well as those of nearby

Cornwall, are infamous for the rogues who light false fires to lure ships to their doom. The idea is for the wreckers to profit by looting the stricken ship, kidnapping and ransoming the crews. I cursed myself loudly.

Then I heard the beat of hooves. I looked up.

'*Anws blewog*!' I bellowed.

I was staring into the face of a unicorn!

The Bandit Queen

For long moments I was unable to move, paralysed by surprise and alarm. I half suspected I had lost my sanity. Then I gradually realised that it was a fake unicorn: the horn was part of an elaborate headdress and the beast was a normal, if rather large, horse.

The rider who sat astride it was a woman!

Her long, wavy black hair streamed in the breeze and her eyes glittered in the moonlight. I didn't miss the fact that she held a carbine in one hand, an anachronistic wheel-lock model.

Behind me I heard Scipio Faraway say, 'Hello again, Senhorita Luísa! I am delighted by this chance encounter.'

She smiled. 'Chance or destiny, Dom Scipio?'

He bowed. 'Perhaps both.'

I stumbled to one of the driftwood fires, warmed myself with its merry flames and said, 'You know her?'

Scipio nodded with a twinkle in his eye. 'Allow me to introduce you to Luísa Ferreira, the Bandit Queen!'

He approached the horse and kissed the extended hand of the mounted beauty, who murmured something in Portuguese to him, perhaps the lines of a poem. He responded in a similar manner. I was clearly the witness of a story far too secret to be written down in full, but I had entered midway through the tale, at a late chapter.

That's how I felt at that moment; but the mere fact that Scipio knew her didn't mean my own skin was safe, for how could I be confident that even the smallest part of the affection toward the wandering hero she failed to conceal in her expression would be extended to me? In truth I was merely a sidekick, for want of a better word.

My clothes steamed as the heat bathed them. I felt the life return to my weary, sodden bones. I took an interest in my surroundings and saw armed men crouching in the dunes, obviously her followers. The beach stretched to the north in a straight line as far as the eye could see, but to the south it soon terminated in a rocky headland.

'Ask her where the real Buarcos is,' I said.

Scipio said nothing in reply.

She flared her nostrils indignantly. 'Ask me yourself! I speak English, French, Spanish, Catalan, Latin and a dozen other languages! The answer to your question is that the village is on the other side of the headland, but it can't be reached along the beach. You first have to climb into those hills and descend again. An arduous trek.'

Scipio removed his hat, smoothed his hair and said to me, 'This beach extends all the way to Aveiro and is extremely isolated, so it's the perfect location for Luísa's profession.'

'What does she intend to do with us?'

Luísa looked at Scipio; a spark flashed between them. They smiled in a manner that was both wistful and wise. I understood at once that no pale imitation of passion had once existed between them, but only the deepest and truest mutual desire. I had already come to the conclusion that Scipio wasn't a man who treated affairs of the heart casually, and yet neither was he gullible enough to believe that love really was the ultimate truth. I felt the fields of magnetic force between these two, and a pang of envy jarred my own heart, like an elbow striking the corner of a desk. Then I cleared my throat with a contrived cough, breaking the spell and returning us all to the same sombre, dim reality.

'She has different plans for us,' Scipio said.

I puffed out my cheeks. Bandits traditionally keep hostages and try to ransom them. If no ransom is forthcoming, the hostage is dispatched out of the world. Was it my fate to be martyred thus? I doubted anyone would pay for my release; my prudent editor, Ben Gordon, wouldn't ransack *his* pockets on my behalf: that was certain. I wondered how my end would be arranged. To be tied to a stake for the rising tide to drown occurred to me as one option, and I grimaced.

Luísa whistled, and her men swarmed down from the dunes. I counted 20 ruffians, the optimum number for a bandit outfit, too few to create logistical problems but too many to encourage bounty hunters. I expected rude leers and obscene comments, but they were polite and deferential. It seemed that Luísa Ferreira was the more civilised sort of bandit and hated boorishness in her followers. They crowded around me but none offered a threat or even a menacing look.

'You shall be guests at my camp!' Luísa announced.

'For how many months?' I cried.

She frowned, and even in the uncertain glow of the spluttering fires I saw the appeal of her clashing eyebrows as they arched together, dark and alluring, as were her liquid eyes.

'One night only, I'm afraid. Or do you plan to enrol as one of my men? The initiation ceremony is somewhat uncomfortable, and in fact we don't require any extra help at present.'

Scipio guffawed; he couldn't help but enjoy my discomfort, and yet his pity would have been worse, and I'm sure he honoured me by refusing to take me seriously at that point, by showing more solidarity and empathy with the bandits than with me. It meant he was treating me as an equal, a fellow man, not as a weakling too sensitive for prolonged exposure to the harsh realities of the human cosmos.

I smiled at my own folly. He was a good role model and his presence gave me the strength I needed to act in a manner closer to my own notion of what a hero should be in word and deed. I took a deep breath, adopted a nonchalant tone and said, 'One night is sufficient for me, Senhorita, and if it turns out to be my last on Earth, I will insist that it couldn't have been spent in more agreeable company.'

Scipio nodded at this; I had proved myself.

'Very nicely spoken,' said Luísa, 'but I don't intend to kill you; unless you are suffering from some advanced medical condition, I see no reason why this night should be your last.'

She flicked the reins of her horse and the fake unicorn began trotting toward the dunes. Her men extinguished the fires, hefted the glass panes onto their shoulders and followed her at a brisk pace. Scipio and I strode side by side in their wake, and I had absolutely no desire to escape whatever awaited me in those hills of sand. We undulated our way down the tortuous paths, skirting a large crater and passing into a wood of cork trees. In a large glade we found the camp, a scattering of huts and cotton hammocks around a large fire pit.

There was also a stout long table that could easily sit a ravenous tribe in comfort, and it was laden with tankards and jugs of wine. A man with glasses who looked nothing like a bandit stirred cauldrons, pots and pans over the fire with a selection of wooden spoons. He wiped his brow with his apron and muttered a greeting.

Luísa said, 'This is João Seixas, our cook. He used to be a lawyer but decided that becoming a real bandit was more moral. Yet he's not built for strenuous activity, so we gave him the culinary duties! Sometimes I think that cooking for our entire band is more physically demanding than going forth with pistol, musket and knife!'

João called out his agreement with this sentiment.

Luísa dismounted and tethered her horse to a stake. It browsed without complaint the tough marram grass.

'Sit down, my guests! Partake of our hospitality!'

I sat next to Scipio, poured myself a goblet of wine, while my stomach rumbled in response to the cooking smells. Scipio drank with less abandon to the dictates of appetite and asked, 'What was that crater we passed just now in the dunes? A meteorite?'

I grew excited at these words and said:

'One of those damn rocks from the sky holed my ship! There must be an entire storm of them up there.'

Luísa took her place opposite Scipio.

'No, it wasn't a meteorite. A weird aircraft passed overhead and one of the more impatient bandits fired at it. To take revenge, it circled back and dropped an unusual bomb on us.'

'A crater that large? An enormous bomb, surely!' Scipio glanced up at the sky, as if able to read the invisible spoor of the aeroplane in the chilly night air. 'Too heavy for a plane!'

Luísa nodded. 'Normally, yes, but this device was small and strangely shaped. Clearly it's a new kind of weapon, more powerful than anything seen before. It missed our camp, of course, but we weren't able to bring it down with our bullets. I didn't blame the man who fired the first shot. It's understandable that when a vulgar pilot disturbs the peace by buzzing like a gigantic wasp directly overhead, we'll try to silence it. In fact the fellow in question gets an extra ration of wine. Pedro, where are you? Come and introduce yourself! Pedro Marques!'

A tall man with wavy hair that was the colour of the moon approached the table and bowed. He had been stood at the fire pit, joking with João Seixas. 'At your service, Dona Luísa.'

'Tell Scipio and his friend what the plane was like.'

Pedro rubbed his chin. 'It was a monoplane that had floats and wheels under it. The bomb was released from the right wing; the left wing didn't have a bomb under it, but some struts revealed that one had hung there at some point. The colours were—'

I jumped up. 'That must have been what struck the ship I was on! So it wasn't a meteorite after all! Some scoundrel of an aviator dropped a bomb on me! If I ever catch hold of him!'

Pedro waited for me to calm down, then he resumed his description of the aerial intruder. 'The fuselage was painted red with a wide green stripe and the emblem of a rising sun.'

Scipio said, 'They sound like the national colours of

Bessarabia, which I believe has just declared itself independent, or rather *part* of the country has done so, the east bank of the Dniester River in fact. I wonder what the Bessarabian air force is doing here?'

'Surely such a rogue state doesn't possess a fleet of aircraft? That's an absurdity worthy of Jules Verne!'

'Ah yes, the famous essayist and historian...'

'The writer of *fiction*,' I said.

But Scipio was smiling gently, and a strange chill went through me as I realised he was at least half serious. So was the world filled with wonders that had previously escaped my attention? Eccentric inventors creating an array of bizarre machines, explorers travelling by airship across forbidden lands, men firing themselves out of the mouths of giant guns into space? I could scarcely credit this scenario!

I felt something press against the back of my chair. A long head rested itself on my shoulder. The Bandit Queen's horse had wandered over, tired of nibbling tough grass. Then João Seixas used a ladle to beat time on the cauldron as a substitute dinner gong and Luísa brandished her own spoon like a weapon and winked at us.

'Time for supper at last, gentlemen!'

The Morning After

I recall a feast of prodigious proportions; then with reeling brain and my stomach full I collapsed into the nearest hammock. Scipio had imbibed far less alcohol than me; he disappeared into Luísa's hut. I remained outside, swatting mosquitoes, too tired and drunk to be jealous of his luck. Luísa Ferreira was every man's dream girl.

I woke with a headache that soon vanished.

We said goodbye before noon and began walking across the dunes at a diagonal calculated to bring us back to the beach. Then it would be a nice walk northwards to Aveiro, and from that town we could catch a train to Oporto − a city the praises of which *Monsieur* Faraway still frequently sang. I was looking forward to seeing the old quarter, the Ribeira, on the edge of the river, and wandering the alleys.

But it was not to be. I still haven't visited that city.

It took us until late afternoon to reach the lagoons south of Aveiro. The beach became a narrow sandspit at the end of which was an iron bridge to take us into the outskirts of the town.

But something in the lagoon distracted us.

It was an aeroplane on floats.

The fuselage was painted in the colours of Bessarabia.

It bobbed peacefully at anchor.

'That's the plane of the rascal who bombed me!' I fumed.

Scipio nodded. 'Indeed, Mr Griffiths, and the pilot seems

to be dozing on the shore. Shall we say hello?'

We stood above the sleeping villain and I was sorely tempted to wake him with a kick in the belly, but Scipio dissuaded me; simply casting our shadows over him and lowering the temperature on his peaceful face was enough to rouse him from dreams.

He blinked at us. 'Who the devil are you?'

'Never mind about that,' said Scipio. 'The important thing is that you are going to kindly explain to my friend here exactly why you dropped a very powerful bomb on his ship.'

The sleeping man raised himself to a seated position. 'My own sailing vessel was raided by pirates. They stole it and left their own behind. I was so furious I destroyed the derelict.'

'That schooner wasn't a derelict,' I spat through gritted teeth, 'for the simple reason that I was still on it!'

The fellow shrugged. 'I didn't know. And I don't care.'

But Scipio was rubbing his chin.

'What do you mean by saying it was your own ship that was taken by the pirates?' he demanded. 'You didn't have any ship; you had the plane over there. You can't control both!'

The pilot laughed. 'The clipper was a new kind of ship, developed for the use of the Bessarabian navy; there's none other like it in the world, but I'm sure the idea will catch on. The deck has been modified so that planes can take off and land on it while at sea. It's called an *aircraft carrier* and it'll revolutionise warfare! I took off on a practice flight, but when it was time to return I discovered that the clipper no longer belonged to my side. I could hardly land on a deck full of pirates! So I vented my frustration on the schooner and obliterated it —'

'Then you flew here? After dropping your other bomb?'

'I was running low on fuel and needed to lighten my load. Somebody took a shot at me, so I fought back.'

Scipio asked, 'What's your name, young man?'

The pilot answered with a sneer, 'Mihaila Adrian. I'm not Bessarabian by birth, but a Romanian from Bucharest. After the First Balkan War last year I became disillusioned with the attitude of the Great Western Powers who attempted to manipulate the peace treaties with the Ottomans to their cynical advantage. I heard about a radical band of separatists who thrived beyond the Dniester — an anarchist group — so I went to join them. To force the European 'powers' to take us seriously we had to impress them with a show of strength. It's the only thing they respect. We hired the services of a freelance military adviser, the best in the business. He designed both the aircraft carrier and the special bomb.'

'What were you doing far out in the Atlantic? Surely the Black Sea is closer to your sphere of influence?'

'The military adviser told us to be more ambitious.'

'What did he recommend to you?'

Mihaila said, 'An invasion of the Azores; we intended to colonise and exploit the islands in the name of the Bessarabian Syndicalist Republic! I was perfecting my bombing run when the pirates appeared and ruined our schemes! A great opportunity lost!'

'What is the name of your military adviser?'

'Jukka-Petteri Halme. Do you know him? He alarmed me when I met him, but he's certainly a strategist of genius! He told me that the screams of dying men are like oxygen to him.'

I began to say ironically, 'A pleasant sort of —'

Scipio interrupted me by snapping his fingers. 'I knew *he* would be up to his dirty tricks again!' He turned to face me. 'This Jukka is one of the most dangerous and diabolical men who have ever walked the surface of our planet! I locked horns with him 13 years ago, during the Boxer Rebellion in China. He invented a decapitation machine that came within an inch of removing my own head from my shoulders! He wanders across the globe spreading death and destruction. I would welcome the chance to put a permanent stop to his antics!'

'I assume he's still in Bessarabia?' I said.

Mihaila shook his head. 'He left Tiraspol in a hurry. The last I heard of him was that he had crossed the border into Romania and was working for King Carol's government. A Second Balkan War has started and there will be plenty of "oxygen" for him.'

'*Pwdin blew!*' I cursed.

Scipio rested his hand on my shoulder. 'I'm sorry, Lloyd, but I won't be able to give you a tour of Oporto now. This news changes my immediate plans. I'm going to Romania.'

I blurted out impulsively, 'I'll come with you.'

Scipio smiled down at Mihaila. 'We need to borrow your aeroplane. I am sorry we can't afford to pay for it, but I'll do my best to ensure that it reaches Bucharest in one piece. You may collect it there, if you wish. So farewell, my idealistic friend!'

Mihaila grumbled but didn't attempt to stop us. We used his inflatable dinghy to row ourselves into the middle of the lagoon; it was too much effort to deflate it and store it in the rear of the aircraft, so we allowed it to drift back to shore. I climbed into the passenger seat and Scipio took the controls. He seemed familiar with the principles of powered flight. With a series of coughs the engine shuddered into life and the wooden propeller began turning. Scipio muttered:

'He wasn't lying; we're low on fuel.'

I looked at the gauge. 'How far do you think we can go?'

'Probably only to Viseu, a village in the hills, but I'm sure we can get petrol there. If not, we'll have to travel to Romania the old-fashioned way, by mule. I hope that won't happen!'

I expressed my appreciation of the joke with a chuckle.

But he frowned at my reaction.

Then it occurred to me that if anyone was capable of crossing from the Western extremity of the broad European landmass to the Eastern in such an uncomfortable fashion, and furthermore enjoying the experience as he went, that man was Scipio Faraway!

The Demonstration

The generals stood together and waited while the Finnish mercenary took his knife and cut off a thin slice from the small lump of ice. Then he shut the door of the refrigerator and carried the sample to the mouth of a weird device that resembled the musical instrument of an insane demon, a cross between an immense trumpet and a nightmarish lute; the bronze horn was strung with resonating wires in the pattern of the most evil spider's web it might ever be possible to conceive.

Adjacent to this peculiar contraption was another almost as strange, an engine of a highly unusual kind. Although it bore some resemblance to an ordinary internal combustion motor with no fewer than a dozen cylinders, it was plain that a wholly original mind had been responsible for modifying major aspects of the basic pattern. The 12 pistons drove a compressor rather than a standard propeller and fed a combustion chamber connected to a sequence of optimally arranged exhaust nozzles. The thermal reactive force thus created would be immense.

Professor Bogdan Velicu sat on a chair in the corner of the laboratory. He was pale and weak and his white coat was ventilated in many places by thin cuts; he had come under Jukka's malign scrutiny too many times and his life force was ebbing away.

Jukka placed the sample in the centre of the web.

Then his gnarled hands operated switches and levers on a console and he licked his lips as the power hummed.

'What is happening?' one of the generals asked.

Jukka replied, 'This apparatus is a spiritual energy converter and I've connected it to a motorjet. I plan to run a static test for you. You'll soon see what power is at my fingertips!'

The general grumbled, 'Spiritual energy? But—'

'It exists!' cried Jukka. 'Don't doubt that for even an instant! Men die and their souls break free of gravity and sorrow. They are blown like chaff by the solar wind off the surface of the planet and into deep space. Spirits are like the vapours of a combusted gas; they obey the Coandă Effect and are attracted to nearby surfaces. Yes, I've read his notes. You let a genius slip through your fingers, gentlemen!'

The generals murmured among themselves.

One of them said, 'What does any of this have to do with the fragment of ice vibrating on that artificial web?'

Jukka adopted a thoughtful pose. 'For some reason the shard of ice in that refrigerator is suffused with spiritual energy in a highly concentrated form. I don't know why this should be, but I can make a guess. Perhaps it is all that remains of an iceberg that sank a crowded ship. Many hundreds of people died because of it; their ghosts were released into the aether, but because of the Coandă Effect they were attracted to the nearest contoured surface, namely the iceberg itself!'

'Yes, but as the iceberg melted, the ghosts would be freed one by one and now there should be none left.'

'That's not how the phenomenon works, gentlemen. After the impact, the ghosts circled the original iceberg at a certain speed, unable to detach themselves from it, but with clearance between each individual. Then the iceberg shrank, but the Coandă Effect remained; the phantoms continued to orbit it, for they had no other choice, but now they were packed closer together. The souls of every man, woman and child who drowned in that collision are doomed to rotate around the shard until the very last crystal of ice turns back to liquid water!'

The generals blinked in stupefaction. Velicu rocked unsteadily on his chair and whispered. 'It's wrong—'

Jukka threw back his head and laughed. 'This world is still an enigma, despite the efforts of science! *Why* should the souls of the dead behave in the same manner as exhaust fumes? Once I knew a witch-woman; I think she would be able to tell us the answer, but she's not here. She dwelled in a misshapen walrus-tusk cabin on a remote beach on the Gulf of Bothnia, near the island of Hailuoto, and that's where I met her. I tried to steal her secrets and I killed her familiar, a raven with blue eyes, and she vowed to tie my bones in knots with magic!'

The generals exchanged nervous glances.

Jukka continued, 'Ah, those Finnish witches! They are the worst in the world. Into a massive iron cauldron she cast herbs, gizzards, powders and other diabolical ingredients and she bubbled them into a foul brew over a driftwood fire! But I was cleverer than she; I was hiding *under* the liquid, holding my breath with my lungs fit to burst; and I had a crossbow in my hands, loaded with a barbed bolt! Slowly my flesh boiled but still I waited for the right moment. Then she leaned right over with a ladle and I let her have it in the face! Into her vile skull lodged the bolt and I surfaced like a salted leviathan, overturning the pot and putting the fire out. I was cooked nicely, gentlemen, like a potato!'

His shoulders undulated with hideous mirth.

'What will happen to the souls that are converted into energy?' asked one of the generals with a frown.

'Pure energy, gentlemen, pure! There will be nothing left! No sacrifice is greater than to forsake the chance of eternal life for the cause of victory in this war! Fools and cowards may object that these innocent souls didn't volunteer for the honour, but that is a minor detail. Behold! Witness total conversion of spirit into power...'

And Jukka flipped a switch on the console.

The vibrating web began to glow. The speck of ice vanished in a flash of utterly intense colour, but a colour not in any human spectrum. Then a communal scream that soured the blood rose from the mouth of the horn and the generals recoiled in horror, but Jukka laughed scornfully at them and drank with both ears the despairing wails of those who felt their souls being obliterated; souls that should have been immortal, souls that if lost were gone forever. And the energy released was fed into the compressor of the motorjet engine in its frame.

'This is the foulest blasphemy!' wept Velicu.

Jukka stepped toward him, his knife glittering. A quick stroke and the penultimate segment of the professor's heart was dangling between thumb and forefinger of his free hand. Velicu sat back down. Inside he was now a lattice, barely functioning, running on the absolute minimum of organic matter needed to stay alive; another mistake and his entire visceral system would collapse like a deflating jellyfish. Yet he was grateful; his soul was untouched, in one beautiful piece.

With a roar that muffled even the awful screaming, the tethered engine shot off the desk and smashed right through the wall of the laboratory. A cloud of brick dust settled around them. They peered through the hole and saw the engine scraping itself to pieces on the road, knocking pedestrians down like skittles; soon it was gone.

Despite his misgivings, one of the generals applauded; then the others joined him. Jukka bowed theatrically.

'Imagine an aeroplane powered by such an engine! And imagine such an aeroplane armed with a gun I have recently perfected that puts one of my old machines to a new use; you will see for yourselves! I will reduce the entire Bulgarian army to pulp!'

He threw up the segment of Velicu's heart and caught it on his tongue. Then he smirked and bowed again.

'You wish to receive payment now?' asked a general.

Jukka nodded. 'Yes, why not?'

The general barked an order and an adjutant entered the

room; he held a struggling girl in his arms. He let her go, and with huge eyes she stared wildly at her surroundings. The Finn approached rapidly and ripped her bodice apart with his bare hands, exposing her firm young breasts. To the disgust of the other generals and the disbelief of the assistant, he roughly rubbed his stubbly chin over her nipples. She struggled and cursed, but to no avail. Then Jukka slapped her into silence, picked her up and balanced her on his shoulder. He paused.

'Are there any deep wells near here?'

The Letter

Fuel for the plane proved easy to obtain in Viseu, and Scipio was confident we could travel the entire distance through the air. As long as I live, I will never forget that flight! We proceeded in a series of hops from one tricky landing to another. It was necessary to refuel regularly and sometimes the engine needed spare parts; something was always going wrong with it. As we flew, Scipio talked about the numerous advantages of Henri Coandă's motorjet and expressed his wish our own aeroplane was powered by one, but I guessed he was happy enough.

Our route took us first to Madrid, then to Barcelona and over the sea to the island of Mallorca, to a landing near the quaint village of Deia, where decades later a novelist by the name of Robert Graves would pen *Count Belisarius*, one of the finest historical novels ever written. From Mallorca we flew to Alghero in Sardinia; then across the Tyrrhenian Sea to Rome and over the Italian peninsula to the Adriatic, where we weathered a bad storm. By this time we were famished as well as weary, so Scipio decided to land in the Croatian city of Split.

'A chance to buy a newspaper too!' he said.

'I doubt *The Western Mail* is available. Though it does pay for special correspondents in various countries.'

'Something local will suit me better...'

'I thought you didn't trust journalists?' I replied with a

laugh. It was a jest he took without rancour, but I knew his desire for news had a serious purpose behind it. We needed to know how the Second Balkan War was progressing; if Romania was suddenly annihilating the armed forces of its opponent without much resistance, then Jukka-Petteri Halme was almost certainly behind it. I don't mean to imply that Romania wasn't capable of winning without his help, but the First Balkan War had been a long, hard slog, as struggles in that corner of Europe always tend to be. Rapid gains in *this* war would be uncharacteristic and thus a clue as to the presence of the dreadful Finn and his scheming.

One thing I had noticed at all our landings was the way I was greeted with increasing interest by the people we had dealings with. In Madrid, in the Casa de Campo, I had been virtually ignored; in Barcelona, people did look at me from the corners of their eyes, but only that; in Mallorca I was stared at openly; the same in Sardinia; and by the time we reached Rome I seemed to be an object of enormous appeal; and yet, so far, nothing had happened to make me feel concerned.

To pass the time, Scipio answered my questions about his life. Then he asked his own questions about mine. He was an extremely cultured man, as I believe I've already stressed, and kept me entertained with poems and songs and riddles in a dozen languages.

Below us was the port of Split …

We landed in the harbour and moored against a stone jetty. The beauty of Mihaila Adrian's plane was that it was equally at home in the sky, on sea or on land. A true Vernian machine, it reminded me a little of the vehicle used by the villain Robur in *Master of the World*. I was smiling to myself at memories of that book as I followed Scipio Faraway up a metal ladder to the top of the jetty. A man was waiting there for us. He handed something to Scipio, who had his back to me.

Then the stranger walked rapidly away.

A second later, Scipio turned to me and handed me a crumpled letter. I was astounded to see that it was addressed to me! Narrowing my eyes in quiet amazement, I read it through.

Dear Lloyd!

Greetings from your editor! I wonder if you have forgotten me? I hope not. I certainly haven't forgotten you.

I'm very disappointed with your attitude and actions. When you failed to return from Hugo Bloat's residence after your interview with that most august and noble gentleman, I was dreadfully worried that you had suffered a lethal accident. What would *The Western Mail* do without its finest journalist, I asked myself? I wept for many hours!

Yes, I don't mind admitting that I was overwrought with nostalgia and grief at the thought you might be dead. Naturally I made enquiries; I went in person to Mr Bloat's house. He had no idea what had happened to you, but I found him to be an extremely fascinating person, severely misjudged by his peers and the general populace of Porthcawl.

In fact, in the following days we became firm friends.

Indeed, it soon went further than that.

When he received a report from a man in his employ, a certain Captain Tom Alaerts, that he had taken aboard a new crew member, and that the name of the sailor in question was identical to yours, he didn't neglect to pass the information to me! I was grateful to him. In return I confided my suspicion that your motives weren't pure. Correct me if I'm wrong, Lloyd, but I don't believe you decided to change your career from journalist to buccaneer; on the contrary, I'm convinced you planned to write a story about your little jaunt as a pirate and do your best to discredit poor Mr Hugo Bloat.

That was very despicable of you, in my view.

We still think this is your plan.

Anyway, Mr Bloat offered to put up a large reward for your safe return and I accepted his superb generosity in this regard; but it seemed to me that the 'safe' condition was a little too stringent.

So I persuaded him to alter it to 'dead or alive'.

Many people contacted me in the hope of claiming the reward but they had nothing credible to reveal; they were just desperate for money. Other candidates promised to seek you out and bring you back, but most wanted the reward in advance. Fraudsters! What is the world coming to? There was only one serious applicant; his name is Rolfe and he seems keen to succeed. Of course I gave him my blessing and waved as he set off.

He'll probably face stiff competition on the way!

Not only did I advertise the reward in *The Western Mail*, you see, but I made sure it was printed in every other newspaper in Europe. Mr Hugo Bloat's money can achieve wonders. I know you'll appreciate my thoroughness in this business. I sat back and waited for results.

Before long, reports reached my desk.

You were recognised in Mallorca, Sardinia and Rome. I was notified on these occasions by telephone and so I opened an atlas, found a decent map of Europe and worked out your likely route; then I telephoned ahead to one of my agents in Croatia and he wrote this letter for me. He was the chap who delivered it to you just now. You probably are wondering why the envelope was so bulky? I won't keep you in suspense. It's because I included an explosive device with the letter. It's quite small but deadly enough.

When has it been set to go off? Good question! Approximately 20 seconds after the envelope is opened.

And that's right about ... now!

Goodbye and the very worst of luck to you!
Yours truly,

Ben Gordon

The Arrival

I shrieked but the sound was swamped by a dull roar. The letter bomb had exploded! Yet I felt nothing; there was no pain or blood and my brain was still inside my skull. What had happened?

Scipio turned to me. He was covered in water and seaweed.

I blinked like an electrocuted fish.

He explained, 'I had a hunch something wasn't right, so I opened the package for you; the letter was harmless enough and I passed it on, but I wasn't impressed with the accompanying "gift", so I dropped that into the sea, just in time as it happens!'

'*Cer I ware gyda gotsen dy fam-gu!*' I exhaled.

'Pure Welsh poetry indeed!'

'Well, I'm a marked man now,' I said.

'Come, Mr Griffiths, let us buy some fuel. I suspect we're running out of time. We ought to obtain food too. It's a long way over the mountains of Bosnia, Serbia and Romania.'

'I could do with a strong coffee, my friend!'

'Wait until Bucharest; the cafés there are scarcely inferior to those of Paris. You'll see! Come on now!'

And so I saw very little of the sights of Split.

Back in the air, we had the benefit of thick cloud cover as we climbed above the first range of mountains. Unseen far below, the wildest regions of Bosnia thrummed with the hoofbeats of bandits and brigands in their quaintly colourful costumes; then we crossed into Serbia. I thought I now smelled the stench of war, but that was surely an olfactory illusion, blood and smoke in the mind's nose, so to speak, rather than in my real nostrils. I covered my face with a pocket-handkerchief. Through a narrow break in the clouds I saw we were directly over the Morava River. Scipio told me that we required another fuel stop.

We landed outside a town called Zaječar and I was nervous as we got out of the plane, but there was no fighting here: we were far north of the main theatre of war, which was Macedonia. We successfully haggled for fuel and returned to the skies. Scipio flew all night. I felt guilty that he had taken this responsibility entirely upon himself, but this simply wasn't the time or place to give me flying lessons. Shortly after midnight we passed over the border into Romania, and when the sun rose on the following day I was greeted with an astounding sight.

The clouds had dispersed and below us spread the true wonderland of Wallachia, with picturesque villages nestled in the Carpathian foothills. I enjoyed this spectacle as the sun warmed my face. There was no evidence of war or carnage down there either: the scene was tranquillity itself! But I didn't relax too much, because the greatest ordeal still lay ahead.

The hours grew old in contemplation. Scipio began a gradual descent, and on the horizon I saw the towers and houses of a city.

Bucharest at last! The fabled Paris of the East!

Incidentally, I've never understood why places must be compared with other places instead of with themselves, but that's not something I intend to discuss further here. Time is short!

Scipio narrowed his eyes. 'Something big is happening.'

We were flying low over the city, and he pointed down into the tangle of streets. I couldn't see anything remarkable at first, then I realised that a large crowd had gathered in one of the parks. I learned later that this park was actually named the

Gradina Cişmigiu and was a delightful relic of the Turkish occupation of long ago. In the centre of the park was a large lake and in the middle of the lake was a —

'What a bizarre aeroplane! Look at its engine!'

'Yes,' said Scipio, 'and it seems to be armed with a very peculiar gun. Let's take a closer look at it, shall we?'

As we swooped lower and nearer, I was astounded that not one head in the mob turned to regard us. Then I saw they weren't real people but only a collection of shop mannequins, rows and rows of them, arranged like an invading army at the south side of the park. They were dressed in tattered uniforms and carried dummy weapons, but there was something not right. I confided my suspicions to Scipio.

'You're perfectly right,' he said. 'Those aren't Romanian uniforms but *Bulgarian* ones. Why dress a phoney army to resemble enemy soldiers? I wonder if this is a military exercise?'

I clicked my fingers. 'Of course! Practice for a Bulgarian invasion! It seems extreme. From what I've heard of the progress of the war there's no chance Bulgaria can ever reach Bucharest, let alone overrun the city! The Bulgarian army is having great difficulties even holding on to territory in its own country! But look there —'

The remarkable plane in the lake shuddered into life. It had no visible propeller and took off almost vertically. The pilot was a bulky figure who exuded menace even at this distance.

'Jukka Halme! I recognise him!' cried Scipio.

'How can we engage him? Our own aircraft is unarmed!'

'We can't. We must land first.'

At the north end of the park sat a group of generals on folding chairs. I hadn't noticed them until now. They *were* dressed in the correct uniform and I surmised they had gathered to witness and judge the demonstration that was about to take place. I imagine they gave it full marks when it was finally over. I have never beheld anything so devastatingly awful! Jukka's plane banked steeply and he dived at a shallow angle toward the army of mannequins. I expected him to strafe them with his nose-mounted gun but when it clattered into action, not one of the fake Bulgarians fell down. It seemed to me that Jukka had failed.

'What an imbecile! Every bullet missed!'

But Scipio shook his head. 'His gun doesn't fire bullets! Take a proper look, Mr Griffiths, and remember!'

I did as I was bid. Then I saw that the odd gun had been discharging a stream of cogs, bolts, nuts, wheels, screws and other metal components and that these individual parts were all fitting neatly together in front of the mass of blind and unfeeling soldiers. It seemed the gun was somehow assembling a machine at long distance, but what kind of machine? As the last component spat out of the mouth of the barrel, I heard Jukka's shout of exultation before he turned his plane again in a wide arc and landed it on the lake. Then he stood up in the cockpit to watch his work. I stopped watching him and observed the result.

Every cog had slotted into its rightful place; every wheel turned on its proper bearings; every rivet was tight.

The thing that stood in front of the ranks of soldiers was a cylinder of iron mounted on many legs. It had many arms and each arm terminated in a scimitar. Suddenly it pounced! The sharp blades flashed. Dummy heads sprang from dummy necks. Like a storm of steel, a vortex of vengeance, it charged through the Bulgarians, lashing out, the arms moving so fast they became a blur, the spindly legs stamping prone bodies, the mindless rage of the thing beyond all description.

Scipio Faraway rubbed his neck and winced.

'What's wrong?' I cried.

'Nothing much, Lloyd. Merely that I've seen that decapitation machine before! Jukka Halme never liked wasting an earlier invention, but he has excelled himself this time! He has combined the old with the new to build a weapon of truly ferocious power!'

'I would hate to see it employed against living men.'

'You were lucky not to.'

'What are his next plans, Scipio?'

'Until now, his decapitation device has been too bulky to be of use in warfare, but it seems he has finally developed a method of transmitting it in pieces at high velocity. He also has a plane capable of flying fast, high and acrobatically enough to avoid anti-aircraft fire and deliver his weapon to the front line. He's a genius!'

'The generals seem pleased with the outcome!'

'I know Jukka. He will have told them that he intends only to eradicate the Bulgarian army, but in fact he'll do his best to remove the heads of all the civilian inhabitants too. We must stop him. Romania can win this war cleanly, without *his* devilish tricks ...'

The Ending

Scipio searched for a suitable place to land. It was not possible to land in the park itself, for there wasn't enough room on the lake; and the streets in the vicinity were too narrow to use as runways. We finally put down in a spacious square south of the old town. Scipio hailed a coachman, and with scarcely a pause for breath we jumped aboard and directed the old fellow to take us to the Gradina Cişmigiu.

The *droshky* we sat on was comfortable enough, but I was bemused by the method of letting the coachman know whether we wished to turn right or left. He wore a kaftan sprouting two cords and we pulled on one or the other as he lashed his black Orloff horses to faster speed. Scipio explained that the fellow was a member of the Skopţi sect, religious dissidents who ritually castrated themselves because they believed the generative organs were the source of all sin. Needless to say, they castrated themselves only *after* they had fathered successors…

Scipio appeared to know Bucharest well. He pointed out various sights as we passed them. 'That hostelry is called *Hanul lui Manuc* and we can find good rooms there later. It was founded by an Armenian a century ago and is the most delightful place to stay in the city.' And a little later: 'See that fine tavern? That's the *Carul cu Bere*, and when this dreadful mess is over we'll go there to slake our thirst!'

We stopped at the gates of the park, paid the coachman and ran inside. I didn't pause to worry about the consequences, I simply followed Scipio. I trusted him implicitly. A pale man waved his hands and cried, 'Stop! The park is restricted! I saw you land. No-one else was looking but I saw you! You aren't allowed to enter this —'

Scipio glowered at him, and the man retreated.

He was a feeble guard indeed!

We surveyed the situation. Jukka was standing on dry ground, talking to the generals. Then he turned away from them and opened the door of a refrigerator that was standing to the side, but one of the generals asked a question and distracted him. Scipio frowned, stepped forward and shook the pale man. 'We want information!'

The pale man spluttered, 'I don't deserve such treatment. I'm not well, not well at all! I didn't want to guard the park; they wouldn't even give me a pistol for the task. I'm Professor Bogdan Velicu and I don't belong here. He's evil, I tell you, evil! It's not my fault. I did everything I was told, but he still took my organs away from me!'

Scipio released him. 'What's Jukka doing now?'

Velicu answered, 'That first flight was merely to demonstrate his gun and decapitation device. He used ordinary fuel in the engine of the plane because he can't afford to waste the special fuel. There's only a tiny piece left! He has persuaded the generals of the viability of his weapon. He will now insert the special fuel into his modified engine and use it to reach the front line at unbelievable speed, and then he will chop the Bulgarian boys into gobbets of quivering gristle.'

'Special fuel? In that refrigerator, you mean?'

Velicu nodded, and before I rightly knew what was happening, Scipio was running toward the generals. Nobody noticed until he reached them and there was a struggle near the refrigerator. Jukka stood back with eyes that were inscrutable and then he smiled. The generals shouted orders and adjutants came and seized Scipio.

'I must help him!' I bellowed, but I didn't move.

Velicu plucked my sleeve and pointed. I saw Jukka approach the open door of the refrigerator with a swagger; he reached in and picked up some object too small for me to discern.

Then he walked with it to the side of the lake.

His plane was moored there. He opened the cover of the fuel tank and dropped the contents of his hand through the hole. He replaced the cover and climbed into the cockpit. He cast off the mooring rope and started the engine. It screeched and thundered.

The generals and the adjutants turned to look.

Scipio Faraway slipped away!

He ran back and joined me. Velicu groaned.

'You failed!' I whimpered.

But Scipio merely smiled and said, 'I might be able to take you for that glass of beer sooner than you think.'

Jukka's plane rose at a steep angle. The Finn was laughing, and even at this distance we caught a few of his words. 'I will slaughter every citizen of every city, town and village in Bulgaria ... Then I will return and treat Bucharest in the same manner ...'

'He's truly insane,' Velicu stammered.

'Watch,' said Scipio.

The engine of the aircraft coughed. It sputtered. It died. The plane was now at an altitude of several thousand feet. The Finn's expression was lost beyond the range of eyesight, but Scipio had taken a naval spyglass from an inner pocket of his black pea coat.

He studied the situation, passed the spyglass to me.

Jukka was screaming and laughing.

At the same time! Horrid!

The plane stalled. It fell like a dead vulture.

Somewhere far to the south it crashed. I prayed that nobody had been killed in the collision, apart from Jukka, of course ... A thin curl of smoke spiralled into the sky.

Scipio said, 'Probably a good idea to take our leave.'

'I couldn't agree more!'

We hurried out of the park back in the direction of the tavern. I think I must have been in shock. My brain was spinning and the next thing I remember is sitting at a pavement table with a glass of foaming beer in my hand. Scipio drank his own down and ordered a glass of vermouth. The waiter asked if he wanted ice with it, and I'll never forget Scipio's strange answer. 'No, I have my own, thank you.' He was a constant source of amazement to me, that mysterious sailor without a ship.

When the vermouth arrived, Scipio dropped a tiny piece of ice into it. I blinked as it melted quickly to nothing. *Monsieur* Faraway swirled his glass and tasted the mixture with delight.

'I don't understand anything,' I confessed.

Scipio smiled. 'It's simple enough. When I reached the refrigerator and saw what was inside, I had a sudden inspiration. I exchanged what was in there for an object I had on me that looked identical. My substitute turned out to be very bad fuel, however.'

'You trickster! What was it?' I asked.

'A diamond, ' said Scipio, 'given to me by the grateful inhabitants of a village in Sierra Leone. That's all.'

While I sat there, musing on the peculiarity of life, a drone disturbed my peace. For an instant, I thought that Jukka Halme had somehow come back to life, that my head was still destined to be removed from my poor shoulders by his infernal contraption.

But in fact it was a different plane, *our* plane!

Scipio stood as it approached us. 'That Velicu fellow is piloting it! He must have taken note of where we landed. I wonder what he wants? Soon find that out!' He used his spyglass to get a closer look. 'There's murder in his eyes. He's coming for us!'

'I wonder why?' I blurted naively.

Scipio said, 'He hated Jukka and was happy to see us defeat the Finn, but Velicu is no traitor; he's a patriotic Romanian and he considers us to be saboteurs. After all, we *did* destroy Jukka, who had been hired by the government of King Carol. I feel sorry for him up there. He's in a moral maze and there's only one way out. That plane isn't armed, so I surmise he intends to crash it into us —'

'A suicide attack?' I was incredulous.

'Why not?' grinned Scipio.

'My dear friend, this is the 20th Century. Suicide attacks belong to an older, more barbaric age, surely?'

'All the same, I think we're in danger…'

Velicu was still climbing. It was clear he intended to put the aeroplane into a steep dive from as great an altitude as possible. He wanted as much momentum as he could get. I guessed that the entire tavern would become rubble in the aftermath of his attack.

Up and up he went, finally reaching the apex of his curve. Shaking his head, Scipio lowered his spyglass.

'Drink up, Mr Griffiths, while you can!'

I did so. Too fast perhaps.

For now a new buzzing assailed me. I thought my ears were deceiving me, for the drone of the engine seemed to come from *behind* me. I shook my head, but the effect grew more pronounced. Finally I couldn't resist a glance back over my shoulder. I reeled at the sight. An aircraft skimmed the roofs of Bucharest, a fantastical craft decorated with filigree designs, with elegant curved wings and a bearded pilot dressed in robes. Was this sight the result of too much beer?

The exotic pilot looked down and waved.

'Salaam, *Monsieur* Faraway!'

'Hello again, Rais Uli!'

'I appear to be a few degrees off course!'

'Yes indeed, Rais Uli.'

'May I perform a service for you?'

'If you would be good enough. The pilot in that other plane hopes to send us to the next world.'

'Leave him to me. Farewell, Scipio!'

I gasped in disbelief and rubbed my eyes as the exotic pilot levelled an ornately carved musket of improbable length, aimed carefully and pulled the trigger. I saw Velicu's plane falter. The professor was dead. His corpse pulled back on the control stick and the pride of the Bessarabian air force headed out of the city, while the Riffian equivalent continued on its long, utterly remarkable way to Tibet.

'The Barbary Corsair,' explained Scipio.

I frowned. 'Yes, of course. His aircraft has no propeller.'

Scipio winked. 'Let's go.'

'You want to give me a tour of Bucharest?'

'I think that's a superb idea. There are many places worth seeing near here. We'll begin with the Royal—'

The sound of *yet another* engine interrupted him.

'What can it be this time?' I cried.

Scipio said, 'Sounds like a pulsejet to me.'

I looked up. At the end of the street a bicycle came into view, but one with a very unusual quirk. It was powered by a homemade jet engine! An automatic feeder dropped grenades into a combustion chamber. The man who sat astride it wore equally crude armour and carried a lance; he was a curious parody of an ancient knight.

I sighed and turned to Scipio.

'Permit me to introduce you to Mr Jason Rolfe.'

'He's going to charge you.'

'Will you help me survive the encounter?'

Rolfe slammed down his improvised visor and accelerated his lunatic machine toward me. His lance was aimed at my chest. A second before it made contact, Scipio stepped in front of me, seized the point and pulled. The lance came out of Rolfe's grip, and as the bicycle passed our table the sailor casually swung the pole like a monstrous club. The butt struck the automatic feeder and damaged it.

Grenades fell into the combustion chamber at a ludicrous rate. With a yell of terror, Rolfe accelerated away. He was soon lost as he struggled to steer through the warren of streets. We watched as he failed to apply his brakes; his engine was stuck at maximum thrust. Scipio said, 'If he can stay on the saddle and find a way to cross the Bosporus, he might reach the Himalayas before Rais Uli!'

We laughed together, like old comrades.

I had an impulsive thought. 'Will you come back to

Wales with me? I could do with your assistance against Ben Gordon and Hugo Bloat. I have a feeling our fates are still linked.'

Scipio considered my proposition and finally said, 'I understand there's a Welsh resistance movement against the English? If that's true, I'll come. I always support the underdog ...'

'But first a brief holiday in Bucharest?'

'Yes, yes, I think so.'

And throwing back our heads we laughed.

PART TWO: DISTANTO

THE GARGANTUAN LEGION

The Lance

The first European invaders of Mexico arrived in 1517 on 4 March after a hazardous voyage from Cuba. They were Spaniards, and the captain of that expedition was Francisco Hernández de Córdoba; he had three ships under his command. The original intention was simply to sail from Cuba to the nearby Isla de la Juventud in order to procure slaves. A huge storm blew the little fleet off course; and when land was sighted it turned out to be the impressive Yucatán Peninsular.

His ships cautiously followed this unknown coast until they reached a spot where a stone pyramid reared above the trees. This was a surprise for Córdoba; his inability to assimilate the fact that sophisticated civilisations might exist so far from the Old World led him to refer to the pyramid and the city it served as *El Gran Cairo*, as if they were a Moslem creation. So it was that Mayan buildings first came to the attention of Europeans. And truly those Europeans were intimidated.

But Córdoba was a typical soldier of his times, a *conquistador*, and he failed to see any merit whatsoever in refusing to make landfall and claim the entire region for the Spanish Empire. He ordered his fleet to anchor as close as possible to shore. Then he made preparations to lead a force onto the beach. The inhabitants of the strange city hurried to the sands to stare and marvel at the Spanish vessels; and some of them launched canoes and paddled out to greet the peculiar visitors.

Córdoba assumed these primitives would regard him as a god, but this was a foolish fancy on the part of the captain, for the Mayan race were far less superstitious than the other tribes the *conquistadors* had encountered in the Americas; unknown to the captain, the Mayans had seen Spaniards before. Although Córdoba's crew were the first European invaders of this domain, they weren't actually the first visitants. Two shipwrecked sailors had preceded them by half a dozen years.

In 1511, a ship under the command of Diego de Nicuesa floundered in heavy seas and was smashed to pieces while sailing to Hispaniola. Taking to a longboat, the survivors drifted for many days. Finally they washed up on the Yucatán shore and staggered inland. There were soon apprehended by the locals, and most of the castaways were sacrificed immediately; the others were enslaved. Those who were enslaved were worked to death, all apart from the toughest pair of the company.

Gonzalo Guerrero and Jerónimo de Aguilar were their names, and they preserved their lives through luck and sheer stamina. Guerrero impressed his captors with his bravery and strength. Not only was he set free, but he was made an honorary Mayan and eventually became a minor chieftain in his territory. Both men were living close to *El Gran Cairo* while Córdoba fancied himself the first Spaniard to gaze on the pyramids and houses and inhabitants of this mysterious civilisation.

The Mayans already knew that the Spaniards were men, not gods, but nothing of this was suspected by Córdoba, whose strategy was still to act like the avatar of a terrifying divine force. But he waited patiently on the deck of his ship for the curious canoes to reach him, and tried to communicate with the occupants with crude sign language when they arrived alongside his flagship. He was reasonably successful in his efforts. Strings of green beads were lowered down into the canoes.

The hour was late; the sun was setting. The Mayans made

it plain that they would return the next day, and it seemed best to Córdoba to wait until the resumption of daylight before attempting a landing. The night boiled in the sweats of anticipation, as Córdoba wasted slow tropical time in his cabin, playing at dice with a few officers. At last he dismissed them and went to sleep. Dawn appeared on the horizon shortly afterwards as the signal to rise and oversee developments.

The Mayans began gathering on the beach. Now they were numerous indeed and armed with slings and bows. Nonetheless they maintained the friendly manner of the previous day. They paddled out to Córdoba's ships and invited the *conquistadors* into the canoes to be ferried ashore, and the Spaniards accepted the offer without hesitation, for they too were armed, with muskets and crossbows. Córdoba carried a lance he had borne from Spain, a weapon precisely as tall as himself.

As soon as the canoe that held him reached land, Córdoba called to his priest to give him the crucifix. The priest was horrified. He had forgotten to bring it! Córdoba scowled and paced the sand in dismay, uttering curses into his beard. For without a symbolic planting of a crucifix in the ground, the domain couldn't be claimed for Spain. The priest cowered, then came out with a notable suggestion. A crucifix, he claimed, could be created on the spot, improvised from available materials.

Córdoba regarded this idea as a fine solution to the crisis. Into the soft sand he stabbed his lance, then bound his own musket to it at right angles with lashings of cord. Kneeling before this rough simulacrum of the most true and holy cross of their faith, the *conquistadors* pledged to occupy the land in the name of God and the King of Spain. Then they stood and eyed their hosts warily. The Mayans kept smiling, offered to lead the Spaniards to the city and feed and entertain them there.

Half expecting an ambush, Córdoba and his troops allowed themselves to be guided into the jungle. Mayan warriors were hidden in the branches of trees; they dropped stones on the heads of the invaders, who relished a chance to fight. Crossbow bolts pierced flesh; the stink of gunpowder and blood drifted through the forest. The Spanish were outnumbered. Mayans fired arrows with tips that shattered on contact into the *conquistadors*, and these fragments caused an excruciating death.

The order to retreat was shouted. The invaders hurried across the sand back to the canoes, with arrows, darts and stones felling them as they ran. Córdoba was closely pursued by three warriors. He tripped and sprawled on the beach; his sword was flung out of reach. Now his enemies howled in triumph as they bore down on him. But he reached out, felt the shaft of the improvised cross. Hauling himself to his feet, he swivelled the musket and pulled the trigger. There was no need to aim.

The flint sparked and the weapon discharged with an incredible sound, a roar of fury and callous joy. The projected ball passed through the torso of the first pursuing warrior and also penetrated the second. The third lost his nerve at this sight, turned and ran. Staggering and screaming, Córdoba reached the nearest canoe and was soon paddled back to his fleet with the other survivors. The ships subsequently returned to Cuba. And so the first invasion of Mexico was a convincing failure.

For several days, the lance remained where Córdoba had thrust it, but the ruler of the city finally decided to claim it. The moment he plucked it, he realised something about it had changed. The crucifix is a symbol of a particular type of holiness; the musket is a symbol of war. The vibrations when the weapon was fired had passed into the lance, and in some manner the primal energies of holiness and war were now blended: the lance was saturated with both qualities simultaneously.

When the Spaniards returned years later to do a better job of conquest, the ruler of *El Gran Cairo* gave the lance to Gonzalo Guerrero, the castaway who had converted to the

Mayan cause. Guerrero worked as a tactician for the Mayans. He showed them how to defeat the invaders in skirmishes, for he was familiar with the thought processes of the *conquistadors*. The mystical lance was carried by him into dozens of successful battles but eventually the Spaniards proved too stubborn to defeat.

What happened to the lance in the aftermath of Guerrero's death is an unsolvable mystery, but presumably the Mayans took good care of it, for it reappeared almost three centuries later in the hands of Miguel Gregorio Antonio Ignacio Hidalgo y Costilla y Gallaga Mandarte Villaseñor, a man better known as Miguel Hidalgo and generally acclaimed as the godfather of Mexican independence. There was surely Mayan blood in his veins, an arterial connection with those brave warriors.

The lance became also his symbol and totem, a lever to break open the manacles of the Spanish Empire; thus its destiny continued in new hands. Tired of the impositions of the occupiers, Hidalgo raised a fierce army of peasants dedicated to revolution. Onward they marched. Stopping at the Sanctuary of Nuestra Señora de Guadalupe in Atotonilco, Hidalgo affixed an image of the Virgin to his lance and cried, 'Death to bad government!' Then he rushed his troops into battle joyously.

His insurrection was eventually crushed by the Spaniards, but Hidalgo had murdered the moral authority of the occupiers, and a short time later, Mexico was truly free. The lance vanished. The dusty decades sighed into the past like the pages of an old book. Mexico was an independent nation now but it acquired a pack of dictators. Each dictator was overthrown and replaced with another; at last, in 1910, there was a revolution that brought a bloody and justified end to this sequence.

This famous revolution was the work of such men as Emiliano Zapata, Pancho Villa and Francisco Madero. At first all went well with them. The new government attempted to put right the wrongs of history, to improve the miserable living conditions of ordinary people; but cruelty is never so easily cheated as that. A sly counter-revolutionary general by the name of Victoriano Huerta employed assassination and sabotage to install himself in power. Then he resurrected the repressions.

Huerta had all the delicacy of a cactus, and yet his regime was greeted with relief by most of the major world powers. He allied himself to Japan and Germany; and an arrangement with Paul von Hintze, the Ambassador of the Kaiser, ensured that in the event of a World War, mutual aid would flow in both directions. But disillusionment with Huerta soon set in. Poor organisation and a violent skirmish with United States marines in the port of Veracruz helped to propel Huerta into hell.

His abysmal government lasted from 18 February 1913 until 15 July 1914 and then he fled, his ministers scattering in all directions. One of his most fanatical followers happened to be in possession of the mystic lance. He was Mario Granieri, son of an Italian immigrant, and instead of taking refuge in the backwaters of Central America, he developed an audacious plan to sail to Spain, invade and conquer that noble country; but to do so by stealth. He believed the lance would aid him.

The Tavern

It had been supremely educational and enjoyable travelling across Europe in the wise company of Scipio Faraway; but anyone who crossed borders at that time couldn't fail to notice how clouds of war were gathering, and because clouds of war are always storm clouds, I won't deny that I pulled the collar of my coat symbolically higher around my neck as we reached the magnificent city of Dresden. My reflexes often made Scipio grin. We found a cheap hotel and then he said:

'Look here, Mr Griffiths, you'll have to excuse me for tonight. There's someone I want to see who lives here.'

'An old flame perhaps?' I smiled.

He nodded. 'A girl I once had a connection with. The daughter of the last authentic alchemist in Germany.'

'Alchemy! You don't approve of that nonsense?'

'It depends,' he answered.

'You never fail to amaze me. Surely, trying to make artificial gold is the proper occupation of charlatans?'

'That's not what real alchemy is about, Mr Griffiths, but I don't care to argue such topics at the present time. I'm interested in the girl, not in what her father did. I promised to visit her if I happened to be in this town, and now I'm here and must keep my word.'

'Go ahead. I'll be fine on my own,' I said.

'I'll see you tomorrow morning. Then I'll show you the sights of this incredible place. Until then, farewell!'

And off he went, his black pea coat buttoned to the throat, his creased cap tilted at the angle always described as 'jaunty'. He looked just like the adventurer he was. I had no doubt that the girl in question would swoon into his rough arms the moment he appeared. How many damsels around the world had given him their hearts? Hundreds? Thousands! Certainly I was envious, but I was also acutely aware that I could never compete with him, so I smiled with resigned tolerance.

The hours passed slowly. I started reading a book, a volume loaned to me by Scipio. *Candide* by Voltaire. But I wasn't in the mood for whimsy and polemic, however accomplished. Even the amusing wordplay failed to satisfy me. I grew pensive. We have all grown pensive at times in our lives, its roots spreading through our brains, its leaves bitter with anxiety. That's wordplay too. I closed the volume.

Our journey overland from Romania back to Wales was half done. As historical events seethed around us, it was becoming increasingly difficult to travel without harassment from border guards. War was certainly on its way, perhaps within the next few months. I shuddered and lay on the bed, staring at the ceiling. It was growing dark outside and I was bored. At last I decided to go out and entertain myself.

I had no map and no guidebook, and I didn't know anyone who lived there, but my advantage was that I was Welsh. Even the most belligerent of the locals would probably fail to recognise my accent. If accosted by a mob of patriotic ruffians, I would simply deny my British nationality and speak in Welsh. That might seem a cowardly recourse; but I'm a survivor, not a hero, not a skilled fighter like Scipio.

I wandered the streets alone. A city of incomparable grace, Dresden. If only I hadn't already visited so many other cities of incomparable grace! I hope you appreciate the wistfulness of that comment. Europe was packed with monumental grace in those days. I turned down a narrow alley. Fogs poured down it, having overflowed the banks of the cold river. Losing my way in the soupy labyrinth, I

RHYS HUGHES

chanced on a tavern, pushed my way within. I ordered a stein of beer and sat at a table.

Another man was also seated at that table, hunched in the shadows. In the flickering firelight only part of his face was visible. I studied it with a frown. He turned to meet my gaze. I jerked in surprise. It was Scipio! This coincidence wasn't so weird really; it was logical that he might choose to meet his girl in a tavern. I hoped he didn't think I had followed him! Then I realised that he had changed his clothes. Not only that: he had managed to grow a thin moustache and lose a finger!

RHYS HUGHES

Shipping Out

It was awkward sitting there in silence, so I said, 'Didn't you find her? Or maybe she didn't want to see you?'

'I beg your pardon?' he answered slowly.

Acutely embarrassed, I tried to make amends for my clumsiness with the offer of buying him a beer. 'No thanks, it's time to go back,' he said politely. 'I've drunk enough,' he added.

I drained my own brew, wiped my mouth on my sleeve. 'As you wish. Nothing much to do at the hotel, though.'

He frowned. 'Hotel? I'm referring to my ship.'

'Ship? You've acquired a ship? That was quick!' I was overjoyed for him. He had been without a vessel for far too long; and for a man with brine flowing in his veins, that's a situation only marginally preferable to losing all his limbs and senses. 'Well done!'

'Yes, of course I have a ship,' he said in a puzzled voice.

'Let's leave at once, in that case!'

We stepped out of the tavern together, into the fog, which had clotted into a yellowish froth that lapped the walls of the houses on both sides of the narrow alley. Visibility was reduced to the distance of one's own hand in front of one's face; the streetlamps were ghostly haloes, indistinct, eerie and somehow menacing. But he set off with a confident step and I trusted his judgment entirely. His instincts hadn't let me down yet. The twists and turns of the maze ahead were considerable, but I assumed he was heading unerringly in the direction of the river.

'You never cease to impress me, *Monsieur* Faraway...'

'Are you quite sure about that?'

'Indeed. How can you doubt my sincerity?'

'I doubt anything I'm permitted to.'

'Ah yes! A joke, of course!'

He shrugged and I felt his shoulder rub against my own, for I refused to wander too far away from him in this creamy murk. We continued like that for perhaps half an hour. I couldn't smell the river but it had to be just ahead of us. Where else would a captain choose to moor a ship? But up to a lonely old door he went, fumbled in his pocket for a key, opened it wide and stepped into a narrow bare passage.

The passage led to a spiral staircase. He climbed this and I followed. It was utterly mystifying. The river couldn't be upstairs! Or could it? Right at the very top, another door opened onto a flat roof. We were on top of a tall building, perhaps an apartment block or factory, I couldn't tell which. Despite the elevation, the view was negligible. Just colourless lights, very vague, in the congealed fog. For a dreadful moment I wondered if reality itself had dissolved back into nothingness.

This idle fancy passed as I realised that my companion was climbing a rope ladder. I couldn't see the top of it, and the illusion was strange, as if he was engaged in climbing onto the other side of the sky like an angel or steeplejack employed by the gods, but presumably it led to another roof. The building I stood on was clearly higher than I had supposed. I watched him vanish into the almost tangible clouds; after a moment of loneliness, I followed him. I'm not expert at climbing such flimsy ladders; it swayed like the pendulum of an over-wound clock.

It was longer than any rope ladder dangled from the side of any ship in my experience; but that experience was fairly limited, despite my travels, and so I clenched my teeth and continued upwards. Suddenly the sky was solid. A roof of metal above me! I was at a loss to account for this, but it made no difference to my ascent, for the rope ladder went through a hatch that was open. I hauled myself up and through the hole. I was exhausted by the climb and sprawled like a dying fish.

While I rested on the floor, the captain reeled in the rope ladder, shut the hatch, locked it and strode over to a console that resembled a forest of levers. I was clearly on the bridge of a ship, but it was a vessel of unusual design.

'*Monsieur* Faraway…' I began.

He ignored me, strode to the porthole with a megaphone.

Opening this window and raising the cone to his lips, he bawled, 'Cast off!' to some unseen accomplice below.

There was a violent lurch. I clung to the floor more tightly.

'Is the river in flood?' I gasped.

The captain turned to look down at me. Then he offered me a hand and pulled me to my feet, laughing as he did so. The vessel steadied itself, but I was grateful for a chair he offered me. I sat down firmly and watched as he busied himself with the levers on the console. Now I felt the throb of a powerful engine in the very substance of the hull. Through the extremely large portholes directly ahead, I could discern nothing at all. Just fog and pale glows. Not a good time to set sail!

I repeated my question. The captain turned and said, 'The river? What do you mean? Is it some sort of riddle?'

'By no means. The current seems strong, though.'

He smiled. 'The only currents that concern *this* ship are currents of air. I have no interest in the river at all. Only if we are forced to come down in it will I pay it any attention. What's the matter? You seem to be quivering with fright! Or perhaps you are sick?'

I shook my head and forced a grin, but doubtless my expression wasn't healthy. For I had only just realised what kind of ship I had come aboard. Not the regular sailing kind.

129

Not one of those. If I jumped out a window, I would fall a long way before landing.

Unbelievable as it sounds, I was on an airship!

Distance Is No Object

'Scipio!' I cried. 'What has got into you?'

The captain looked at me sharply. He rubbed his jaw with his damaged hand, the one with the missing finger, and for a moment he frowned with a twinkle of ferocious amusement in his eyes. Then his rage, if that's what it was, subsided and he merely said:

'Why do you call me by my brother's name?'

Had I not been seated in a chair, I would have toppled over in surprise. I had made a ludicrous mistake that would change my life forever. 'You mean to claim you are Scipio's twin?'

'Triplets we are, the Faraway Brothers, not twins. I am Distanto. Now it's my turn to enquire who *you* are.'

'Distanto? Distanto Faraway!'

He slitted his eyes again and said, 'You have the same name as me? Although I accept that this world is full of bizarre coincidences, I really don't believe that statement of yours.'

'No, you misunderstand. I am Lloyd Griffiths.'

I explained exactly who I was in fine detail, giving him an account of my work as a journalist, my meeting with *Monsieur* Scipio, our adventure in Romania, and the fact that I had received the shipless sailor's pledge to aid the struggle of my own people against the English. Distanto nodded at this and waved a hand for me to continue. He continued adjusting levers, steering the dirigible through the fog.

I told him that I wanted freedom for my nation; and yet, with evil war between Britain and Germany likely in the next few months, I was having second thoughts about stirring up trouble back in Wales. Far more ethical to postpone my dreams until the conflict was over! In fact I regarded it as my duty to fight a rampaging Kaiser.

He asked me why I thought this, and I told him.

I had always admired German culture, but the expansionist designs of the current regime were intolerable. The Hun would stamp Europe into a black mush if given the chance. The Welsh must join the English and put aside their ancient bitter grudges. This temporary rapprochement applied equally to the valiant Scots and Irish.

'You are quite the pragmatist,' he observed.

'The Kaiser is a tyrant,' I said.

Distanto replied calmly, 'I share your dislike of that mildewed dictator and certainly I'll aid my own country, France, in the event of an invasion, but I don't consider myself hugely patriotic. It's more the case of a choice between two bad options: I'm obliged to choose the least bad of the pair. I wonder if the same thoughts are going through your mind at this moment when you compare me with my brother?'

I scarcely knew how to respond to this cryptic remark, but fortunately he didn't appear to require an answer. He said, 'My navigator fell to his demise a few nights ago; I require a replacement. When you followed me out of the tavern and through the city, as if urged by destiny, I decided to take advantage of your unfathomable persistence and pressgang you into the vacancy. The post is now yours.'

'Navigator!' I blurted. 'But I'm untrained!'

Distanto smiled thinly. 'It's not difficult for a clever fellow to learn the rudiments on the job. Since the accident, I've been doing the calculations myself, but I'm already fully engaged steering this vessel, and frankly I'm overwhelmed with work. There are books on the subject in the navigator's cabin, which now belongs to you.'

'Don't you have any other crewmen who might fill the

role instead? I know you have accomplices; an unseen person cast off the mooring ropes when you shouted down the order.'

Distanto waved a dismissive hand. 'He was just a local I hired for that specific task after I landed. I fly alone now; but it's simply not safe to fly this way for long. The job is yours.'

'Very well, I accept, because I have no choice.'

'Thank you, Mr Griffiths. But what's the stink that rises from you? It's unlike any odour I've encountered —'

'I suffer from a rare fungal infection,' I explained.

'It's not unpleasant actually.'

'In no way does it hamper my competence.'

'Good. That's reassuring. Plot a new course, please. There are charts, compasses and other instruments over there.' He pointed with the stub of his severed finger at a table in the corner. I rose and went over to inspect the enigmatic tools of my new trade.

I found Dresden on the first map. 'Where are we headed to?' I asked, as I shuffled through the other charts.

'Brazil,' he replied nonchalantly.

'*Cachu planciau!*' I blurted.

'No doubt a vulgar curse in your own language?'

I nodded mutely and he smiled with approval and heaved a chuckle. I understood how different he was from Scipio. I'm not saying he was less brave, less resourceful or even less cultured; but he had a coarse strain in him that the other brother lacked. Whether I would feel more comfortable in his presence as a consequence, or less, remained to be seen. But for the meantime, my thoughts were elsewhere.

'Brazil's in the southern hemisphere!' I gasped.

'Most, not all,' he corrected me.

'And why are we going there, *Monsieur*?'

'Because distance is no object.'

I winced at this facile retort, and it seemed he shared my disgust with it, for he sighed and added quietly:

'To pick up the rest of my fee. Dom Daniel paid me half in advance; I completed his commission, and so I go to claim the other half. I don't fly this airship just for my own amusement. I am in business. I advertise my services to anyone in need of them. Even an airship captain must eat, Mr Griffiths. I was paid to fly to the Arctic and that's what I did; now I'm on my way back to Brazil, as arranged.'

'The Arctic? Is that where you lost your finger?'

It was an indelicate question, certainly, but it escaped my lips before I might hope to restrain it. And Distanto wasn't offended at all. He laughed and shook his head. 'Hardly! You suppose frostbite was the cause? I was the agency of its removal, Mr Griffiths. When I was a boy I was told by a fortune-teller that I had no fate line.'

I closed my eyes and remembered Scipio, his brother. 'So you decided to carve one into your own flesh, into the palm of your hand? In order to control your destiny! Is that correct?'

'Yes indeed. But I used a hatchet and missed!'

A violent shudder went through me. It lasted only an instant but I was profoundly affected by it. Desperate to change the subject, I asked about Dom Daniel, his client. And he told me. Dom Daniel, it so happened, was a mad genius, a prophet of sorts, a man who dreamed terrible dreams of a future blighted by the pollution of industry, of a coming age when greed and rapacity would despoil our planet. These dreams were so powerful it was impossible for Dom Daniel to sleep peacefully; so he had resolved to cheat the nightmares as best he might.

Distanto continued, 'He believes that within the next hundred years or so, the forests will be mostly gone; that humanity will have rendered our environment poisonous and ugly. Our race is fated to consume itself into oblivion. Such is his particular creed.'

Bicycle Interlude

While Distanto related the story of the strange Brazilian who had engaged his services, a different visionary was crossing into Persia. The eccentric inventor Jason Rolfe was mounted on a bicycle with a pulsejet engine; he had already crossed Europe on the device, dressed in a suit of homemade armour; he had also traversed the length of Turkey. Now he was entering a realm even more exotic and evocative.

Once he had held a lance in his hands, a lance similar to that planted in a Mexico beach by Francisco Hernández de Córdoba centuries earlier; but it had been snatched from his grasp when he attempted to transfix Scipio Faraway while the mariner was patronising a pavement café in Bucharest. He was unarmed as a consequence; and in the brigand-infested parts now to be cycled through, that was a disaster.

So he planned to make himself a substitute. Unable to dismount from his machine because of its astounding velocity, he had to devise a way of manufacturing the weapon while in motion. Far from being an impossible task, this could be achieved with only a little resourcefulness; and Jason Rolfe had no shortage of that. Already he had learned to eat and drink on the saddle, to collect food as he zoomed.

Although he attempted to remain on paved roads as much as possible, there were times when he had to veer off and proceed over the untamed landscape, whether to avoid wild goats or grosser hazards. The roads in this part of the

Near East weren't much smoother or easier than the open country anyway; and his bicycle was a stout one, with superb suspension and vulcanised tyres of extreme durability.

Often he passed through forests and orchards. Fruit sometimes fell into his lap; other times he was able to reach out and grab it as he passed. As for quenching his thirst, the rains were sweet, and the visor of his helmet was an inverted beak that channelled them into his mouth. Mr Rolfe's odd expedition wouldn't fail for lack of nourishment, that was certain, even if it was destined to come unstuck somehow.

Over the Zagros Mountains he went, into Persia; and through secretive groves he raced, blossom-heavy branches lashing his face like the scented whips of resentful djinn. With a gauntleted hand he broke off some of the straighter branches, bound them together with the cord he carried in a box bolted to the crossbar between his knees. Also in this supply chest was an extremely vicious knife, a camping tool.

This blade formed the head of his new lance; and a formidable weapon the end result was! Fully 30 feet long, it jutted in front of the demonic bicycle like the horn of a mutant unicorn, glinting with dew or moonlight, a deterrent to any bandits he might encounter! And it would serve also as the agency of his vengeance, if by an unlikely chance he encountered me a second time, the bounty still on my head.

How curious to make a lance from scratch like he did, from whatever materials came to hand! We should contrast his actions in this regard with those of Mario Granieri. Remember him?

Mario was the follower of Huerta who fled Mexico and sailed to Spain with the fabled lance of Córdoba in his possession. When he arrived and established himself, he decided to perform an unwise experiment; for he had fallen under the spell of alchemy, poor Mario, and believed he could improve the power of the lance. Specifically, he thought he might turn its head into gold, an amazing status symbol!

And so he melted down, in a crucible, the metal point

that history had already imbued with a remarkable propensity to create change. The steel bubbled and squeaked in the ceramic vessel; and Mario danced around it like an uncoordinated devil-worshipper …

The European Desert

We finally broke out of the fog on the southern side of the Alps. This was a relief, for I had started to feel like an imprisoned angel, surrounded only by solid whiteness, the walls of a grotesque celestial jail. Of Germany and Switzerland I saw nothing from the air; only when we crossed into France did the weather allow a spectacular view.

I took great delight in gazing at the meadows and towns far below; but I wasn't permitted to shirk my responsibilities. Distanto made sure I paid close attention to my calculations and route-plottings. Too many airships had gone missing because of slack navigation in recent years; he had very little desire that his own should do so too.

And yet there were times when he would engage the autopilot, set the engine to the minimum speed and attempt to show his friendlier side. He wasn't an especially likeable man, but I soon realised he was inept rather than misanthropic; his social skills were negligible, but he didn't have an obnoxious soul. This is still my judgment.

He told, for instance, the tale of Dom Daniel with relish; but there was no mockery in his tone. That Brazilian gentleman had spent the majority of his decades, from youth to old-timer, collecting the seeds of plants, for his ambition was no less than the preservation of the complete flora of the South American jungles. It was this collection, carefully sealed in flasks, that Distanto had flown to the far north.

'But that's no place for tropical vegetation!' I cried.

Distanto laughed at my naivety.

'Mr Lloyd, the world is full of surprises; despite my experiences I am still constantly caught out by it. Dom Daniel had come into ownership of a rare atlas. I forget who drew the maps inside it. Possibly it was the work of Hippolyto Joseph da Costa, the mystic. That name is nagging the back of my mind. The atlas was peculiar.'

'In what way?' I challenged.

'One of its engravings showed an Arctic island that was no less fertile and balmy than the Amazon forest. How so? It was warmed by volcanic activity, by steam and maybe magnetism; I can't vouch for the latter. The perfect nursery for his project! His seeds might be preserved there during the inevitable ecological disaster; in some future age, a more enlightened race, having learned its lesson, would discover the stash and thus be able to repopulate the blasted earth with beauty. A worthy dream or fancy for any man, don't you agree, my friend?'

I arched my eyebrows at this. '*Haliad hallt!*'

'Another curse? You want to know if the island was real? Yes, it was. It exists there, far to the north of Novaya Zemlya. Lush it is, an anomaly beyond any other on our entire globe.'

'And did you leave Don Daniel's seeds on it?'

'That's what I was paid to do.'

'A successful mission then, *Monsieur* Faraway!'

He smoothed his moustache.

'Not exactly, Mr Griffiths. After I secreted the first batch of seeds in a suitable location, I saw a commotion amongst the trees that already grew there; and I'm sorry to report that a dinosaur appeared and swallowed the sealed flasks one by one; this was an unforeseen eventuality. I could do nothing to prevent it. I didn't bother to deposit the second batch of seeds after that; they are still on board.'

'You will return them to Dom Daniel?'

'I will, but I still intend to claim my full fee from him. Dinosaurs weren't part of the deal. My vessel is unarmed and I wasn't paid to bag a trophy. I flew out of that prehistoric Eden as fast as helium bags and diesel engines could take me! I saved my skin.'

'A dinosaur! Surely you jest?'

'It looked like a triceratops, but I'm no expert.'

I had nothing to say in reply. I was too dazed. Perhaps he mistook my silence for contempt; he made a new effort to be friendly, and I realised even more acutely how desperately he needed a navigator. So I had some power over him; good to know this!

He said, 'Do you play billiards? There's a table in the recreation area. Yes, this gondola that dangles from the airship has more than one room! Later I'll challenge you to a game. I'm a master at the sport, but not vain enough to suppose I'm invincible.'

'Yes. I look forward to that, *Monsieur* Faraway.'

'Good. Proceed with your work.'

Across France we went and into Spain, following the east coast of that country toward the point where Europe and Africa loom close for a kiss or bite, depending on your political outlook. We veered inland, for I was making constant adjustments to our course, and soon we were in Almería, the only genuine desert on the European mainland. Yellow bleakness far below, scoured rock and dry riverbeds.

I rubbed my eyes. 'Are we in Africa already?'

'Not yet, Mr Griffiths. This desert is a sample, a taste, of the wastes that dominate the Maghreb. But still it is Spain, essentially Spanish in all its quirks; and down there, if you search hard enough, you will find *tapas* and flamenco, siestas and *Señoritas*.'

'Yes, I believe you; nonetheless it is strange.'

'The Almerían desert is partly of man's making. As Dom Daniel said, humanity is the despoiler of the Earth.'

'How can men create a desert?' I demanded.

'By diverting water, Mr Griffiths.'

'I understand. Reckless engineering projects?'

'The little water that does exist in the region is pumped to commercial greenhouses where enormous fruits are grown all year round. So Almería is a productive enough place; unfortunately the old towns and villages are depopulated. Thirst drove the inhabitants out. Some roughnecks refuse to leave and manage to survive, but generally it's a lonely corner of Europe. Having said that, what do you see?'

I opened the nearest porthole and poked my head through. 'Some kind of settlement, but it's not on my map.'

'Charts aren't always right, Mr Griffiths. My airship is running rather low on supplies, and soon we will be over the open ocean; this might be a good opportunity to land and restock.'

'On enormous greenhouse vegetables?' I smiled.

He nodded without obvious irony. 'The avocado pears grown here are bigger and perhaps more intelligent than many human heads. Yes, I think we ought to descend. I shall vent gas.'

I resisted the temptation to comment on this.

Down we went, and when we were only a dozen feet above the surface, he shouted, 'Cast out the anchor now!'

I did so. The iron implement landed on the desert floor with a muffled thump, bouncing and catching a barb on a cactus. Then Distanto ordered the lowering of the rope ladder; he climbed down first and I followed. On firm ground again, I stretched my limbs happily. The dusty settlement lay a mile or so to the south. We trudged.

We were equally dusty when we entered it. We passed beneath a crude arch made of planks badly nailed together. There was no pavement on the other side of the arch, just red earth.

The flag sagging on the flagpole didn't look right.

A typical Almerían village?

Hardly. It wasn't what I had expected. Not Spanish in character at all. The houses were made of planks and the single street was deserted save for horses tied up outside a saloon.

This saloon had swing doors. Tumbleweed rolled in front

of it. A pot of beans was bubbling within and the aroma was emerging in beckoning wisps; that's what my nose told me.

'No shops,' I remarked. 'Nowhere to buy vegetables.'

Distanto said, 'Let's go inside.'

We stepped into the saloon. Faces turned to stare at us. Men with long, drooping moustaches and hats with extremely wide brims stopped eating stew and playing cards. The bartender had a bottle of tequila in his hand but he was no longer filling glasses.

'Good afternoon,' said Distanto cautiously.

Then I realised something …

What fluttered on the flagpole outside was the *Mexican* flag.

A fat man stepped close to us.

He wore two bandoliers on his chest and his moth-eaten brown poncho was thrown back to reveal them. He also had a belt around his waist and holsters suspended from his hips, and in the holsters were revolvers. With slow, threatening movements, he inserted a cigar stub between his stained teeth, took a match out of his pocket.

Then he tried to strike a light on my cheek!

The match failed to ignite.

'Your steenking chin ees too soft, hombre!' he said.

Much laughter. Trouble!

The Syndicate

Kindly picture to yourself a rotting mansion in the dunes near Porthcawl. You know the one I mean. Newspaperman Ben Gordon, my former boss, and the evil Hugo Bloat, owner of the building, are huddled in the highest room. Since getting to know each other on my behalf, they have become inseparable, assisting each other's schemes. They still want me dead, but that's not the only plot that occupies their attention. At this very moment, in fact, they are planning a series of bomb attacks that they can blame on the Welsh Nationalists, not only to discredit the independence movement but also for financial reasons; Bloat has shares in English companies who are buying up land and resources in Wales, while Gordon wants a scoop to increase sales of *The Western Mail*.

They work well as a team, these two villains …

Having put the final touches to the details of their bombing campaign, they sit back and chuckle. 'And next?'

'Why not return our attention to Lloyd Griffiths?'

'Oh, *him*. Why I ever endured —'

'Come now, Mr Gordon, you weren't to know he was going to turn out despicable when you hired him. You probably imagined he would make a perfectly fine journalist. And so he did.'

'Humph! He has a conscience; I can't stand that.'

'Let's eliminate him then!'

They discuss many potential methods, including poison,

traps, trained beasts, but nothing seems suitable. Then Mr Bloat winks. 'Still a bounty on his head, isn't there?' he asks.

'Of course! But nobody has claimed it yet...'

'Let's withdraw it and use the reward cash to hire assassins instead. A single professional is more effective than a hundred amateurs. I wonder if you quite know why that should be?'

'Tell me, Mr Bloat, I'm listening attentively.'

'So you are, my dear Ben Gordon. Well now, a single professional has no wife to distract him. Ha!' The tears of mirth that fall from his withered eyes are oily. And he slaps his thigh.

'A good joke, very original. And yet all the same—'

'What is your precise objection?'

'Don't misunderstand me; I regard the suggestion of hiring an assassin with a surge of glee and awe in my bones. But we have no idea where Mr Griffiths currently might be. Why don't we hire many assassins, one from *every* country in the entire world? That way, it doesn't matter where he is, or where he goes. He'll still be got!'

'Ingenious! Brilliant! Yes, that's the solution!'

Never underestimate that pair ...

They have the resources to make discreet, effective enquiries through the channels of the criminal underworld; to advertise secretly for experts in murder; to transport the men and women thus recommended from any part of the globe to that mansion in the dunes near Porthcawl. And while they wait for the hired killers to arrive safely, Gordon and Bloat focus on their other projects, the bombs and embezzlements of a normal workday, for they are bellicose and versatile.

And within a month, the final assassin arrives.

By ship, train, horse, motorcar they have come, and also by aeroplane, even by submarine in one instance.

There are 195 countries in the world.

The assassins occupy the ground floor rooms; the furniture and carpets are mouldy and foul, but it's only a temporary arrangement. Gordon and Bloat are standing at the top of the rickety staircase at the end of a narrow hallway; they send down their voices, without following them in person. I wouldn't be flattered at the description they give of me, if I was present to hear it, though I admit its accuracy.

'Lloyd Griffiths must die! Without a jot of mercy!'

'We will kill him!' is the reply.

There are 197 assassins in the house; neither Ben nor Hugo notices the discrepancy.

The Great Work

Alchemy is more than just the chemistry of fools and primitives. Properly done, it's a mystic art that manipulates archetypal symbols of the soul and creates transcendent answers from arcane formulae. Mario Granieri was a true devotee of the discipline. He was forever playing with his retorts and flasks and bellows in his basement workshop. Although the processes of the ancient masters are extended metaphors, it doesn't hurt to experiment with real substances, with fire and metal.

When Mario melted down the head of the lance of Córdoba and added various elements to the bubbling sauce, he wanted only to turn the blade into gold, as I've already explained; but in fact something went wrong, or maybe it went right, and he ended up with three separate slivers of metal. Try as he might these wouldn't recombine; the lance head had partitioned its miraculous qualities, split them off from each other. One fragment was gold; the other two were black and brown.

He subjected these three shards to scholarly scrutiny, tested them with the objectivity of an authentic empiricist; the vibration of the musket, on that long ago beach, had blended into one substance the spiritual essences of holiness and war, and now he, the clever Italo-Mexican, had separated them again. The gold piece was pure holiness; the black, pure war; but as for the brown, that remained a mystery. What to do with these shards? He still needed a lance, for he was a soldier.

There is a tradition amongst the Italians of unusual weapons. Some of the curious devices that can be obtained from craftsmen in that land have an Arabic origin; the scissors dagger, for example, that makes a gash big enough to post a letter in; or the theft-proof sword with a blade so curved it slashes its own owner. *Signor* (or *Señor*) Granieri wanted to incorporate all the shards into his new lance, but a lance with three blades isn't a lance anymore; it's a trident. That didn't matter.

He designed a trident for himself, but it was no ordinary fork. It was a flick trident, the blades concealed inside the shaft. A quick motion of his wrist and out they would slide! When the weapon was ready he practised with it until he was adept. The trio of blades sprang out simultaneously, a variety of glints at the tip of the stout pole, three points with considerable penetrative power. Holiness, war and a surprise! This trident pleased him so much that he often caressed its length.

It certainly might be argued that Mario had misunderstood and warped the true intention of the alchemical arts. Many alchemists are very eager to stress that the processes involved are concerned with inner change and development; it was Jakob Boehme, influential in the late 16th and early 17th Century, who did most to encourage later initiates to regard alchemy as solely an inner discipline; the complex formulae and elaborate recipes were, for him, merely mnemonics on the long path of mental and spiritual evolution. But Boehme's influence wasn't entirely universal. Some others persisted with practical, messy alchemy.

And although most work done in this field was wasted effort, let every sceptic be reminded that Tiphaigne de la Roche, one of the brotherhood, invented photography more than 60 years before its 'official' discovery and did so entirely through alchemical methods! Mario Granieri loved his basement workshop. He was forever mixing elements and purifying them or trying to hatch something from the flames of his furnace. He believed that this ancient art might help his intended revolution succeed; that gold made here, in his own house, would fund the overthrow of the legitimate Spanish government. He was an optimist!

But he was also a nervous man. Huerta had never been popular abroad, and anyone associated with that dictator couldn't expect too much support or even sympathy from the general populace of the European nations. The soft intellectual elites would shun him. Mario felt tainted; his taint was an itch over his righteous skin. Mexico had gone mad, in his view, tricked by the blandishments of prissy radicals. A brand new Mexico, superimposed on a decadent Spain, would revitalise the faith of those who preferred the stability of strong regimes! Such individuals did exist even in Europe, he felt certain; the problem was finding them.

He crouched over his crucible, spooning molten iron.

He wasn't alone in his basement. He had assistants; women dressed in the bodices and skirts of harlots, flowers behind ears, stockings glistening in the light of his arcane fires. They washed his receptacles for him, gave him whatever he called for, typed his notes. In their spare time they made a little extra money upstairs, in the saloon.

When Mario first arrived in Spain, he had been nothing more than one more refugee, alone and poor. But he had a tongue of gold. Some say this was also a product of alchemy; a golden tongue from which flowed words that were very persuasive. He found a remote region where he might have peace and quiet for the scheme he had in mind; the desert of Almería. He soon attracted followers among the dispossessed people of the abandoned towns. They willingly converted to *Mexicanism*, wore gladly the ponchos and sombreros, drank deep of the fermented cactus juice, strummed large guitars and puffed Mariachi on trumpets.

Ay caramba! Ay ay ay ay ay! Arriba, arriba!

Mario ordered; they obeyed. Rapidly and happily they constructed this village for him, a perfect replica of an obscure Mexico pueblo. And as for Huerta? Mario had once been utterly loyal to the tinpot but had outgrown him now. If Huerta turned up, Mario wouldn't reject him outright; but the former dictator would have to know his place. There was a vacancy in the stables. Mario was the boss, the master …

His trident stood propped in a corner. He continued to spoon.

The door opened; through it came two figures and his chief henchman behind them, his pistol prodding spines.

'Boss, I caught thees pair sneaking around inside the saloon. I theenk they are spies. Look at thees ugly gringo! His steenking chin ees too soft to strike a match on! Shall I keeel them?'

Mario Granieri turned to stare at Distanto and me.

The Stealth Empire

'Whatta mistake to make, spying on me!' roared Mario, throwing down his spoon and glowering. 'No-one must know about this village. We aren't ready yet to make our move!'

'Shall I keeel them, boss? Shall I? Pleeese!'

'Not yet Pancho Henchman!'

The barrel behind me seemed to sag in disappointment.

'May I speak?' asked Distanto.

'No, gringo, you may not!'

Mario approached us, inspected the aviator carefully, sneered and gave me the same treatment. '*Cabrones!*'

'With respect, we are explorers, sir,' I said.

He cuffed me across the cheek.

'Whom do you work for? For the King of Spain?'

I shook my head. 'No!'

'Who then? For Zapata and those pigs back in Mexico, those socialists and traitors to the natural order?'

'Not them either,' said Distanto calmly.

'Then who?' bellowed Mario.

'For ourselves alone,' crisply replied Distanto.

Mario sighed, wiped the sweat of the furnace from his brow, smiled an awful smile and said, 'No matter.'

I misunderstood his comment. 'You'll let us go?'

Mario and Pancho Henchman burst into a laughter so despicable I can only describe it as 'yellow', the colour of rotting teeth. Then the alchemist spat on the floor and lectured us.

He told us about his schemes, his dreams, his hopes.

Obviously he intended to kill us!

Otherwise he wouldn't have said a single word.

But why he decided we should hear about his plans in detail before we died is a puzzle to me. Maybe he missed having an audience; the denizens of his village doubtless had heard it all before. I tried to pay attention, but I wasn't a model pupil and my mind was on other things, especially on the stark fact of my impeding destruction.

To my chagrin, Distanto seemed genuinely intrigued.

He asked intelligent questions.

Mario replied politely to some of these, but it was plain he didn't really care for his monologue to be interrupted too often. He explained the need for a new Mexico in Europe, a stealth empire, for it would be established in a host nation like a parasite, taking over from within. He envisaged that all future colonial adventures might be run in this manner. Having created a Mexican village in a remote locality as a base, it remained for him to set up a secret administration capable of doing everything the government of Spain did, in parallel. Then with a sideways flick of his followers, the old regime would be displaced, superseded.

'And Mexico, the *real* Mexico, will have moved to Europe. The maps in the atlases will need to be redrawn. Here is the Iberian Peninsula, they will say, and it contains two countries...'

'Portugal and Mexico,' I mumbled.

'Yes, gringo! For an idiot, you do have brains. Ay!'

'You forgot Andorra,' said Distanto.

Mario blinked unhealthy lids. 'What was that?'

'Andorra is an independent country on the Iberian Peninsula. And let us not neglect Gibraltar,' added Distanto.

Mario turned pale. His rage was so extreme that his legs shook and his knees knocked together like massive castanets. 'You dare to correct me! I am outraged by your insolence! Pig!'

'The truth is never insolent,' I muttered unwisely.

'You will die now! Spies!'

He clicked his blistered fingers. 'Pancho Henchman! I command you to take these devious swine outside.'

'Yes Boss. Shall I remove their steenking heads?'

'Do that, by all means!'

And Pancho Henchman jabbed his pistol into my back.

Distanto tried to distract our captor.

'You say that maps in atlases will be redrawn after your macrocosmic political alchemy turns Spain into Mexico; but in fact I have evidence that they need to be redrawn anyway.'

Mario narrowed his peepers. 'What mean you, hombre?'

'Have you heard of Hippolyto Joseph da Costa, a Brazilian sage? The maps he drew aren't normal ones.'

'Yes, I know him! He was an alchemist too!'

He gestured at Pancho Henchman to desist from executing us, at least for the time being. Distanto continued, 'If Hippolyto's geography is right, there's one country on the globe that still hasn't been officially discovered by outsiders. It's an Arctic Island that despite its northern latitude is warm enough for tropical life to thrive.'

'What is this island named, hombre?'

Distanto twirled his moustache. 'Hippolytomia.'

Mario laughed, his eyes watering.

'Indeed, indeed. I have heard of it and the man who named it. He was a mason as well as an alchemist and geographer; not a mason who builds walls, but one who rolls up a trouser leg and keeps secrets. A freemason! I have nothing against that lot; but tell me, have you ever heard of Sadegh Safani? Yet another alchemist...'

'I must confess that I haven't,' said Distanto.

'A Persian fellow. Perhaps he is still alive, I don't know. According to him, there are actually *two* countries on the surface of the globe that still haven't been officially discovered. The Arctic island is one. The other lies in a secret valley in the Himalayas.'

Distanto gazed at his shoes. 'I didn't know that.'

There was a lengthy pause.

Mario sighed. 'Your attempt to distract me has failed. *Qué pena*! But before I send you to your deaths, allow me to reveal the rest of my plan. I have made contact with likeminded individuals throughout Europe. This continent is crammed with malcontents who loathe the softness of the old governments and their liberal platitudes. In Italy, homeland of my fathers, a movement has come into existence that calls itself 'Fascist'. Its members are a strapping bunch of grim toughs!'

'You plan to ally yourself with them?' I asked.

'Not merely with them,' Mario replied, 'but with many other societies that are similar in style and purpose. Every European state seems to have at least one group of this kind. A sign of the times, no doubt! Letters have passed to and fro between these disparate groups. We have all resolved to work together; to aid each other overthrow, one by one, the pale, cowardly fools who currently rule in our midst!'

I frowned. 'Rule in the mist?' For some indescribable reason I thought of gorillas. Wearing crowns. Peculiar!

'In our *midst*,' said Distanto, wincing slightly.

Mario continued, 'We will deal decisively with every state in Europe. Together our alliance will overthrow unworthy kings and presidents and prime ministers and other morons. Our combined army of strongmen will form an invincible legion of doom!'

'I see. When does this begin?' asked Distanto.

'It already has!' shrieked Mario.

'And Spain is the first battleground of the greater campaign? Does this mean that foreign fighters are here?'

'Not yet. They are on their way right now!'

'I'm a journalist and maybe I can write a story about this,' I offered as a pathetic attempt to preserve my skin.

But Mario wasn't tempted to accept. He shook his head. 'No, you will die. Both of you. Wouldn't you like to know how? You will be forced to participate in a Wild West shootout.'

'What will happen to the winner?' Distanto asked.

'He will be hung,' smiled Mario.

'And if we refuse to fight each other?' I cried.

Mario's smile vanished. 'Then you'll be impaled alive on a cactus and left for birds to peck slowly. But if you agree, you will be given revolvers with only one bullet in each chamber.'

I turned to Distanto with a horrified expression, but he winked at me. I understood that he had formulated a plan of escape. I trusted him. No less resourceful than his brother, was he.

Flock Of Assassins

Assembled in the house of Hugo Bloat, the assassins wonder why it was necessary for them all to make the difficult journey there, merely to listen to a simple instruction that might have been conveyed by letter, telegram or telephone. 'Lloyd Griffiths must die!'

But when payment is good enough, they are willing to tolerate the odd behaviour of patrons; and Bloat and Gordon have offered them thrice the going rate. They are satisfied. They depart the house, each one intending to track down the victim in his or her own way.

These assassins are individuals, preferring to work alone.

But public transport in Wales is dire.

Because of infrequent and unreliable services, the pack of assassins is unable to disperse. They must all wait for the same bus; it's the only one that day. So the assassins remain clustered longer than any one of them had planned. And they converse with each other while they wait. Then, seated on the bus that trundles slowly from Porthcawl to Bridgend, they begin to enjoy and appreciate the companionship.

Before the vehicle reaches Bridgend, they have all decided to remain together, to work as a team. Incredible!

They board the train at the station and rattle down the rusty line to the city of Cardiff. From here they catch a ship to Bristol; and in Bristol, in the harbour, one of their number stands on the crumbling stone quayside and gingerly sniffs the air. This assassin is hairy and uncouth. He walks with a stoop and carries a gnarled club in one massive fist. His senses are preternaturally keen and he stinks badly.

He smells of sabre-tooth tiger fat!

Some of the more cultured assassins whisper together.

'Who is he? From whence comes he?'

So sharp is his hearing that he turns towards them and rasps, 'Me from land that have no name in my own language. In yours is sometimes called Hippolytomia. Lies far beyond snow and ice. Me called Unkoo. Land of my birth very dangerous. Monsters!'

'Fascinating,' comments the assassin from France.

'Very,' concurs the assassin from China.

'How did you manage to leave your island, Unkoo?' asks the assassin from Lithuania. 'If it's so remote?'

'Unkoo hide inside airship. It come down, hatch open, man come out and put some objects on the ground. Me climb through hatch when he not looking. Conceal myself under billiard table. Man come back, airship rise up, fly south. Land again. Me get out.'

'And where was that?' wonders the Egyptian assassin.

'Dresden. Nice city. Unkoo like!'

'Ah indeed, a gem of a place. Delightful and charming!' says another assassin, surely the one from Germany.

Unkoo resumes sniffing the air. 'Me catch scent!'

'What of?' asks the Dutch assassin.

'Lloyd Griffiths, our target!'

'How is that possible?' asks the Russian assassin.

'Unkoo recognise it. Back in house in the dunes, me sniff stair carpet, pick up pungent odour. Me wonder what make it. Hugo Bloat explain that Lloyd Griffiths visit his house once, that the journalist smell like that. So I think our victim has fungal infection of some kind. Me can smell it now. Lloyd Griffiths has been here too!'

'That's logical,' approves the assassin from Siam.

'What would he come *here* for?' wonders the assassin from Ethiopia. The answer is provided by the assassin from

Argentina, who is sipping a *yerba mate* gourd, and who drawls:

'Must have caught a ship from this harbour.'

'That's right!' cries the assassin from Ceylon. 'There's no explanation that makes sense other than that one.'

'Then we must get on a ship here too,' roars the Irish assassin, 'if we are to stand a chance of finding him.'

'Might as well!' concludes the assassin from Cuba.

'Let us get aboard this vessel,' suggests the Australian assassin, as he notices a liner docked nearby that is accepting passengers. A murmur of assent greets his proposition. The pack of assassins crosses the gangplank and takes up residence in the liner.

Meanwhile back in the house in the dunes ...

Hugo Bloat and Ben Gordon are buttoning up the final button of a suit that is extremely unconventional in style and size. It's big enough for both of them to fit inside. And that is precisely how they wanted it made. The fact of the matter is that money can buy almost anything; and a tailor who is asked to design a suit twice as wide as normal won't bat an eyelash if a wad of cash is thrust into his visage.

Bloat and Gordon had been getting on well. So well that they began to despise their own separateness. Why couldn't they occupy the same body, like conjoined twins, but without the health issues? They had decided to become one person instead of two. There might have been an alchemical basis for this desire. For was it not the legend of the Fountain of Salmacis that featured the fusion of two into one?

They had consulted the best doctors in Wales, thrusting cash in faces best qualified to dream surgical dreams.

But an operation to graft them to each other, artery to artery, nerve to nerve, bone to bone, was impossible to perform without killing them. For one thing, the blood types were incompatible. Gordon was Type B; Bloat was Type X^2+Y^2. And so that particular dream was extinguished. Making the best of the situation, they resolved at least to fuse *metaphorically*; but to symbolise this mystic union properly they would live in the same suit, Ben on the right side, Hugo on the left …

Does this seem eccentric to you?

It was a more eccentric age back then, when grotesque war was on the verge of smashing Europe to bloody shards! Honestly. Think of a bowl of thumbs. That's weird, isn't it? Yes, but not as weird as the Kaiser! Take it from me, who was there at the time.

Anyway, Bloat and Gordon are now encased in one pair of pantaloons, one shirt and one jacket. It takes the duo only a little practice to perfect an efficient gait. They walk down the rickety stairs and back up again. Easy! Then they sit down on a comfortable sofa, get up and sit back down, just to experience the sensation. It operates fine, this single identity. Thus it is time for the next stage of the merger.

A single name instead of two separate names!

Hugo Bloat and Ben Gordon.

From now on they shall be one individual.

Hubengo Gordbloaton!

Yes, that is marvellous, that is dandy!

With diabolical joy, monolithic square shoulders shaking with mirth, a bass drone of laughter splutters forth from this improvement on the basic human model, Mr Gordbloaton…

Talking about spluttering, that's exactly what Mr Jason Rolfe's engine was doing as he coasted along the southern shore of the Caspian Sea; but there was nothing wrong with the machinery. Pulsejets always splutter as they work. This part of Persia is cooler and softer than the deserts further south, and Jason was enjoying the dappled sunlight. To his left sparkled a series of wavelets on the inner sea.

To his right rose the mighty Elburz Mountains, the dwelling place in the ancient Zoroastrian religion of the *Peshyotan*, an immortal assistant of the *Saoshyant*, who is the one who will bring about the final renovation of the world; but Jason cared little about such things. He was relaxing on his saddle, slumped as far back as feasible. Sleeping in the saddle without falling off was a most tricky tactic.

He approached an isolated castle; a tall structure perched

on a crag. As he passed near it, something fell from the battlements. A man! The fellow had been leaning too far over, curious to observe the bicycle. Down span this unfortunate, to his certain doom, but lo and behold!, he landed not on the hard ground, but on the bicycle.

And yet the impact didn't unseat Mr Rolfe.

Nor did it kill the newcomer.

The vast sack of supplies that bulged directly behind Jason cushioned the fall of the man and saved him.

But he was stuck on the speeding machine …

Mr Jason Rolfe looked back over his own shoulder and said, 'Do you speak English? I am an inventor.'

'Yes, I do. I learned it in Tehran University.'

'Ah, so you are a scholar?'

'Indeed. I am Sadegh Safani, an alchemist.'

'They teach alchemy as an academic subject in this country? I'm quite astounded to hear that. As you can see, I'm marooned on this bicycle until it runs out of fuel. But there's a lot of fuel remaining; and I suspect I'll end up drowning in the Pacific Ocean.'

'Oh, but that's very far away! Surely you exaggerate?'

'I wish I did, but I don't.'

Sadegh nodded thoughtfully. 'Well, it's just as inconvenient for me to balance here like this. I'm sure there must be a way of stopping the device and dismounting safely! Let me see.'

'Are you cogitating the problem?' asked Mr Rolfe.

'I am. Wait, I have the answer!'

'Pray reveal it to me, sir.'

The Persian leaned forward and whispered into the explorer's ear. This wasn't an easy thing to do, for Jason still wore his knightly helmet; yet the words of the alchemist were clear.

'There's a country east of here mostly unknown to outsiders. Long ago I went there; when I was young. It's hidden away in the Himalayas. Every side is guarded by a high mountain.'

'Is it accessible by bicycle?' asked Jason Rolfe.

'No, but that's to our advantage. Listen carefully. If you steer directly up the side of one of those mountains, your velocity will start to decrease until eventually it reaches a speed low enough for us to jump off without breaking our skeletons into crumbs.'

'But we'll be stranded at a great altitude!'

'True, but then we can descend the *other* side on foot, into the country that almost nobody knows about ...'

'Will they welcome us there, Mr Safani?'

'I have no doubt of that.'

Higher Noon

Distanto stood at one end of the single dusty street. I stood at the other. A classic scene from any Western dime novel you care to name. Slowly and determinedly, we approached each other. My Colt revolver was holstered and my fingers undulated above its handle like spiders' legs. An audience had gathered to watch our fatal sport.

Mario Granieri began whistling. It was a heartbreaking tune; it had all of Mexico in it, the knife blue of the skies, the circling vultures, and yet it was somehow redolent of spaghetti. His Italian blood kept coming to the front of everything he did, the rascal!

My brow was bathed in sweat. I stumbled.

I was scared. I expected to die.

There was no way I could beat Distanto Faraway in a shootout without cheating. I had never seen him fire a gun, but I had a feeling about him, a feeling identical to that which his brother Scipio had given me; he was an expert with a vast range of weapons.

Step by step the distance between us narrowed.

'Don't draw unteel you can seee the whites of his eyes, hombre!' cried Pancho Henchman in an ironic tone.

Mario stopped whistling. He fished a rusty harmonica from his pocket and puffed a melody even lonelier.

Distanto was so close I could see his expression.

He blinked rapidly! Dust in his eyes?

No, it wouldn't be that; with the Faraway brothers there was always an unorthodox reason for all behaviour.

Then I realised that he was signalling to me.

Morse Code! With eyelids!

I had learned to read this code as part of my journalistic training. Even now, everyone who writes features and news items for *The Western Mail* must be *au fait* with dots and dashes.

His message was simple but breathtaking!

He'd formulated an escape plan.

The details shocked me; but I trusted his judgment.

Mario honked a minor chord.

Distanto and I squared off, maybe 20 paces apart.

He stamped his foot thrice!

That was the signal for me to draw and shoot.

I did so. And so did he!

Blam! A double blast. A double echo down the street.

Horses near the saloon snorted.

Distanto's skill at billiards was put to good use now. My bullet met his bullet at the midway point between our two barrels. His bullet acted like a cue ball, deflecting mine at a prejudged angle. Can you imagine the mind it must take to calculate that?

The brain of that airship captain was glorious.

'Good shot!' I screeched.

But my congratulations were premature. Even geniuses make errors! I don't mind stating that Distanto's effort was out by a few degrees. Instead of puncturing the heart of Mario, the deflected bullet buried itself deep in the neck of Pancho Henchman.

Who collapsed with a groan into the dust.

Mario dropped his harmonica.

'Pancho Henchman is dead! Take his place, Pancho Lackey!'

A new henchman ran up, nodding.

Mario gave vent to his fury. He pointed at Distanto and me. 'You will both die immediately! Not by the bullet, the rope or even the cactus, but by the trident. I'll fetch it now!'

And he ran back into the saloon and down to his workroom. The trident was still resting in the corner. He snatched it up and hastened out into the glare of sunlight. 'Die like pigs!'

I looked around, wondering if we could make a run for it; and Distanto was clearly thinking the same thing. There was nowhere for us to flee, for we were surrounded by a semicircle of angry Mexicans, a semicircle that was turning into a tightening noose.

'Our guns are empty now,' I said sadly.

'Do you know how to fight with bare hands, Mr Griffiths?' Distanto asked. I shook my head despondently.

'Not my own,' I admitted. 'What about you?'

'I'm a black belt in Jujutsu.'

'Will that suffice to save us, I wonder?'

'Probably not from Mario.'

'We never did get to taste an avocado as large as a human head. That's one regret I'll take to the grave!'

'I doubt we'll be buried in a grave, Mr Griffiths.'

'What will they do with us?'

'Feed our bodies to the dogs and centipedes.'

'The despicable villains!'

I have already explained where the deflected bullet went, but doubtless you are wondering what happened to the cue ball bullet? It didn't do any damage to anything, merely embedding itself into the wooden wall of one of the nearby buildings. Thought I should clear that up before Mario puts an end to my life forevermore …

He shook his trident under a cloudless sky. 'I want your blood to spill in the sand, amigos. That's where it belongs! The gold point of my trident is holiness; the black is war. I will jab at you with the latter! The qualities of the brown point are unknown.'

'The steenking sand ees thirsty!' chortled Pancho Lackey.

'I'll slake it soon enough!' Mario's nostrils flared as he added, 'Death is the best condition for you two!'

I disagreed with him about that; but who am I?
Merely a fungoidal journalist.
A Welsh one at that!

Gathering Storm

From every corner of the European continent, from every secret alcove, niche and cranny came the fascistic volunteers to the dread cause of the hubristic Italo-Mexican, *Signor* (or *Señor*) Granieri. In black, brown and green uniforms they marched onwards, chins mostly square and shaved, windswept fringes at 45° angles on thunderous brows. All of them were committed to power, strength, blood, iron, purity, race, honour, war and inequality. They were thugs and ranters.

From Romania came men with bags of soil around their necks, earthy reminders of the magical force of their homeland; from Norway came the descendants of Vikings, who still believed that Thor and Odin were gods fit for humanity; from Ireland came mystical warrior-poets who sang and jigged away each twilight; from Bohemia came men with sneers sharper and deadlier than daggers; from Hungary, Germany, Poland, Croatia and Estonia, they came. From everywhere.

Even from Lichtenstein, Luxembourg, San Marino.

Not forgetting the Papal Lands!

Due to some quirk of timing, they all converged in a narrow mountain pass over the Pyrenees. Recognising each other by a prearranged salute, a matter of clenching one's fist and biting down on it, they combined forces to cross into Spain in a single mass.

Towards Almería they went, kicking up dust clouds.

The peasants who witnessed this influx shook in their sandals, if they could afford sandals, or trembled in bare feet if they couldn't: they didn't try to oppose them. Armed with weapons of all types and ages, including maces, swords and halberds, this gargantuan legion was a hideous sight, a grotesque invasion of motley maniacs.

Europe had gone mad; the world was utterly insane!

Contrast this scene with another ...

A liner packed with assassins has finally reached its destination, which happens to be Santander in Cantabria, a region of Spain. Though cramped by the voyage, these assassins disembark flexibly enough. Led by Unkoo the ape-man, they proceed toward Almería, pausing only while he sniffs the ground. Armed with weapons of all types and ages, including rapiers, throwing stars and hatchets, this gargantuan legion is an appalling sight, a grotesque invasion of motley maniacs.

Did you spot the difference between the two armies?

I didn't. And I'm a professional writer; Lloyd Griffiths is my name, but you knew that already. What's yours?

It's almost inevitable that the two legions will collide!

But what will happen then?

I have no idea. Nor does Hubengo Gordbloaton.

Nor does Mario Granieri ...

At the very moment in time that all this is happening, Dom Daniel in Brazil is seated at his study window staring out at the jungle. The sounds of a saw and an axe disturb his reverie; the majestic trees are being felled all around him. He sighs at this destruction, for soon his beloved country will be a wasteland of stumps and starving animals. He has done what he can to save the flora of the rainforest. His sad thoughts turn to daydreams of that implausible Arctic island, that paradise concealed among icebergs and snowfalls; unknown Hippolytomia.

Unlike Distanto, he has never actually been there.

So his daydreams aren't coloured with the crayons of experience; they remain abstract, archetypal, wondrous.

The atlas of Hippolyto Joseph da Costa featured notes scribbled in the margins in that alchemist's hand: his discovery of the anomalous island had been an accident. He had lived there for a year, had fathered a child by an ape-girl; nobody would ever be aware of the fact, but Hippolyto was the ancestor of Unkoo, which is how that hairy assassin was able to pick up the languages of the civilised world so easily. The tongues of our own culture were already locked in his genes.

But we didn't know much about genes back in 1914.

The atlas said nothing about dinosaurs.

It's inconceivable that Hippolyto could have lived there without seeing at least one of those awesome beasts. They dominated the island, roaring and stamping all over the place, leaving footprints on the beaches. So his silence on the matter suggests self-censorship. If he regarded them as too ridiculous, he would have feared ridicule from readers of the atlas. Had I been in his position, I too would have said nothing about them. Once lost, an honest reputation is difficult to recover.

Curiously enough, Hippolytomia is extremely similar in all its aspects to Alirgnahs, the land hidden away in the Himalayas that both Mario and Sadegh have mentioned. Alirgnahs is not technically an island; but it acts like one in every particular, for it is ringed by mountain ranges as difficult to cross as the waves of a tempestuous sea.

There are dinosaurs there also. Hairy yeti too.

Only occasionally visited by outsiders, Alirgnahs is currently host to a brave man from the Rif region of Morocco.

Mulai Ahmed el Rais Uli is his name. A hero.

He arrived by motorjet aeroplane.

Despite the excellence of its design, the engine had faltered, had given up in mid flight; his craft had stalled. He managed to glide it to a ruinous landing on the hard-packed snow, saving his own life but utterly wrecking the aircraft. He was marooned in Alirgnahs!

But he was not entirely without resources. He had his long musket, so long that it might serve as a scabbard for Jason Rolfe's improvised lance; and with this he could hunt dinosaurs for food. He had his kettle and a wad of mint tea; always refreshing. He had also a radio transceiver, and with that he planned to send a message to friends.

His first concern wasn't to summon help. Rais Uli was a different kind of man from those who weep and blubber at every fantastical setback. All he wanted was to reassure them he was safe.

And so he laboured to set up his transceiver, to erect an aerial.

Inquisitive tyrannosaurs had to be warded off!

He had plenty of ammunition for that …

Because this world of ours is a place of startling coincidences, please make no mistake about that, Sadegh Safani, the man who had named and mapped Alirgnahs, was rapidly approaching its borders. Jason Rolfe, his new friend, was proving to be a pleasant travelling companion. All across Persia they had rolled, through the lands of the Jafar Khan, into the wilder domains of Afghanistan. Fruit still fell.

They would have reached the Himalayas in good time had not a weird accident befallen them. Jason took a wrong turning and ended up getting stuck inside a waterwheel. Round and round it went at ludicrous velocity, accelerated to a hitherto unheard of rate of revolutions per minute by the spluttering pulsejet engine of his bicycle.

The engine pushed the bicycle; the bicycle turned the waterwheel. The most bizarre disaster imaginable for any cyclist! The riders had no choice but to wait for the wheel to shake itself apart and set them free again. This would happen much sooner than you might expect, for the wooden wheel hadn't been constructed to endure such treatment for long. Nonetheless it meant a delay in their arrival at Alirgnahs.

To pass the time more agreeably, Sadegh lectured Jason in alchemy. It might be worth detailing his lectures here, but unfortunately I wasn't there to hear them, and so I am ignorant of the finer points of his discourse. But it seems likely he talked about the blending of substances and soul energy to create the philosophical egg, which might then be hatched into a chick of perfect wisdom ripe for raising into an adult bird of omniscience. That is an oddly extended metaphor, by the way.

Sadegh's vast turban probably sparkled with dew and windfallen fruits and nuts. His dark eyes twinkled no less compellingly. He touched on the mixing of holiness and war; surely this was a coincidence. Such a fusion couldn't be undone, he said, without leaving a residue. Jason wondered at the qualities of this residue. Sadegh grinned at the back of his questioner's neck and said, 'It is dark brown in colour and its properties are unusual. I'll describe them for you now. They are —'

The Point

Mario strode over the sand, swinging his trident. A fluid movement of his wrist and the three blades flicked out of the end. Distanto stood still, eyes narrowed, lips compressed; I stepped back a pace, but my retreat was still blocked by the Mexican mob behind me.

'I'll just use the *war prong* to deal with you!' Mario cried.

There was nowhere for us to run.

'What shall we do?' I whimpered; and for an instant I felt disdain for the airship captain. I felt sure Scipio wouldn't have gotten me into this mess. But that was unfair, the bitter reflections of a journalist about to die in an awfully painful manner; Scipio wasn't really much more competent than his brother. Distanto turned to face me.

'Relax. I'll think of something,' he said blandly.

Mario raised and aimed the trident.

'Hurry, *Monsieur*!' I hissed.

Suddenly Distanto bawled, 'Don't let him stab you with the war prong. That's the black one. Impale yourself on one of the others first!' And with a reckless laugh, he rushed forward.

Mario was caught by surprise. Before he could lower his trident, it was already receiving the body of Distanto Faraway. The holiness prong, with a sort of deflating hiss, slid into the diaphragm of the oncoming pilot. The blood was less than I might have expected. Fixed there, on the cruel barb of the point, Distanto was safe from impalement on the war prong, for he occupied one position that other blade could never reach. Turning to look over his shoulder, he croaked:

'Come on, Mr Griffiths! Cheat him of victory!'

I saw the wisdom in his words.

But he had left me with the brown prong, the one of unknown quality. What if the effects of that blade happened to be even worse than those of the war prong? The gamble didn't fill me with confidence; and yet it was worth taking, for the war prong was certain doom, but this one … With a laugh far less reckless and convincing than Distanto's,. I flung myself onto it. Mario was unable to twist it away because Distanto prevented him. So I transfixed myself solidly and groaned.

Something was activated in the shaft of the trident.

Some battery or other power source …

The shaft glowed as the energy stored within it pulsed into the blades. I felt it flood my body; it filled me up on the inside. It wasn't pleasant but it wasn't utterly foul either. It was brown light; a mundane contrast to the golden light that now suffused Distanto.

Steam rose from the trident shaft. Mario yelped.

He let go and it quivered next to him, the weight entirely supported by the two bodies of its willing victims.

Then the last pulse of energy was drained from it.

The trident was empty; we were full.

Mario studied us carefully. He placed his hands on his hips and shook his head in a style that was the essence of negation. Then he cried, 'You tricked me! Whatta mistake to make!'

'Why was it a mistake?' queried Distanto serenely.

'Because now you die!'

'But we were going to die anyway, weren't we?'

'You will die by the gun …'

And he stamped back into the saloon and returned with a rifle. I think it was a Winchester repeater, but I'm no expert on firearms. He aimed it at Distanto and dribble poured down his chin. He was so furious that he'd lost control of his saliva glands.

I stood next to Distanto and turned my face away. We were still stuck on the prongs of the trident; probably fatally. But it didn't appear we would be given a chance to bleed to death.

Mario intended to shoot us before that could happen!

Then Distanto did something.

He smiled with the tranquillity of a cherub.

He lifted one hand to his chest and touched his left nipple. I felt rather uncomfortable at this display of self-love; but I had misjudged him. Not a decadent of that sort was he. Gripped between first finger and thumb, the nipple rotated. He tweaked it and kept tweaking it. Then I noticed why. A strange object was shimmering into existence directly above his head, an outline that slowly acquired solidity.

A circle of light. A halo! A halo on his head!

Truly he had absorbed the outflow of the holiness prong in full! As he continued to tweak, the halo grew brighter and brighter; he was adjusting its glare, turning it to maximum!

I was unable to bear the radiance any longer!

Nor was the rascal Mario!

The Italo-Mexican scoundrel dropped his rifle and covered his eyes. I felt a tug deep inside me, insistent and agonising. Distanto was moving, taking the trident with him; and me with it. Pancho Lackey blundered in futile loops, colliding with the minor henchmen. No-one was able to see anything in that glare, a scream of visible intensity that exceeded by far the power of the midday sun. I felt a wrench. The trident was out, thrown aside by the airship captain's fingers.

'Run, Mr Griffiths! Back to my vessel! Quickly!'

To make such running possible, he turned his halo down again. Along the single street we scampered, past the flagpole, under the arch of planks and out into the badlands of Almería.

Shots rang out behind us. Puffs of dust appeared.

At this range, accuracy in shooting was impossible, but Mario fired at us anyway, hoping for a lucky strike.

Although I was almost out of breath, I still managed to

groan, 'Won't we bleed to death in a few minutes?'

'There's a first aid kit back at the airship,' said the captain.

He exuded an air of abnormal calm.

I found this very exasperating! And I said:

'You are packed with holiness now; and that's all well and good. You have the charisma and tolerance of a saint. Fine, *Monsieur* Faraway, fine. But what about me? Poor old me!'

'What about you, my friend?' he beamed.

'My energy isn't golden like yours. I am full of brown light. So what's *my* talent? Any ideas? What's mine?'

Suited To The Task

Hubengo Gordbloaton is anxious for news. He is impatient to know if any of his assassins has succeeded in killing me yet. This is a standard worry for anyone who commissions a murder. Another worry creases the double brow of the sartorially amalgamated man. What if an assassin turns out to be untrustworthy? He might receive a phone call from, say, the Javanese assassin, claiming that a *kris* knife has sundered my spine, only to learn later that it was a lie. Not every assassin is honest. Men who hire them often pay for a 'hit' that never actually happens. And where does one complain when an assassin is guilty of breach of contract?

No court in the land, however corrupt, would touch such a case. There is no compensation for the victim of substandard wrongdoing; not even in Wales would redress be available. And Hubengo detests the idea of being cheated, despite his wealth. He must have evidence of success. To cavort and gloat over my cadaver is his desire!

'Must be a way of securing evidence,' he says.

'I agree,' comes his own reply.

'But what's the answer, Mr Gordbloaton?'

'Not sure yet, Mr Gordbloaton!'

'Will you attempt to think of one, Mr Gordbloaton?'

'Certainly, dear fellow, I shall.'

Hubengo is always very courteous to himself …

His monolithic square shoulders hunch as he devotes

himself entirely to the task of solving the problem. These shoulders are so square and so flat that dust has mounted on them; indeed a crow has made a nest on the left one, for it's the kind of stable platform unavailable in the twisted trees of the dunes outside. Hubengo runs through all the options in his bilateral mind. Then he clicks his thumbs!

'A matter transmitter, that's the answer!'

'Does such technology exist, Mr Gordbloaton? The year is only 1914 and we are on the verge of a war.'

'Yes indeed, Mr Gordbloaton: the war to end all wars! But I believe a matter transmitter *is* a feasible option for us, for I seem to recall reading a newspaper article somewhere about a genius who claimed to have already designed, fabricated and tested one.'

'Now I remember, Mr Gordbloaton! That article was published in *The Western Mail* by no lesser a personage than me. Nikola Tesla was the name of the genius; or was it Oliver Heaviside? One or the other. Funnily enough, it was Mr Lloyd Griffiths who wrote the piece. He was asked to produce a series of essays on overlooked and neglected inventors. He did one on Jason Rolfe and another on Karl Mondaugen. The third was Tesla and the fourth was Heaviside. I'm sure Tesla is the relevant one! With his aid we can obtain a matter transmitter.'

'Very good, Mr Gordbloaton. Let's contact him!'

'One moment, dear fellow … What use will a matter transmitter be to us? You haven't explained that to me.'

'Ah, my apologies, Mr Gordbloaton! Well, with a matter transmitter we can project ourselves through the airwaves at a particular frequency in the form of an invisible wave. When we reach a receiver we'll reconstitute ourselves as corporeal beings. The moment one of our assassins slices up Lloyd Griffiths, we can beam ourselves to the site instantly to witness the kill. The perfect insurance against fraud!'

'I like the sound of all that, Mr Gordbloaton. But—'

'What's your objection, dear fellow?'

'None of our assassins is equipped with a receiver.'

'True, true, that might be an issue … But Tesla claims that

an ordinary radio receiver can pick up the signals of his matter transmitter. So perhaps we simply need to instruct each assassin to drag the body of Mr Griffiths to the nearest radio station after the fatal blow. Then they can contact us from there and we'll immediately arrive.'

'That makes perfect sense. But how do we inform our assassins of this instruction? They might be anywhere.'

'Advertisements in newspapers around the world.'

'Ah, the same way we put the bounty on Mr Griffiths' head. Brilliant! How I adore you, Mr Gordbloaton.'

'I love you too, dear fellow.'

'Nice to be in the same pair of shoes, isn't it?'

'Delightful, Mr Gordbloaton.'

And so they make preparations to contact Nikola Tesla and engage his services. Tesla is no longer the underrated figure he was back then; all the efforts of Edison to damage his reputation ultimately failed. Anyone who knows the story of early 20th Century scientific and engineering progress holds Tesla in high esteem; but when Hubengo contacted him, he was an outsider, an eccentric individual, shunned by the mainstream; a visionary condemned to obscurity and neglect.

Tesla arrived at the house in the dunes alone.

Hubengo Gordbloaton greeted him with two glasses of wine, red and white, one in one hand, one in the other.

Tesla didn't choose between them. He drank both.

'You have two heads,' he said.

'Better than one, that's why,' explained Hubengo.

'I suppose so,' Tesla agreed.

He was an amazing fellow, this unfairly neglected inventor, Croatian by birth. His ideas were so far ahead of their time that time itself would run out before they happened. Some of his projects were so epic in length and scale that their endings were influenced by their own beginnings. He was, for instance, the first fellow to envisage the wireless transmission of massive amounts of energy over vast distances. He designed a device that could destroy the planet with continuous earthquakes; another that could keep reversing our planet's magnetic field so rapidly that Earth became an immense electric motor with a power output sufficient to nudge Mars and Venus off their orbits into the sun.

Yet another was a time machine that went into the past at precisely the same speed that time goes forward, one second per second. Tesla drained the last drop of wine and asked:

'So you are interested in matter transmission?'

'Yes, I am,' confirmed Hubengo.

'You do realise that the operation sometimes goes wrong?'

'Really? In what manner, Mr Tesla?'

'If, for example, an object somehow got into the transmission capsule with you, it would alter the matrix.'

'The matrix? Please speak in normal talk.'

'When your molecules are broken down and converted into energy – a process similar to that of alchemy – they form a "soup" that scientists prefer to call a "matrix", because it sounds better. This matrix must remain pure if possible, so that the energy can be perfectly reconstituted at the receiving end of the transmission. If a seemingly insignificant object, for instance a dandelion seed, got inside the matrix, when you arrive at your destination you would be no longer just a man.'

'We would have some dandelion properties too?'

'Exactly! You'd be a hybrid!'

Hubengo Gordbloaton digested this news. 'Well, that's really not such a bad outcome, is it? There are many possibilities there. The properties of a dandelion! We don't sneeze at such ideas, Mr Tesla. Indeed no. But for the present moment, our priorities are elsewhere. We want you to build an ordinary matter transmitter for us.'

'It will cost you lots of money. It's tricky work.'

Hubengo reached into a pocket of his large coat and pulled out a wad of banknotes and thrust it into Tesla's face, rubbing it over his nose, chin and cheeks, trying almost to push the high numbers printed on each piece of paper through the pores of his skin.

'Money is no problem for me, Mr Tesla. Oh no!'

Tesla nodded. 'Then I accept.'

Hubengo asked, 'How long will it take, the installation?'

'A few days. A week at most.'

'Come in, come in; you may have the spare bedroom.'

Tesla hesitated on the threshold.

'What's the matter?' demanded Hubengo.

'The words *spare bedroom* fill me with uncertainty and fear. It's well known that lonely houses are haunted, and that the owners of such places always reserve the scariest room for guests. Why they do this, I can't even begin to guess. But that's what they do.'

Hubengo replied, reasonably enough, 'Very well. I shall use the spare bedroom and you can have mine.'

This compromise is acceptable to Tesla.

'More wine!' he suggests.

My dear tolerant readers! You may have noticed that the telling of this scene has changed from present to past tense. The reason for this is that I am in no position to write with care.

I am currently limping across a desert with a bunch of Mexicans right behind me. Bullets are zinging past my ears. Both of them. If I had other ears elsewhere on my body, bullets would doubtless be zinging past those also! Distanto has pulled ahead slightly. The airship can be seen in the distance, and it's a welcoming sight, believe me!

Ignoring this digression completely, Hubengo said, 'Would you like a tour of my private museum, Mr Tesla?'

Tesla squinted in the gloom of the mouldy house.

'Explain what kinds of exhibits you have, Mr Gordbloaton,' urged Mr Gordbloaton, with a dramatic gesture.

'Ornaments from all over the world,' said Mr Gordbloaton.

'Any mandolins?' asked Tesla.

Hubengo arches his eyebrows. 'What did he say?'

'He wants mandolins, dear fellow.'

'Mandolins, eh? Yes, I have those. I have several.'

Tesla said, 'Where do you want it?'

'Where do I want what?' returned Mr Gordbloaton.

'The finished matter transmitter.'

'Ah, I see! I have a very powerful normal radio transmitter. Will you connect your machine to mine?'

'Certainly. It'll cost you extra, though.'

Hubengo threw open a secret door to reveal an entire room crammed with bundles of cash. Then he laughed.

And Tesla laughed too; but not quite as loudly.

Conflicting Rascals

Distanto Faraway puffed up the last ridge; I was trailing behind him. It wasn't far to go, but I was weakening rapidly. To my astonishment, the airship captain paused on the brow of the ridge. Clearly he was able to see something on the far side that I wasn't.

I staggered and stumbled to his side. Then I paused too.

The plain beyond was thick with rascals.

Even from this distance, it was obvious that they were of a militant and intolerant bent. The black, brown and green uniforms seemed some warped echo of the prongs of Mario's trident. Distanto squinted for yet another minute and finally remarked:

'If we run, we can reach the airship before them.'

'Are you sure?' I muttered.

'Yes. They are twice as far from it as we are; and we are slightly less than half as weak as they. Hence ...'

I was in no mood for mathematics. I nodded.

We had no choice but to run on anyway; for Mario Granieri, Pancho Lackey and the other Mexicans were gaining on us. For the first five or ten steps I kept pace with Distanto, then he inevitably pulled away, and I was left to my own company again.

Stuffed with brown energy, I lurched onwards.

My vision was clouding over.

My eyes were like Welsh skies. Visibility was that poor!

185

Death was coming for me, I knew.

Many different fashions of death but all with the same purpose: behind me, a bullet; in front of me, a stampede of rascals; within my own frame, a gradual leaking away of lifeblood.

Despite my pearly-misted eyeballs I saw that Distanto had reached the bottom of the dangling rope ladder.

And now was climbing it with a gibbon's skill!

Something in this sight prompted the rascals to a frothing fury. With a single shout, they started running toward the airship, wielding maces and swords and halberds above their heads.

Some of them had automatic pistols also!

Most were festooned with daggers.

They shouted in a variety of languages; and then it became obvious to me who they were. The gargantuan legion Mario had mentioned! Killers, brutes and chumps all of them! Heavies with no mercy. Lovers of blood, racial theory and ignorance. Enemies of reason! Stampers on all that was good about humanity: for I was still naïve enough to believe that humans aren't entirely a damned species yet.

Distanto had reached the top of the ladder.

He pulled himself through the hatch. Then his head emerged again in an inverted position and he bellowed:

'Come on, Mr Griffiths! You can do it, my friend!'

This encouragement helped.

But not very much, to be brutally honest ...

Hardly at all, in fact. Ah well!

If this account were a work of fiction rather than a sober telling of the truth, I would have reached the ladder safely. I would also have managed to climb it and attain the security of the airship gondola. Then the captain, bless his heart and hat, would have cast off the anchor; and away to peace and liberty would we have floated.

That's not what happened, I'm sorry to say.

The savage scoundrels caught me.

They reached me before I reached the airship.

And they stabbed me to death with fascistic daggers! Cut to ribbons, I was! Made mincemeat of, poor me!

Lloyd Griffiths: shredded journalist anyone?

I recall globules of my flesh being flung away from my skeleton. Then I remember brown light pouring out …

Distanto was vainly trying to save me. He had had an idea.

He had decided to use his halo.

But not in the manner he'd already employed it.

He tied a rope to it. Then he cast off the anchor. Up lurched his vessel, just before the first villain could reach the rope ladder. Using the halo on the rope as a lasso, he cast and snagged me around the neck. Pulling with all his might, he drew me upwards like a bag of bones without the bag. It put the frenzied villains into an even greater frenzy! An unexpected gust of desert wind pushed at the airship.

I trailed behind the bulk of the thing, halfway in elevation between the ground and the gondola. All my flesh was gone. I was a skeleton and held together only by tendons and sinews.

I've never known the difference between those biologic items, tendons and sinews; I have no desire to learn.

But at that very moment, they kept me in one piece!

A skeleton and yet still alive? Weird!

But that's me. Plus I'm Welsh.

Distanto would have continued pulling me up, I'm sure, but he had to go and attend to the steering; otherwise we might have just gone round in circles. So I remained suspended at the midway point, the maniacs below me howling and saluting in a delirium of frothing rage, so bewildered by my escape that they forgot to shoot me with their automatic pistols. Dolts! But they weren't the only actors in the drama.

A shot *did* ring out; and with deadly accuracy too!

It severed the rope holding me in place.

Down I tumbled, limbs jerking.

Who had done this? Mario or one of his henchmen?

No, they were also paralysed into inaction: they had spotted something that froze their muscles with alarm.

Another gargantuan legion!

A gargantuan legion no less diabolical than the one that had flayed me alive. The legion of hired assassins!

It had arrived successfully in Almería ...

Unkoo was in the vanguard.

He raised his club and whooped in his own language.

One of the assassins directly behind him, I believe it was the one from Jamaica, lowered a smoking carbine.

As my greasy bones clattered on the parched ground, I comprehended the reason for the rope severance.

The assassins needed my body as evidence.

Hubengo Gordbloaton wouldn't pay them a farthing if my body wasn't available. Seeing it reduced to a skeleton, they had assumed I was already dead; they didn't want Distanto to fly off with me! Hence the sniper. The triumphant shrieking of this new mob would have frozen the blood in my veins, had I any blood or veins left.

'Let's retrieve his corpse and put it in a bag!' opined the assassin from Namibia. 'Anyone have a bag?'

Nobody did. 'But I have a sack,' said the Tajik assassin.

'That'll do,' was the consensus.

But the first gargantuan legion, the one comprised of fascistic fighters, even though Fascism as an authentic political movement was barely in its infancy, saluted itself with stiff-armed phallic salutes and said, 'His body belongs to us! We chopped it up.'

'Finders, keepers,' said Unkoo in his primal wisdom.

'Don't you dare!' came the reply.

'What will you do if we do dare?' demanded Unkoo.

'Try it and find out,' was the response.

'Bloody will!' snapped Unkoo.

Sprawled like a dog's dinner, or maybe a bear's breakfast, I managed to lift my skull and watch the outcome of this exchange with my sockets, which seemed to work as well as my eyes had done. There was going to be a battle between the two forces!

Assassins versus Fascists! Who would win?
I didn't think it mattered much.
The outlook for myself wasn't too bright.
'*Spwng dorth*!' I cursed.

The Legion Of Legions

Mario Granieri had recovered his Italo-Mexican composure by this time and was watching the pre-battle preparations with intense interest. These pre-battle preparations mostly consisted of strutting and sneering. At an arbitrary moment, some unknown intelligence, perhaps the mass mind of the gestalt mob, decided that the required amount of ritual posturing had occurred. And then real violence began!

The blades of swords flashed, because that's what they are designed to do. The sharpened curves of axes chopped the leg wood of men who knew what it felt like to be a tree for just an instant. Scimitars, pikes and knives were blurs of death in the agitated scene. Assassins yelped; fascists wept! Well-matched were they, the opposing sides, and the sand of the only true European desert gulped cherry mouthfuls

Bright the blood of fighters! Dim their dying eyes!

And other poetic observations …

I am a journalist, a star writer for *The Western Mail*, but even I had no stomach to put into words the clamour and stench of that localised war; a war of dark honour and twisty morals. I also had no stomach for anything else; and no liver, spleen or kidneys.

Unable to see everything I wanted to see from my sprawled vantage, I rolled over and clattered to my knees.

I felt lighter, more awkward in physical form.

Clearly it would take some time for me to adjust to the

fact I now had a skeleton's body instead of my own, even though that skeleton *was* mine. Does that make sense? Or am I raving?

A severed head bounced past me, blinking furiously.

It belonged to the Swiss assassin.

Another followed it, knocking into it like a croquet ball. This belonged to a proto-fascist from Macedonia.

In the heat and dizziness of battle, a heat and dizziness almost exactly superimposed on the already excessive heat and dizziness of the desert, it was difficult to focus properly. Combatants shimmered; everything was a mirage. Even the mirages of men were fooled by yet more mirages. Such a nightmarish tableaux! Like a labyrinth of distorting mirrors with a blind man at the centre instead of a Minotaur.

The clash of steel; the zang of bullets; the ululation of tongues, not all of them still connected to mouths!

And Distanto high above, anxiously waving at me through a porthole. He didn't leave me, bless him; he was just as noble as Scipio deep down. I may have given the impression he was seedier and darker than his brother in character and manners, but that is merely because I too misjudged him. Don't take everything I say at face value.

My own face had no value at all. It was chopped to bits!

And who would buy a chopped face?

Not even soup kitchens have a use for such a thing!

The battle raged and doubtless would have continued to rage until the participants were all slaughtered. But crafty Mario Granieri didn't care for that to happen. He saw opportunity here.

He called to his henchmen to go back to the settlement and return with a cannon – he had been keeping it in reserve for emergencies like this. They did so, Pancho Lackey leading them. It squeaked on its wooden wheels as the Mexicans dragged it up the ridge.

Mario had taken his position there, where the full battlefield could be seen. The cannon was parked next to him. He ordered gunpowder poured down the barrel. Then a stone cannonball was inserted and rammed home. The fuse was inserted and Mario cried:

'Fire the first shot across their metaphorical bows!'

Pancho Lackey struck a match.

The fuse hissed. The cannon roared like an amplified ox.

Blaaammm booom!

In a hissing arc rose the sphere.

And then it curved down again, smashing a hole in the ground. At the vibration of its impact, some of the fighters fell. Others fell because their feet had been chopped off. But Mario achieved the desired effect. All the antagonists stopped fighting at once.

They looked up toward the ridge at him …

As the smoke cleared, Mario made a megaphone with his hands. Then he called out in a rich, sonorous voice:

'Killing each other? Whatta mistake to make!'

'Whom, then, should we be killing instead?' asked Unkoo, his apelike voice full of displaced jungle irony.

'Not me, that's for sure!' retorted Mario hastily.

The assassins and the fascists waited to hear his words, for it was plain by his stance he intended to make a speech. And that's what he did. Italo-Mexican eyes shining, he declaimed:

'Look at you! Magnificent men and women, but mostly men, for there are always fewer women attracted to militant groupings for some reason! It gladdens my poor heart to marvel at you. Yes it does, with your bloodlust and your rampaging viciousness! I am a simple man, a humble man, and I have only one ambition in life. Namely, to take over Spain and rule it like my onetime associate, the tyrant Huerta. You probably don't know him. It doesn't matter if you do or not, for he is beside the point. But what I want to say now is this: why not *combine* forces? Surely two malignancies are wiser than one? Think about it please!'

The two groups stared at each other, calculatingly.

Mario saw this and added:

'Together you can achieve so much more than on your

own! Together you can take over the entire *world*!'

Unkoo was the first to respond. 'Unkoo say yes!'

There was a massed cheer.

Mario swelled with joy. He bawled out:

'No longer shall there be two ordinary gargantuan legions! From this moment on, there will exist only one super-gargantuan legion! And that's you lot! And I will command you!'

The bloodied and bruised fighters began dancing.

Mario held up a hand for restraint.

'Before you celebrate overmuch, my friends, let us remember that this union must be washed in blood and pain to sanctify it! What better way of performing this profane baptism than by grinding to dust your first enemy in your new capacity as a single unit?'

'Agreed! But who is that enemy? Tell us who!'

Mario pointed directly at me.

'Him! Mr Lloyd Griffiths, the Welshman!'

'*Pen pidlan gawsog*!' I breathed softly. I was amazed that Mario knew my name. I didn't recall revealing it to him. Maybe he had learned it from some unorthodox alchemical process.

I was on my knees; I jumped to my feet. I clicked all over.

'Get that skeleton!' trumpeted Mario.

Suddenly, the legion of nasties was bearing down on me! They wanted to pulverise me.

What could I do? There was only one option.

Yes, I had a desperate plan.

Actually it wasn't really a plan; just a reflex. My survival instinct was still strong, even though I was technically already dead. The anchor cast out by Distanto still lay on the sand. It was attached to its cable. I grabbed the end of the cable and started swinging the barbs of the iron implement around my head. It whistled angrily.

Faster and faster it rotated, generating a circle of doom with me at the centre. Nobody could step inside it!

My   enemies   shuffled   ineffectually   beyond   the circumference of hissy iron. One fool stepped over the threshold and the anchor battered his skull to a flatness never intended by nature. He slumped and died; but still did I continue to spin the black mass. When I say 'black mass' I'm not referring to devil worship. It's just a practical piece of anchor-description. Anyway, I was dimly aware of Distanto steering the airship until it hovered directly over me. This was very encouraging.

But I couldn't stand there indefinitely, swinging that heavy anchor, for even skeletons get tired; there had to be some other way out! Then I knew what it was. I altered the angle of my swing, cast the anchor up, snagged the airship with one of its cruel barbs!

The point punctured the skin of the canopy …

Helium gushed out; propelled by this discharge the airship zigzagged through the torrid sky like a deflating toy balloon. If you have attended a child's party, you'll know what I mean …

I was still clutching the end of the line. Up I went!

Dragged behind the airship, I was flung about over the landscape. The escaped helium was everywhere; sucked into the lungs of the villains and desperadoes below, it made them squeak at each other like mafia mice. In my relief to be free of their evil machinations, I forgot that Distanto's halo was still around my neck, training its own rope. The end of *this* rope was dragging over the ground, leaving tracks in the sand like those of a snake on its way home. Very unfortunate!

The end of this other rope passed near Mario Granieri.

Who reached out and snatched it.

And then yanked it hard.

I assume he hoped to dislodge me and bring me back down to earth; if that's what he intended, he was cheated of his desired outcome, for harder was my grip on the anchor cable than the power of his tug. True, the halo tightened around my throat; I might have choked to death had I owned an uncrushed windpipe, but my neck was bare vertebrae. Still the helium gas poured out of the hole in the airship …

195

And that airship pulled me onward, my hands still gripping the anchor cable; and I pulled Mario off his feet. Higher we went, and so it happened that the grotesque Italo-Mexican became a more closely integrated part of my fate! Distanto struggled to control the airship; I struggled to keep hold of my cable; Mario struggled not to lose his grip on his rope. All three of us went sailing off together eastwards.

'Blast them out of the sky!' Mario screeched down.

His followers reloaded the cannon.

This time they used grapeshot, but the pellets only struck the rudder of the craft. No opportunity for a third volley; we were out of range. With a final fling of his authority, Mario cried:

'Pancho Lackey is an idiot! Pancho Poncho, take over!'

A blade slid between the ribs of Pancho Lackey and the wielder of the knife in question laughed. He was the new chief henchman and he gritted his teeth above the dying body of the man he had just replaced. 'Too bad, amigo, you were a steenking henchman.'

'I speeet on your steenking grave,' croaked Pancho Lackey.

Pancho Poncho wiped his blade clean.

'That's not nice,' he said.

But he didn't press the point. He was the new chief henchman. It was his responsibility to make decisions.

Before he had time to think, an unseen voice amid the crush of bodies cried, 'Let's follow the airship!'

It was a very hairy voice. It had a flavour of snow and ice about it, but it didn't belong to Unkoo. Pancho Poncho blinked. It wouldn't set a good example to the legion if the chief henchman, namely himself, appeared to be obeying the orders of a subordinate.

So he gestured at the retreating airship and boomed, 'Have you been reading my mind? That was my idea too. In fact, I had it long before you did. So now, follow it, hombres!'

The improved gargantuan legion set off immediately.

Massed chaos; a horde of horror!

As for Distanto, he left the controls of the airship long enough to haul me up and through the hatch. I flopped like a bundle of sticks inside the gondola. He closed the hatch, trapping Mario outside. He surely assumed that the Italo-Mexican would eventually lose his hold on the rope, plunge from altitude to the ground and rupture.

But that's not what happened. Mario was strong.

He climbed the rope to the closed hatch. Then he gripped the rivets on the side of the gondola and climbed those too. When he reached the roof of the gondola, he flung himself down.

Like a tinpot on a cool cat roof! Not quite like that.

I'm a skeleton. Forgive me.

The Third Prong

'Looking a bit skinny, Mr Griffiths!'

That's how Distanto attempted to cheer me up after I had recovered my senses enough to work out what he was doing. He was trying to open a sealed flask with a crowbar. I laughed to humour him, but in truth I felt more like weeping. So would you.

'The worst thing ever to happen to me,' I said.

'At least you're still alive …'

'That's very pertinent, *Monsieur* Faraway; but your comment doesn't help to explain the *why* or *how*.'

He stopped what he was doing and mused.

The ends of his moustache were twiddled between his fingers; just the same way he had twiddled his nipple. Well, not really the same way. The moustache was waxed. He muttered:

'Something to do with the brown trident-prong.'

'My thoughts too,' I agreed.

'It had the power to return a dead person to life.'

'Had? Don't you mean *has*?'

Distanto frowned. 'I just have a feeling that it can be used only once. I may be wrong about that, of course.'

'A hunch, *Monsieur* Faraway, is that so?'

'Exactly that, Mr Griffiths.'

'Some sort of Lazarus Effect, so to speak?'

He nodded vigorously.

'That's precisely the crux of the matter. Think about the three points of that madman's trident. One symbolised war; another symbolised holiness. Both war and holiness always *promise to return*. Does this make sense to you? People and institutions that have vested interests in holiness or war are forever predicting warlike or holy events in the near future. Holiness and war are fated to come back.'

'I follow you so far,' I admitted reluctantly.

'So now,' he continued, sitting on the flask he wanted open, 'it seems to me that the third trident-point, the brown one, the one that stabbed into your flesh, represents that quality of "returning". You have returned. Not as a ghost or a zombie, but as you are.'

'And yet without a scrap of flesh,' I sneered.

'That doesn't matter,' he said.

'Your explanation sounds highly contrived.'

He wagged an admonishing finger. 'No, no, Mr Griffiths. If this were all taking place in a novel or other work of fiction, then yes, I would say it was contrived! But we are real.'

'I accept your point,' I agreed, 'in nearly the same way I accepted the vicious brown point of the trident.'

Distanto appreciated the symmetry of this remark.

I rubbed my bleary eye sockets.

'In the real world, Mr Griffiths,' Distanto continued, 'all sorts of very bizarre things occur. They aren't contrived, because no guiding intelligence has planned them. They are random events. That you are a skeleton is a harsh fact, not the conceit of some flippant author! The brown light has stained your bones, by the way.'

I scratched my skull. 'No, I believe that is my fungal infection, finally exposed to view. Horrid, isn't it?'

'You still stink like an elephant's trunk.'

'That's what my aroma resembles? No-one ever told me until now. I guess they deemed it kinder to keep it a secret. An elephant's trunk isn't so vile a smell. I feel happier now!'

'Not so fast, Mr Griffiths! You don't yet know what the elephant *keeps* in his trunk. It might be putrefying fruit or disembodied hyena gums. You didn't think I was referring to the beast's nose, did you? Oh dear! But bad smells don't bother me too much.'

'It is a relief to hear that, *Monsieur*. But—'

He anticipated my question. 'What am I doing with this crowbar? I'm trying to open one of the flasks Dom Daniel gave me. It's full of tropical seeds, that's why. I require seeds!'

'What for? You aren't planning to grind them to flour to make an odd kind of bread, are you? I don't need to eat now, by the way. I don't have a stomach or guts or anywhere else to put an appetite. You aren't planning to jettison them as ballast, are you?'

He shook his head. 'We can lighten the airship later, if that proves to be necessary. But first I want to plug the leak in the canopy. We've lost a third of our helium already. As for our steering: the rudder was shattered by the grapeshot and can't be fixed. We are heading east and can't change direction. I don't want to land here.'

'Not in Spain? Where is your preferred destination?'

'Nowhere in Europe, Mr Griffiths.'

'Because of the coming war?'

'You are very perspicacious. Do you know that word?'

I nodded, for I am a journalist.

He decided to test me. 'What does it mean, then?'

'Bathed in perspiration,' I said.

He smirked. 'Wrong.'

I tried again. 'Flavoured like persimmon.'

'That's also incorrect.'

I was too weary and skeletal to make a third guess.

He cried, 'Open at last!'

He had resumed forcing the lid of the flask; it came off and the seeds inside sparkled, or would have done had they been sparkly. He picked up handfuls of them, stuffed the pockets of his jacket; then he retrieved his halo, which rested on the floor.

'Back in a minute or so, Mr Griffiths!'

And he climbed a metal ladder that gave access to a

catwalk inside the canopy of the airship. From this catwalk, the helium bags were accessible to any technician who cared to deal with them. Distanto Faraway was his own technician; he came back down.

'All done?' I enquired casually.

'Indeed so, but my halo is completely drained.'

'What did you do, *Monsieur*?'

'I planted the seeds of the Brazilian rubber tree.'

'What was the point of that?'

'So they would grow over the hole and plug the leak with sap. It's the most ecologically-aware solution.'

'But plants don't grow that fast! It'll take years ...'

'I accelerated their growth.'

'How so, *Monsieur*?'

'With the artificial ultraviolet light of my halo turned to maximum! It has given me a painful nipple and the halo is burned out; but it was worth it. The leak has been stopped!'

I greeted this news with bone-clicking joy.

'You are back in control?'

He smoothed his moustache and replied, 'Not really. The rudder, as I explained already, is broken; but I forgot to mention that some pellets of grapeshot also hit the engines.'

'We are leaking diesel?' I cried in alarm.

'No. But they can't be shut down. The wires that enabled me to control them from this console have been severed. So they're stuck on maximum and we must wait for the fuel tanks to drain before attempting to land; the journey ahead is a mystery tour!'

'What is the capacity of the airship's fuel tanks?'

'They are large, Mr Griffiths.'

'But how far will we travel before they run out?'

He shrugged. 'Hard to say.'

'Give me a rough estimate, please!' I pleaded.

'In kilometres or miles?'

'Miles are easier for me, *Monsieur*.'

'Umpteen thousand.'

Quaint Little Pillage

History is a strange thing. And many strange things, in their turn, become history. Which possibly is why history is a strange thing. Who knows? As a skeleton, I wasn't the same Lloyd Griffiths as the flesh man. My identity was the same, true, but something else had changed, something deeper. It seemed as if I'd been bartered for myself. I realise that's a nonsensical and contorted explanation of the discomfort that saturated me, but I just can't describe it in a meaningful manner.

Events didn't care about that, however.

History had its own agenda.

The new, improved GARGANTUAN LEGION, which liked to spell itself with capital letters like that, followed the airship wherever it flew. Here were fanatics, devotees of unreason, violence and bile; lunatic men, with a few women thrown in, who had shredded the last shreds of compassion and mercy in their own hearts; now they cared only to shred the lives and souls of those they labelled enemies.

But they had many enemies. Most of the human race!

Across Spain, they pillaged!

Over the mountains into France, through Switzerland, Austro-Hungary and Romania, went they. Like Cossack hordes, like rabid wolves, like the worst clichés you can think of, they ravaged, raped and slaughtered! Fired into a frenzy, they vowed to rescue their leader, Mario, and pestle me to a fine dust in a mortar in retribution.

They ran, rode horses, bicycles, scooters! They commandeered boats, goats and carriages. They skated.

Many of them fell in skirmishes with locals.

But they always fought hard.

And won many new recruits!

Pancho Poncho was in nominal charge and yet …

Unkoo led them, unofficially. He made sure my scent was permanently in his nostrils, even when the airship was over the horizon and not visible. His club bashed peasants and lords.

'Unkoo smash! Unkoo crush! Unkoo do other stuff!'

And his followers chorused:

'Follow the ape-man! Death to moderates!'

The only dissident was the assassin from England, who paused to sniff a flower in a meadow with the words, 'Can't we slow down and enjoy the scenery? Look at this buttercup!'

Instantly, a hundred weapons sundered him!

Unkoo screeched with power.

'Onwards, valiant avengers! Doom to traitors!'

'Doom, doom, wise ape-man!'

'Up with atavism! Rationality, go home!'

'And don't come out again!'

Never had a horde swept across any land with so much viciousness. A gigantic landslide in the Caucasus buried half their troops under boulders and grit; but the survivors weren't deterred in the least. There were many of them still, enough to turn any river red; not with beetroot or other such juice, but with blood, the blood of innocents! Having said that, Unkoo did bash beetroots with his club when he discovered them hiding in fields; for he believed that crops were weak.

'True men only munch meat! Plants are scum!'

'Wise Unkoo! Strong Unkoo!'

'Yes, both those things am I! Me is the best!'

'Kill grammar! Syntax too.'

And now you know exactly what they were like … Dreadful people. It was an insane time, an insane world, as

I've said before. Europe was soon to go up in flames, and other lands too, for there was a bitter campaign in Africa that has largely been forgotten. Permit me to tell you about Spicer-Simson and Von Lettow-Vorbeck one day — maybe my next adventure, if I live to have one, will be right there.

The airship flew onwards. Eastwards always.

At last the Himalayas hove into sight. These magnificent snow-capped gods among peaks filled me with awe. I wasn't yet so jaded that I couldn't feel wonder to the roots of my spirit.

Distanto stood next to me at the largest porthole.

'Beautiful, aren't they?' he said.

I nodded. 'Puts it all into perspective, *Monsieur*.'

He frowned. 'Puts what?'

'Our little worldly concerns,' I replied.

'Puts them into perspective?'

'That's what I said.'

'But they don't have outlines.'

'What do you mean?'

'Our little worldly concerns don't have outlines. So they aren't subject to the laws of perspective or to any of the laws of geometry. For example, my main worldly concern is what I intend to do with my life after I retire from captaining airships. What shape is that concern? Is it triangular or a polygon with numerous sides?'

'You misunderstand. A figure of speech.'

'A figure? What figure?'

I sighed. He had defeated and confused me with his fake simplicity; I felt sure it *was* fake. Scipio, his own brother, would never have become involved in such an exchange, and siblings born at the same moment in time could never be so genuinely different. That's what I believed then. I still believe it. My frame sagged.

He slapped me heartily on my exposed spine.

'I've just checked the gauge.'

'Which gauge might that be, *Monsieur* Faraway?'

'The fuel gauge, my friend.'

'And what does it say, if anything?'

'It is almost empty. Yes, that means we will be landing soon. Perhaps on the other side of that range ...'

I squinted through the glass. 'I wonder —'

'What lies beyond them?'

I nodded. He didn't answer. He didn't know.

But Mario, still clinging to the roof of the gondola, knew. He recalled the land that the Persian alchemist Sadegh Safani had discovered, and he recognised these mountains as those that guarded Alirgnahs, that isolated region where dinosaurs and yeti roamed. The Italo-Mexican giggled. He clutched his trident more tightly.

He had brought it with him, the blighter!

On the ground, far away, the GARGANTUAN LEGION still gave chase. Unkoo watched the airship cross the mountains. Then he saw the vessel pause. It had run out of fuel at last!

Slowly, ever so slowly, it descended; the occupants were venting gas. They could fly no further. Thus —

'Onwards! Hasten! We've got them this time!'

The mob responded to his words.

Howled, grunted, shrieked!

Girded their loins!

And charged!

Shangri-La Farce

Distanto looked at me, and I looked at him. 'We're going down now but that wasn't my doing!' he admitted.

'You didn't open a valve to vent gas?' I asked.

'Not yet. How very peculiar!'

There was, in fact, a perfectly ordinary explanation for this; Mario had used the war prong of his trident to puncture the canopy. But this wasn't a random puncture like before; it was done carefully, with two holes at two opposing angles, so the ejected gas didn't propel the airship anywhere. He was happy to descend into Alirgnahs.

Directly below was the wreck of an airplane.

And yet it seemed a pleasant land.

The fields were full of wild flowers and there were plenty of trees with blossom on their branches. It was evidently an aberrant microclimate; the sort of place where nothing much had changed for millions of years. Lush and tropical, a thoroughly misplaced Eden. An even better locale for him to establish a new Mexico than Spain!

It had always infuriated him that a 'New Mexico' already existed in the United States. That wasn't really a Mexico; not like the one he planned! It was a pseudo-Mexico, a waste of sun and shade. *His* new Mexico was the real thing: an older Mexico, redone!

The grotesque spirit of Huerta would live again.

But without the bumbling man.

For Mario now despised his former employer.

Huerta: weak. Mario: strong.

As the airship sank lower and lower, he prepared himself for the leap. The grass looked thick enough to cushion the impact. When the moment came, he chuckled as he landed and rolled. His trident tumbled near him, missing his jugular vein by a finger.

The airship landed safely, but without much grace.

No matter. Grace is overrated.

Distanto and I emerged.

A voice called out in amazement, 'Scipio!'

Distanto blinked thrice.

A man was approaching us. Dressed in robes, his exotic elegance was striking. His beard bristled.

'Wait a moment. Truly, you aren't he! Then who?'

'My brother,' said Distanto.

The man was bewildered. 'You are your own brother?'

'No, Scipio is *my* brother.'

'Then, logically, it follows that you are his.'

Distanto conceded this.

'I am Rais Uli. Who is this skeleton?'

'Lloyd Griffiths,' I said.

'Pleased to meet you. I won't shake hands …'

'I don't blame you, sir.'

Distanto asked him, 'Is that your aeroplane?'

Rais Uli nodded. 'Yes, but it crashed. I've just finished setting up my transceiver. I was about to broadcast a signal back to my home in the Rif, a wild region of North Africa.'

'I have flown over it numerous times.'

'This entire valley,' said Rais Uli, gesturing with his hands, 'belongs to a tribe of warrior yeti. They don't especially like outsiders, but I made friends with them. I am sure I can speak in your favour. Every week they hold a council in yonder caves.'

'When is the next council due?' I asked.

'In about ten minutes …'

Distanto turned to me and whispered, 'That's still not

convenient. We are still in the real world, not in a fiction. It's important that you, and any reviewers out there, realise this!'

At least that's what I think he said. Reading it now, I can see how silly it is. I must have misheard him.

Rais Uli continued, 'Let's go there now.'

'To the caves yonder?'

'Yes. That's where my finger is pointing.'

The three of us set off.

We mounted a short flight of stone steps cut into the side of a cliff. At the top was the entrance to a cave. The yeti had already gathered around a fire. They were drinking a sour beer brewed from flowers, and they glanced up as Rais Uli entered. Fangs gleamed in firelight. Rais Uli introduced us, and he spoke so sweetly that the yeti brows relaxed. Then one of the beasts formally welcomed us inside.

'Sit down, sit down,' ushered Rais Uli.

Distanto and I sat on stone stools. The yeti began their conference. It was in a strange, guttural language that I later learned was called Abomina, and I understood not one word of it; but I picked up a small sense of what was on the agenda from the melodramatic gestures and expressions of the participants. A council of war was what it most resembled; I am confident they debated strategy and tactics.

I sat there for about an hour listening to the grunting babble. Cramps in my leg harassed me. I shifted position on my uncomfortable stool and the action seemed to be greeted with distant shouts of defiance and bloodlust. The yeti who happened to be talking at that moment clammed up; hirsute ears stiffened throughout the cave.

'Invaders,' explained Rais Uli, 'from the outer world!'

We jumped up and looked out.

And I saw the GARGANTUAN LEGION swarming like death lemmings down the inner slopes of Alirgnahs. In the vanguard was Unkoo; he was the point of an equilateral triangle.

Without hesitating for even an instant, the yeti snatched up clubs and spears and other weapons and rushed out to engage the intruders in horrid battle. The yeti loved fighting as much as the enemies they now faced! I was aghast; Distanto and Rais Uli were more composed. Should we go to the assistance of our hosts? That was the question I was discussing in the debating chamber of my own mind.

My companions already had decided the issue.

They hastened out into the fray!

I had no real choice but to follow. How could Lloyd Griffiths ever be taken seriously again as a journalist and human being if he failed to fight in the name of truth, honour and yeti?

There were no spare weapons, so I picked up a rock.

Rais Uli hefted his loaded musket.

Distanto unsheathed a cutlass from some secret pocket on the inside of his jacket. He sliced through necks with the speed and flexibility of a man chopping cucumbers — not that normal men ever prepared their own salads back then, or even ate those prepared for them; it was only 1914. But you know what I mean. Don't pretend you don't. An assassin lunged at me and hissed as he did so; in his hand was a rapier. The point passed through my ribs, but there was no pain at all.

'I'm already dead. You can't harm me!'

And while he gaped in astonishment, I smashed in his face, wiping all traces of his disbelief away. I felt an abrupt elation. I was a warrior too! I danced a jig, just a brief one. Around me the battle raged. Yeti fell down, legionnaires too; blood was everywhere. Locked in death grips, both sets of antagonists refused to capitulate.

And yet, slowly but surely, the yeti began to gain the upper hand; or the upper paw, if you're pedantic.

Distanto wiped sweat from his brow with his sleeve and said, 'Behind you, Mr Griffiths! Duck quickly!'

I did so without questioning the suggestion.

A trident prong grazed my skull!

It was Mario Granieri, the Italo-Mexican reactionary, his foul weapon clutched in both hands, a song of doom on his lips. And now I did a thing that changed my life forever; that allowed me to define myself as a hero. Still lacking a real weapon, I tore off my own leg and used it as a cudgel. My first powerful swipe caught Mario in his face! My second also caught him in his face! My third and fourth too!

And my fifth, sixth, seventh, eighth, ninth, tenth …

I kicked that tyrant to death.

An indirect kicking!

I felt an arm restraining me as I hopped to keep my balance. It was the airship captain, Distanto, and he was whispering words to me. His words were wise. This is what they said:

'Might as well stop when you reach one hundred!'

I did so. I looked down.

Putrid pulp was all that remained of perhaps the most evil villain ever, at least until the next one comes along.

Attaching my leg back onto my body, with some difficulty, I turned to see that the battle was almost over.

Three quarters of the yeti were dead.

But the GARGANTUAN LEGION was practically destroyed. Only ten or 11 fighters were left alive. One of them, in fact, wasn't fighting; I saw how hairy he was. He was the assassin from Alirgnahs! Now it was plain that he had been a spy among them all along. Doubtless his was the voice that had persuaded Pancho Poncho to follow the airship. He had led them into a trap! This made oddly perfect sense.

As for Pancho Poncho, he was grossly infuriated.

'Steenking pigs, all of you!'

Then he swallowed a flung yeti spear.

So did his comrades. Ouch.

The very last living assassin, the assassin from Panama, made a final desperate effort to kill me. He hurled a boomerang my way. The mystery of what a citizen of Panama was doing with a boomerang is irrelevant; I was struck on my exposed temple and hit to the ground. He assumed the blow had killed me. Then he noticed the transceiver set up by Rais Uli. It was impossible for anyone to stop him; he was too agile. He fiddled with the controls, transmitted a message.

'Assassin to base. Target has been eliminated.'

There was a crackle of static.

Then a horribly familiar double voice. 'Proof?'

'Yes, boss; the body is here.'

'Very well. Stand back. I'm coming through.'

The air shimmered greasily.

And a figure materialised out of nothingness ...

Mr Hubengo Gordbloaton!

His massive shoulders shook with monumental mirth as he beheld my prone form. He strode toward me on monolithic legs. When he saw that I wasn't dead, he would probably crush me under those legs; which, as I've just pointed out, were monolithic.

Excuse my writing style. I am a skeleton. I know I've used that excuse already, but it happens to be true.

If you were a skeleton I'd excuse you.

Anyway, Hubengo was almost on top of me, the slob!

Then he stopped and turned.

A spluttering sound had distracted him.

Over the summit of one of the tall peaks that ringed Alirgnahs came a bicycle. It was pulsejet powered!

Only one man sat on it; Sadegh Safani had jumped off. He had tricked poor Jason Rolfe. I'll explain how.

The waterwheel had fallen to bits, freeing the bicycle and its riders. So onwards had gone the pair, right to the borders of Alirgnahs. Up the slope of the nearest mountain they went, the angle increasing every second. Just as the alchemist had predicted, the bicycle gradually slowed; but Sadegh knew they couldn't both dismount; the moment the load was lightened by the first departing body, the velocity would increase again; and the one who remained would be trapped.

He did those sums in his turbaned head.

'Keep her steady,' he urged.

That was a hypocritical thing to say!

Sadegh was a proper meanie.

Just before gaining the apex of the peak, when the speed was only that of a galloping horse, he betrayed Mr Rolfe; he leapt off and rolled in soft snow. He still bruised himself, but he survived. As for Jason: the pulsejet engine vibrated with inhuman joy, as if sentient and aware of its reduced burden, and accelerated the bicycle.

Impossible for Mr Rolfe to jump off now!

So he remained in the saddle …

Down the inner slope he zoomed, lance extended.

His visor clogged with snowflakes.

He couldn't see much.

Just a hazy bloated form somewhere in front.

That would serve for a target!

Mustn't be too choosy.

Hubengo Gordbloaton screamed loudly!

The lance pierced him!

It entered the heart on his left side, snapped and turned 90 degrees and pierced his right side heart too. Then it snapped again and turned yet another 90 degrees, came out of his back. Mr Rolfe was in no position to enjoy his ambiguous triumph.

He spluttered past, still heading eastward.

Distanto waved him farewell. I don't think Jason waved back. I might be wrong about that. I often am.

For instance, years later, I chanced upon a book written by the airship captain himself. It was his memoirs. He mentioned this incident; but his version of events was different.

He claims that Mario Granieri was still alive, that he suddenly jumped out from nowhere and mounted Hubengo Gordbloaton like a knight on a stallion; that he jousted against Jason, trident versus lance. If that's what really happened, I must be a deluded idiot or miserable liar. I'm neither of those things. I'm merely flayed.

Distanto Faraway was a rabid exaggerator.

But still a remarkable man …

We all staggered back to the cave. I warmed my bones beside the fire. I can do that literally. You can't.

Bleakness had enveloped my soul.

Rais Uli noticed my mood. 'It's a normal feeling after war, even when one is victorious. It'll soon pass.'

'After the battle, bowels on thorns,' I said.

'A line of poetry?' he asked.

'Yes. The old Welsh poet Taliesin. I often plagiarise him.'

Distanto said, 'Quoting isn't plagiarism.'

'The way I do it, it is,' I said.

That was me being cynical about myself.

Don't take it too seriously!

The aftermath of this battle was an easier affair than the aftermaths of most battles elsewhere. We didn't need to remove the bodies for burial. A bunch of dinosaurs turned up to dispose of them. The chewing lasted the entire night. Even the bones were swallowed. Hygienic, I suppose. But it wasn't enough for the monsters to dine on human and yeti corpses. They also devoured Distanto's airship.

'How will we get out of Alirgnahs now?' I cried.

Rais Uli said, 'Let's walk.'

Distanto smoothed his moustache. 'On one condition.'

'What's that, my friend?'

'We don't go back the way we came.'

'Suits me,' I said. And it did. I had no desire to return to a Europe in the grip of madness. 'Which way?'

'South,' suggested Distanto.

'South,' seconded Rais Uli.

I smiled and nodded agreeably. 'South it is!'

And that's the way we went.

PART THREE: NEARY

THE APEDOG INCIDENT

The Bone Banana

When men pervert science, terrible things happen. But the most repulsive scientific perversions are those that occur in the biological disciplines. In 1920, a medical researcher by the name of Ilya Ivanovich Ivanov decided that it might be possible to create a chimp-human hybrid. He wrote a brief proposal to the revolutionary government who were then dominating and despoiling the culture and life of Russia.

His proposal was passed with a ludicrous lack of efficiency from one department to the next; and often lost and found again on the way to the bureaucratic summit. At last it came to the attention of Lenin, who read it with a frown and finally decided that it was an idea with some merit. But political pressures were mounting on him; his health was poor. Somehow he completely forgot about the document.

The Russian Civil War was raging; conflicting armies of Reds, Whites and Anarchists were stampeding back and forth across the steppes; there was precious little room in Lenin's bald, ailing dome for scientific matters. But Ivanov's bizarre proposal also came to the notice of Stalin, who found it thrilling. Stalin went over the head of Lenin, squinting against the glare as he did so, and issued an official reply.

Ivanov received formal permission and limited funds to commence a series of experiments. There was an ape sanctuary in Sukhumi, capital of Abkhazia, a republic recently absorbed into the Soviet Empire. The apes had belonged to a wealthy trader called Zander. Now they belonged to the Bolsheviks. Ivanov travelled to Sukhumi to inspect them, but they were all useless. The war had traumatised them.

'I can hardly expect a shell-shocked primate to produce healthy and useful offspring!' he grumbled to himself.

If he wanted to secure specimens in perfect health there was no option but to travel to the original source of the apes. He must travel to Africa! Ivanov made the appropriate enquiries and frittered away in bribes most of the roubles he had been awarded; but extra funds were made available to him. Stalin had charged him with sending regular reports back; he did whatever he could to smooth Ivanov's path.

And so it was that in early 1924 Ivanov found himself a passenger on a steamer bound for French Guinea, for the port city of Conakry. Stalin had arranged this for him. That appalling tyrant rubbed his hands in glee and drained the last drop of vodka in the bottle. A chimp-human hybrid would suit his purposes very well indeed. The more, the merrier! Lenin was on his deathbed. Destiny was muttering.

Stalin saw great potential in an army of humanzees. A special division of obedient subhumans, stronger than men, more malign than apes, armed with rifles and short swords and long clubs. Such creatures could march, swing and lope across Europe, smashing the Western Powers to yellowish pulp. Properly controlled humanzees would be almost unstoppable! Stalin called for more vodka and chuckled heartily.

When he finally reached French Guinea after a rough crossing, Ivanov waited for the greenish tinge to leave his cheeks, a matter of only a few days, and then made contact with a group of communists who had been instructed to assist him. The corrupt priests of a religious mission house deep in the forest were willing to help in return for money. Ivanov set off for this remote locale with all his equipment.

The mission house contained a specialist hospital for the treatment of young women. The priest in charge of the hospital, Father Phigga, shook hands solemnly with Ivanov and whispered, 'Ignore all those who already have children. Impregnate only the virgins. They won't know anything is wrong when they give birth to hairy babes.' And Ivanov agreed this was sagacious advice. He began work immediately.

Nets were strung between trees in the grounds of the hospital; bait in the form of fruit was scattered nearby. After a night of terrible screams and thrashings, a dozen chimpanzees were discovered tangled in the traps the following morning. The females were released; the males were taken into the improvised laboratory that Ivanov had set up behind the altar of the hospital chapel. He operated in solitude.

Secrecy was important to the project. Stalin had warned Ivanov that if any news of what he was doing leaked out and reached the ears of foreign governments, the medical researcher would be killed without any fuss by one of Stalin's numerous assassins. Ivanov was careful to hide the details of his experiment even from his guides in Guinea. Only the meddlesome Father Phigga knew more than he should have.

Ivanov removed the testicles of the captured apes. With the fluid they contained, he surreptitiously inseminated the fittest and most attractive of the female patients in the wards. He told them he was injecting them with a new medicine. There was no need to obtain consent: he was a Stalinist to the roots of his identity. In time, some of the virgins became pregnant. He informed them that the bulges were tumours.

He delivered the babies himself, still maintaining the illusion that this was a radical form of surgery to extract the cancers that were eating them. By this time, Father Phigga had succumbed to a new illness that bizarrely resembled strychnine poisoning. Probably he had caught it from the birds he liked he shoot and devour lightly grilled in the jungle. His grotesquely contorted body was cremated without an autopsy.

Ivanov raised the infant humanzees in a wing of the mission house that was off-limits to everyone but he. The furniture and ornaments there had been the property of Father Phigga. The hybrids learned everything from Ivanov alone. He became the father he had always wished his own father had been, indulgent, patient, merry; stern but not unjust. The humanzees were six in number, healthy, hirsute individuals.

One died in an accident, falling into the piano that another was playing in a wild frenzy, striking the keys with fingers strong enough to snap the necks of men in a moment. The resultant music sounded not unlike some of the less successful *avant-garde* pieces of such contemporary composers as Schoenberg and Varèse. A year later another humanzee died, choking on a narrow shoe it had unwisely tried to consume.

Ilya Ivanov waited for instructions from Stalin. Eventually a message arrived that ordered him back to Russia, his creatures and unspent funds included. It was time for a formal evaluation of Ivanov's work. And so the scientist packed up his equipment; but one of the humanzees escaped in the process. Ivanov went after it with a shotgun, but it had fled deep into the jungle, settling in a village in the mountains.

The villagers welcomed the humanzee, made him a permanent guest in the community. People who assume they worshipped the beast as a fetish need to realign their attitudes; for the men who dwell in the mountains of Guinea are not fools. They knew the humanzee wasn't a god. Nonetheless they made him a sort of minor chieftain, and they carved a massive bone banana in his honour. And called him Fabalo ...

Meanwhile, Ilya Ivanov had sailed back to Russia with the three other humanzees, none of which had real names. They were simply known as Specimens One, Two and Three; for Ivanov lacked the imagination of the mountain dwellers of Guinea. These apes sickened and died while still in transit. Ivanov arrived in Russia empty handed; Stalin sent him into exile in Siberia, where he became a latrine attendant.

Fabalo was the object of the amorous attentions of countless maidens of the forest. Perhaps he was regarded as the epitome of potency. Many were the children he fathered in the moonlit shadow of the bone banana; and soon his family was mighty and strong. His sons and daughters were one third chimp and two-thirds human. Some of these later mated with pure chimps, others with humans; and so the flux of genetic percentages soon made strict accounting extremely tricky.

One day, a member of his tribe went wandering off into the forest and never returned. Fabalo sent out a search party, but to no avail. The rains came and obliterated his tracks. Lost for weeks, the youth somehow made his way down to the coast. He was found by an old sailor with very poor eyesight who gave him a set of old clothes. Dressed like a beachcomber, the lost youth wandered into the city of Conakry.

Now we must turn our attention to another eccentric Russian scientist, a fellow called Filip Filippovich Preobrazhensky. For many years, in his Moscow apartment, he had been experimenting with the surgical insertion of chimp glands into the bodies of ageing men and women; rejuvenation was his main objective. But he had discussed a secret project with Stalin, namely the generation of a dog-human hybrid.

Preobrazhensky had already inserted the pituitary gland of a deceased human into a mongrel dog; and the animal had demonstrated increasingly human characteristics within a short space of time. Now Stalin suggested a variation of the procedure: the transplantation of a dog's pituitary gland into a human. Just to see what might happen. But the maverick scientist was told to procure his own dog and human.

Walking the streets of Moscow in a snowstorm, Preobrazhensky soon found a homeless dog and a homeless man; he brought them back to his cosy apartment. A cloth soaked in chloroform was applied to each; and the operation was performed. When the heavily-bandaged patient woke, Preobrazhensky leaned over him and spoke. But the patient understood not a word. The researcher tried other languages.

Finally, he had success. The patient appeared to know French. 'You are an immigrant? From West Africa maybe?'

The patient nodded. Already part ape and part human, he would soon also become part dog. A man-dog-ape hybrid unplanned by anyone! For he was the lost youth who had Fabalo for a father. Half man, half chimp, half hound, he was perhaps the most curious being then alive on the surface of the planet. And before you object that those fractions don't add up properly, what *does* add up in this world? Answer me that, if you think you're so smart. Bet you can't. Told you so.

The Fungus

I set off with my companions, Distanto Faraway and Rais Uli, with only a tiny amount of apprehension in the cavity where my heart had once been. I emitted a dull brown glow as I walked; this was due partly to the mystic preserving energy that suffused me, partly to the fungus that sheathed my bones. My friends did not shine at all.

We left the forgotten (or unknown) land of Alirgnahs by scaling to the top of one of the peaks that ringed it. Then we turned and looked down on its sweet meadows, the dinosaurs and yeti that gambolled there. Only the powerful stink of the rotting corpses of a recently-defeated invading army ruined the illusion of utopian splendour.

We descended the mountain on its southern slope; it was such a steep climb that Distanto and Rais Uli were forced to hack steps in the ice with their blades. I felt no chill, despite the absence of my flesh; and immunity of that kind was welcome. Yet I cared not to listen to the wind whistling through my exposed ribs and vertebrae.

'Perhaps I ought to clothe myself before continuing?' I wondered. My companions nodded silently at this. Rais Uli had a spare cloak; he gave it to me and I wrapped myself in its indigo folds with contentment. At last I felt the weight of a great responsibility lifted from my sharp shoulders. It was a relief no longer to be frightening.

As if reading my thoughts, Distanto said, 'The

improvement isn't quite as complete as you assume. Your sticklike arms and legs jut out; and your skull-face peeps from beneath the hood.'

'Surely that's more acceptable than being a bare skeleton?'

'You look like the Grim Reaper.'

I appealed to Rais Uli for a second opinion. He said:

'I'm afraid that's the truth, Mr Griffiths. I advise you never to accept a scythe if it's offered to you. Also, try to ensure that you never hold in one hand a rapidly emptying hourglass.'

'Thank you. I'll bear those suggestions in mind. Truly.'

But in fact I was bewildered.

Distanto said, 'We're at the bottom now.'

Right at the base of the lofty mountain stood a weathered old signpost that pointed to the south and proclaimed that India was in that direction. I was delighted by this reminder. Dreams of that exotic realm had filled my head for many years; the country seemed a repository of wonders, magic, adventure. A spicy future beckoned.

We had little money between us; I wondered if I might earn a living in India as a guru. When skeletons dispense wisdom, people are more prone to pay attention. That was my theory.

'What gives you that idea?' retorted Distanto.

'Enlighten us,' urged Rais Uli.

I drew a deep unnecessary breath and said:

'Wisdom exists inside every man; so does a skeleton. Clearly there's a connection between skeletons and sagacity. I am a skeleton. I know what is inside a man, for I *am* what is inside a man. Wisdom isn't inside me; it is on my outside. I am coated with wisdom. I don't need to reach within. I merely scrape some wisdom off my bones like butter from breakfast toast and cast it bountifully into the winds.'

'You have the tongue of a sophist,' commented Rais Uli.

'He has no tongue at all,' said Distanto.

'And no eyes, just empty sockets. How does he see?' Rais

Uli plucked at his beard and I stopped in my tracks.

'That's an interesting point you have raised,' I said unhappily. It was a question that had been bothering me ever since I lost my flesh. The jellies that enable men to process photons into images had been gouged from my face; my empty sockets loomed like miniature cave mouths in the side of a cliff sculpted into the form of a skull.

That simile seems to have gone round in a circle. Forgive my awkward writing style. I'm a journalist for *The Western Mail*. My eye sockets were empty, yet they worked. I wasn't blind!

'He can see just as well now as before,' said Distanto.

'True,' agreed Rais Uli, 'but how?'

Distanto smoothed his moustache. 'Perhaps the fungus that covers him is responsible. Some odd sort of inter-species symbiotic relationship now exists between the man and the mould. After all, fungus is photosensitive. Clearly it sees for him; and in return he allows it to feed on the marrow in his bones. That's my educated guess.'

I was shocked to hear this. 'What will happen when all my marrow is gone?' I squealed. Rais Uli considered the query and finally provided an answer both practical and dreamlike.

'You'll sound exactly like a xylophone, Mr Griffiths.'

'And then the fungus will depart and seek a new host. You'll be just a blind hollow nobody,' added Distanto.

'Your theory is wrong,' I growled.

He arched his eyebrows. 'Really? How so?'

'I'm wrapped up tight in this cloak. How can any fungus see through such thick cloth? Even a mushroom with a telescope wouldn't be able to manage such a stunt. It's ridiculous!'

'As I pointed out earlier, your arms and legs protrude.'

'I am seeing with my hands?'

He nodded. 'And your feet. You can see with any part of your body as keenly as a vulture; or if not a vulture, for I often tend to exaggerate such things, then a gerbil. I envy you that.'

Rais Uli contributed to the airship captain's reverie. 'Ah

yes! You'll be able to peer around corners and into small spaces simply by positioning a toe or finger in the correct place. A marvellous gift! You have become an all-over eye. A total-surface-area spy!'

'Around corners, yes. And also into opaque jars.'

'If you are swimming underwater, you'll be able to raise one hand like a periscope. You can peer anywhere.'

'Up skirts too, if necessary.'

The conversation lapsed. We trudged onwards.

At last I could bear it no longer.

'I'm not a raper,' I said.

Distanto turned to regard me. 'I beg your pardon.'

'You said that I looked like the Grim Raper. But I've never forced any woman against her will. It's a lie.'

'*Reaper*, you fool! There's no such word as "raper".'

And he was right about that.

But I never managed to clarify in my brain the difference between the two terms. Many years later, when I was a very old man, a modern music group who called themselves (I think) the Green Cockle Sect released a song entitled 'Don't Fear the Reaper' and I still imagined it referred to a felon who molested women. Weird.

The Clean Balloon

We kept going until we reached the outskirts of civilisation. The sun had set by this time. Instead of entering the village in darkness and scaring the inhabitants, or rousing their dogs with the smell of my bones, we decided to camp on the banks of a river. In the morning, Rais Uli or else Distanto would make contact with the locals.

The riverbank was bright with clothes pegged on poles to dry. Nobody washes clothes with such vigour and thoroughness as the *dhobis* of India. River washing in India is an artform. These clothes flapped in the breeze of a cool evening. We camped near them; chewing the food the yeti had given us and drinking their petal beer.

I lay down to sleep very drunk and wondering how a being without an appetite, stomach or guts could manage to hold his liquor as well as I had. My dreams were awful. Black dogs came and buried me. Cannibals took me and poked me through their noses. Children snapped me in half, made wishes; used my femurs as cricket bats.

Something was licking my face. A tiger or bear?

No, the tongue was that of a fire.

An inferno was raging!

It was still night but the mad glow of the flames enabled me to witness everything in perfect detail. Distanto had stolen the clothes from the poles and had somehow stitched them together. Now he was throwing logs onto the fire, making it hotter and hotter …

'What are you doing, *Monsieur*?' I screeched.

He lifted a finger to his lips.

'I refuse to be quiet!' I protested. 'Those clothes aren't yours.'

'Priority of need,' he hissed back.

'Your brother Scipio would never lower himself to such a deed,' cried I with passion. 'He had morality!'

'Bah! You and Scipio! Marry him if you think he's so perfect! I had to grow up with that pretentious oaf!'

I fell back in horror at this suggestion. A skeleton marry a man! It was disgusting to my ears. I know that in the more enlightened times in which you are reading this, such things don't matter too much. But we were still prejudiced back then; we were bigots.

'I belong in the skies. Not on the ground!' he added.

'That's no excuse for stealing —'

'Yes it is. Up, up and away for me. Goodbye!'

'How will dry clothes aid you?'

'Are you blind, you all-seeing buffoon? I have made myself a balloon! The heat of this fire is currently inflating it. Soon I shall float free of what I regard as a ball of filth, the Earth!'

This was no lie. The canopy was already swelling.

I went to awaken Rais Uli.

He stirred from his slumber with a groan.

'Are the djinns prancing?'

'No, no,' I assured him, 'but something else has happened.'

He opened his eyes and sighed.

'Your don't have a basket, *Monsieur* Faraway. How will you fly under such a vehicle without a basket?'

'I will cling on,' replied Distanto, 'in a special way.'

'What way is that?' I blurted.

'Tight. It's not ideal, but the ground irks me. I must be free of it again, no matter how great the gamble!'

'Leave him to his folly,' advised Rais Uli.

I nodded and sat down, away from the blast of the furnace. The desert son and I watched the balloon inflate bigger and bigger. Suddenly it rose into the velvet sky, Distanto holding on beneath it. He dangled with perfect confidence, needing only one hand. He waved with the other. The breeze caught him and he vanished.

'He won't get far,' said Rais Uli, 'for the hot air inside the canopy will soon cool; but he's a desperate man.'

'Yes, he loves the stratosphere. He should have been born a cloud, not a human being. I feel sorry for the locals when they discover their clothes are missing. Will they blame us?'

'Probably not me, but almost certainly you.'

'Because I am a skeleton?'

He nodded. 'It makes you a more likely suspect.'

'What shall we do?' I asked.

'I'll go first and speak to them. I'm famed for my eloquence. You wait an hour and then follow; the shock will be less after I smooth the way. It might be a good idea to flesh you out.'

'What do you mean by that, Rais Uli?' I wondered.

'A new face can be moulded for you from river clay. Your bony limbs can be coated in the same manner.'

'But if my fungus is covered, I won't be able to see.'

'We'll leave one fingertip bare.'

This was an ingenious solution to my difficulty and I lay full length on my back while Rais Uli scooped handfuls of wet clay from the riverbank, applying them skilfully to my bones; he made arms, legs and a believable visage for me. When the sun rose, he told me to stand facing it, to dry the clay and stop my fake flesh oozing off me in clumps. I did as he bade and the sun coaxed steam from my gunk.

Rais Uli strode along to the village, which was just out of sight around a bend in the river. I heard nothing, no babble of voices, no cows, nothing at all. An hour passed and my face was baked hard. I flexed my limbs; the clay remained in position. Time for me to follow my companion. My gait was stiff but workable. I reached the village in less than ten minutes. As I entered it, I saw that I was expected.

The village elders sat in the shade of an enormous tree; and they were facing me. Rais Uli was with them. He rose and gestured, smiling. Many of the elders frowned. I felt dizzy as I approached, my exposed forefinger held up before me as if poking an imaginary soft fruit. The smile of Rais Uli never wavered for an instant. I stopped in front of him and felt bathed in the scrutiny of two dozen old men.

'I told them you were ugly, but wise,' said Rais Uli.

'Thank you,' I answered calmly.

'Smile at them, smile at them!' he urged.

I did so. My entire face cracked.

It had been baked too hard. It was an unglazed face.

The cracks widened. The face broke.

In three large pieces my visage fell to the ground.

And shattered into crumbs there!

The elders jumped to their feet, pointing and shouting. I didn't speak a word of their language but the meaning of their words was obvious. 'Not a man but a skeleton! He's a bony freak! We can't have that around here. He must be dealt with severely, eh?'

The Midget

Rais Uli did his best to restrain them; but although he remained a figure of respect to them, his influence was rather limited. He had no power to make them desist from manhandling me.

They trussed me up with cords; and the cords were attached to a stake that was planted in the ground in the tiny central square of the village. It's never nice being tied up by people who hate you, but in this case I feared an extra cruel and unusual punishment.

There was a merchant in the village who knew a little Arabic; thus he was able to communicate the plans of the elders to Rais Uli, who relayed them to me. An execution had been scheduled for that morning anyway. Thus my arrival was seen as fortuitous.

Rais Uli explained, 'There's a midget who lives here, a fellow so tiny that he always looks as if he's stood far away when you are talking to him, and he has been accused of magic.'

'Black magic?' I supposed.

'No, purple magic actually. I'm not sure of the exact difference yet. It's a strange dialect of Arabic that the merchant speaks. Anyway, they intend to kill the midget today. At noon ...'

'What does this have to do with me?' I whimpered.

'They plan to burn him alive.'

'Very well. And yet—'

Rais Uli leaned closer. '*Inside* you, my friend.'

My jaw chattered. 'Pardon?'

'You are a skeleton, a walking cage. They will imprison the midget in the cavity formed by your ribs. Then they will pile firewood around you. The midget will burn like indigestion within you. Worse than indigestion, in fact. For the flames will be real.'

'Can't you do anything to help?' I pleaded.

'No,' he answered simply.

'Will you simply stand back and watch?'

'Heavens, no! What an idea!'

I was cheered by this response. 'What will you do?'

His reply crushed my spirits into a pulp even flatter than the puddle of slime they already resembled. 'The merchant is leaving in an hour for the coast., He plans to take a *dhow* across the Arabian Sea to Oman. He asked me to accompany him. I wish to return to the Rif, my homeland. Oman is closer to the Rif than India, so — '

'You backstabbing traitor!' I sobbed dryly.

'Mr Griffiths!' he chided. 'Where is it written that I, Mulai Ahmed el Rais Uli, am a gentle, kind person?'

'Nowhere, I suppose,' I conceded reluctantly.

'I have been known to boil the eyes of my enemies with heated coins. I once imprisoned an adversary in a giant lute and goaded a mad baboon into playing febrile primal melodies on the instrument until the prisoner exploded. That is the truth of it.'

'Fair enough. Point taken,' I muttered.

'Goodbye, Mr Griffiths.'

'Farewell, Rais Uli. Take care at sea.'

'I shall. Roast in peace.'

And then, with a swirl of his cloak, he was gone. I never saw him ever again; but if you are interested in learning more about him, he does linger in certain history books on certain shelves. Personally I was happy to see the back of him, the filthy barbarian!

The elders came out of the largest hut in the village,

leading a midget on a chain. He squeaked in outrage.

With considerable difficulty, they threaded and squeezed him into me, until he squatted behind my ribs, clutching my bones like the grim bars of an oubliette, the worst kind of dungeon.

He ranted and raved in his own miniature language.

The elders heaped firewood around.

A flame was carefully applied!

'*Anws blewog!*' I cried.

The Mongorgon

The elders weren't as clever as they thought they were. The first things to burn in the blaze were the cords that held me to the stake. I broke free of my captivity and stumbled through the burning logs, scattering them with my feet in random directions. Some rolled through the open doorways of nearby huts and set the huts on fire!

In the confusion and chaos, I was able to make my escape. I ran as fast as I could out of the village. No-one followed me; they were too intent on extinguishing the blaze and saving their homes. The midget laughed and I felt him shift position inside me like a hearty meal. Then he spoke, to my utter amazement, in my own tongue.

Flabbergasted, I gasped, 'You know Welsh!'

'Yes. I'm from Swansea.'

'How is that possible? You are a midget!'

And I voiced other objections.

He snarled back, 'Don't little men grow in Wales too? Of course they do! And I have dark skin. So what? And I speak Hindi, Urdu and Bangla. What's the big deal? I also speak English, French, Spanish and Greek. I'm an engineer and I travel the world.'

'What were you doing in this remote region?'

'Preparing the ground for a railway. That village was supposed to be the terminus of a new line from Patna, but the elders didn't care for such an innovation. I was welcomed when I first arrived, but that environment went sour. False accusations were made against me; charges not trumped up by an elephant but by humans!'

'Yes, we are a despicable species,' I pondered.

'Well now, what's your name?'

'Lloyd Griffiths. Yours?'

'Hywel Owl, it is.'

'Pleased to meet you, Hywel.' I could only shake his hand by groping inside my own chest like an Aztec who plucks out his own heart after he has sacrificed himself. 'Are you the smallest engineer in the business? It must be difficult working with rivets.'

I assumed he frowned. 'How so?'

'A rivet will be to you what a large bun is to me.'

'That's not a problem.'

His tone was so unwavering that I was assured of the fact. Indeed, why shouldn't little men excel at any task they are given? As I said before, the times were more prejudiced back then; we were full of absurd ideas about what was proper and what wasn't. Sometimes, when I remember what the normal attitudes were between the years 1909 and 1986 I am ashamed. In my long life only the most recent decade has demonstrated even to a tiny degree that tolerance is practicable.

'I wasn't always an engineer,' he told me. 'I once was a hunter of that mythical beast known as a Xaratan; but that's a different story for another time and place. Increase your pace, if you would, my friend. I suggest we head for Srinagar, where my railway company has an office. They will be very helpful. Take a right turn here.'

We had reached a dusty crossroads; I obeyed him.

All day and night I trudged.

And the following day too. And the day after that.

For many days. For weeks.

It was a fantastic landscape, an impalement of mountains; raging white rivers full of melted glacier water rushed everywhere, spanned only by an antiquated series of rope bridges. At night we camped beneath large trees twisted to bizarre shapes by fickle winds and the demands of atmospheric imagery. I lit and huddled around fires; for Hywel was a normal man and shivered when cold. Ever had a midget shiver inside you? It's not what I'd recommend as a beneficial event.

I lost count of the days. Eventually we reached Srinagar.

Self-consciously I walked the streets.

Eyes swivelled in sockets.

Fingers jabbed at us. Mouths gaped.

At this precise point, I planned to reserve a paragraph to describe that wonderful city; to mention the sights we saw and the sounds we heard; to give the slightest impression of the colour, chaos, vibrancy of the place. It seemed the least service I might do you, the reader, who have come so far with me through these memoirs. But Hywel dissuaded me. His argument was ingenious. I present it here:

'Any author might pick up a guide book and use that as a source of his information about a city he has never visited. If you describe Srinagar in a detached way, as you have described every location so far, readers will be forced to conclude you never went there. In short that you are a cheat and these adventures never happened!'

It was a valid criticism. I thanked him for his advice.

So don't expect any background details.

I want you to believe I was there!

And thus I was. Hywel too.

Before I withered under the rapacious gazes of the inquisitive citizens and merchants of Srinagar, we turned a corner and saw before us a minor office of the same railway company that employed my tiny friend. It was a drab building but welcome to our eyes. I opened the door, pushed into a dimly-lit room and approached a clerk who was seated at a desk in the far corner of the space. He looked up.

'Have you made an appointment?' he asked.

'No. I am a skeleton,' I said.

'Ask to speak to the manager!' hissed Hywel.

'The manager please,' I said.

The clerk frowned at me, got up and went into a back room. His head reappeared in the doorway a minute later. 'Come through. Mr Higgs will see you in his own private office.'

'Lucky!' squeaked Hywel. 'I know him!'

'Very fortunate,' I agreed.

I followed the clerk down a short corridor to another gloomy room. Mr Higgs was playing with an executive toy, one of those boyish devices that demonstrate the principle of the conservation of momentum between steel balls suspended from a rack. He was thoroughly engrossed in his sport, so much so that the clerk coughed to attract his attention. Mr Higgs frowned at me and said, 'You look familiar.'

I was astonished. 'Really? Have we met before?'

He waved a hand. 'No, I meant that you bear an uncanny resemblance to the famous composer Borodin.'

'Alexander Borodin? But he died in 1887.'

'Exactly, dear boy! All *his* flesh must have rotted too by now.'

And Mr Higgs burst into laughter.

I fumed and opened my jaw to strike back with a deadly insult of my own, but it was the midget, Hywel Owl, who spoke first. 'Mr Higgs, sir! Remember me, sir? It's Hywel, sir!'

Wiping his steamy spectacles on the cuff of his sweaty shirt, replacing them on his nose and squinting, Mr Higgs said, 'Ah yes, Hywel! We gave you up for dead. What are you doing squatting inside that living skeleton? It's not the most dignified position.'

'I was forced into him by malign elders, sir!'

I confirmed his story. 'It's true.'

Mr Higgs remained unimpressed. 'I'm not sure what you expect me to do about it. You didn't come here hoping for another job, did you? That's simply not possible, I'm afraid. You have proved yourself to be unreliable and unpredictable. Our company can't afford to keep incompetents on the payroll; not even tiny incompetents.'

And he giggled again. India had made him insane.

Or maybe he had been even more insane before he arrived, and he had been partly cured by the overwhelming spirit of India, so that now he was only half a loon. But a damn big half.

Hywel Owl stuttered, 'What about severance pay?'

'Half wages for a half man?'

'That's my right. Give me what you owe!'

Mr Higgs remained unmoved. 'Half pay for a half man entombed in a halfwit. Let's see. That makes half of a half of a half. So one eighth of one hour's normal pay. Total: one rupee.'

'I dispute that calculation!' squeaked Hywel.

'Oh dear. There's a clause in your original work contract that specifies that a midget who disputes, while occupying space inside a skeleton, any calculation made near a working executive toy, must forfeit all severance pay and be further liable to a fine of —'

We didn't get to hear the rest of it. I had fled out of the room, down the corridor and through the front door.

'What are you doing?' Hywel demanded.

'We have no money,' I muttered, 'and if we must pay a fine, however unjust, we'll end up in debtors' prison. Better to forget seeking help from those cheats and look after ourselves!'

He saw the wisdom of this. 'Fair enough.'

We hurried through the crowded streets. Men frowned at us; eyes full of mirth or wonder twinkled. We turned a corner into a busy market. The people gathered there called out at us.

'I don't think living bones are welcome,' said Hywel.

'Maybe I leer too much?' I asked.

'Could be. Who knows? I think you should increase your speed. There is an atmosphere of peril here. Let's go to the train station and try to jump on a train. Even if we are caught by an inspector and thrown off, we'll be out of Srinagar at least! Quickly now!'

This was good advice. We passed through the market at a trot. No man followed us, but something did. Something thin and low, sleek and agile. One of the market traders had let it loose. Was it a pet? I turned to glance over my shoulder and I shouted out:

'A mongoose! They've set a mongoose on us!'

Then I saw that it wasn't precisely one of those famous animals. True, it had the body of a mongoose; but it had snakes for hair, little cobras and vipers that spat and hissed viciously.

Hywel cried, 'It's a Mongorgon. We're doomed!'

The Steam Elephant

'*Pen pidlan gawsog!*' I breathed softly, and then I added, 'What the heck is a Mongorgon? Does it truly exist?'

Hywel nodded his head inside me. I felt rather than saw him do it; and the feeling wasn't nice. 'Yes. This is no hallucination. I told you I was an expert on mythic beasts. The Mongorgon has a particularly nasty bite that is fatal to midget-enhanced skeletons.'

'What shall we do? I don't want to die again …'

'Have you died already then?'

'Not sure. An army of proto-fascists did flay me; but I was already full of a rejuvenating brownish energy.'

'That's a tricky one,' he acknowledged.

'Think of something fast!'

'Look! There's the train station!'

I swerved around an ox and bounded to the entrance.

A guard gestured at me to stop.

But I dodged past him, vaulted the ticket barrier and sprinted onto the platform. Yet there wasn't a train in sight! Our hopes of getting a free ride on a locomotive that was just pulling out were decisively dashed. Up the platform I went, and back down it.

The foul Mongorgon was close behind, weaving between the legs and baggage of the waiting passengers. Guards with long truncheons emerged from a hut and came rushing at us.

'This is starting to get intolerable,' I remarked.

'Across the tracks!' said Hywel.

I had little choice but to run that way, praying my narrow feet wouldn't get stuck between the rails. We ran behind a derailed carriage, found that it formed a corridor with another carriage, and that this corridor led into a maze with a constant railway theme.

Soon I was lost in a dismal region of warehouses, rusting rolling stock, iron girders and wooden sleepers stacked in untidy piles. But we appeared to have escaped the Mongorgon and the guards. 'So unfriendly!' I huffed to myself as I thought about them.

I didn't expect a reply to that, but I was bewildered by a snore from my ribs. Hywel Owl had fallen asleep!

I picked my way through this open-air museum of the *now*. There was a peculiar peace about it. The sun went down and in the twilight the hulks of abandoned locomotives resembled the beached hydrogen-whales of the planet Saturn. Or so I imagined! I haven't ever been to Saturn so I can't be sure the comparison is apt. Anyway ...

Beyond the clouds of gnats, just around a bend in the tracks, I saw the trunk of an elephant. It unnerved me.

Elephants are enormous creatures; incredibly strong. Welshmen never feel comfortable in the presence of such magnificent beasts. I wasn't sure what to do next. I couldn't ask Hywel for advice, because I didn't want to wake him. He was clearly exhausted.

I slowed my pace but didn't stop. The trunk waved.

Undulated like a thick snake.

Or maybe like an intelligent one.

I peered more closely. There was something odd about it. As it moved, it made a clashing noise, metallic.

As silently as possible I approached the bend.

The trunk stopped waving. It puckered as if sniffing; it had caught my scent. It pointed itself directly at me. There was silence for half a minute. I watched to see what it intended.

Suddenly it blasted out steam!

A hot cloud that completely enveloped me!

Locomotive Breath

Hywel woke instantly. He howled as he felt himself scalded by the steam and then screamed again as that steam condensed into boiling water. Then he rattled my ribcage violently, throwing me off balance. Far too late now to flee this strange elephant's wrath.

I blurted, 'We are done for. Unless it mistakenly thought we needed a sauna, I think it plans to murder us.'

But Hywel wasn't convinced by my analysis.

Red in the face and dripping, he recovered his senses quickly. 'To the best of my knowledge, Mr Griffiths, no elephant contains steam. Go and investigate properly. It must be a machine of some kind. What is there to lose? We can't return to the station.'

He was right about that. I stepped forward again.

The trunk didn't move at all.

Then I rounded the bend.

A man stood there; and his profile was so recognisable that I chuckled with bony glee and made no effort to mute my mirth. 'Distanto Faraway! I knew you wouldn't get far under that absurd balloon. So we are reunited again for another wild adventure—'

The frown on his brow cut me short. Then I realised my mistake; I had made a similar error before, in a tavern in Dresden. 'Scipio, is it? Yes, I knew it was you. Scipio Faraway!'

The man continued to frown. Then he said:

'Why do you address me by the names of my two brothers? I'm Neary Faraway; I am only part human …'

So this was the third sibling, the last of the triplets!

Hywel said, 'Only part human?'

'Yes, the remainder of me is locomotive.'

This was spoken in so nonchalant a tone that I assumed he was jesting. In the dusk it was difficult to discern details; but as I glanced down, his wheels became plain to see. Just like the wheels of an ordinary train, they were mounted on the rails of the railway. I was speechless. His stomach was a furnace and coals dimly glowed behind the grilled door. The water was stored in his hollow sternum.

'Who did this to you?' demanded Hywel.

'I did it to myself,' said Neary.

'But why, man? Why?'

'Because I like to move with the times.'

'You engineered yourself?'

'Indeed. Choo choo!'

I snapped out of the trap of my stupefaction. With a heel click no less precise than that of a Prussian aristocrat, I declared, 'We are honoured to make your acquaintance, *Monsieur*. I'm scarcely in a position to criticise anyone on the basis of appearance and this is a fine evening. I know both your brothers well and I'm happy to state that the Faraway Brothers are an incomparable bunch of prodigies!'

Neary said nothing in reply. He was beyond flattery.

'Do you have a lamp?' asked Hywel.

Neary nodded and adjusted something on his brow. It glowed and cast a warm pallor over our surroundings. A warm pallor? That sounds like a contradiction, but isn't. The lamp was an integral part of his person, just one among many modifications. Able to inspect him more closely in the light, I noted that less than one third of him remained human. One of his arms was a normal man's arm; the other was the metallic trunk. I nodded and asked between clenched teeth:

'Surely that trunk is less useful than a real arm?'

'Not so,' he replied. 'Not so.'

'Would you care to explain why?' I pressed.

He answered, 'There are more muscles in the average elephant's trunk than in the entire working body of a human being. The trunk is capable of great dexterity. It can snap branches from trees, strangle tigers to unconsciousness if necessary, wrestle soldiers or policemen to the ground and uproot signposts from crossroads.'

'A celebration of brute force,' I murmured.

He heard me. 'Yes. But it is also capable of delicacy and gentleness. I can use it to peel jackfruit, stroke the luxuriant tresses of a dusky maiden and even execute a self-portrait. Elephant trunks are accomplished in war and peace; in science and the arts.'

'Execute a self-portrait? I don't believe you!'

'I will demonstrate,' he said.

I watched very intently, for I didn't think he would be able to hold the end of a paintbrush in such a clumsy-seeming mechanical limb. But I was soon to be shamed. He reached into a cavity with his human arm and took out an old portrait of himself as an unmodified human. I widened my dark sockets at this, for it seemed I was looking at Scipio or Distanto. A youth in a beret lounging with a baguette.

'This painting is already finished!' I objected.

'Yes, a domestic scene. Gustave Moreau painted it. Do you know his work? He was a symbolist. Funnily enough, you resemble him strongly. In fact, the likeness is almost exact.'

I blanched at this. 'Moreau died in 1898!'

He chuckled. 'Precisely!'

'You have deceived me,' I said.

He ignored me, propped the picture against a nearby rock. Aiming the metallic trunk at it, he closed his eyes and squeezed his face, as if he was suffering from dysentery or another gastrointestinal complaint. Suddenly a stream of bullets erupted from the trunk! The picture in its wood frame disintegrated; and the echoes of the gunshots reverberated down the rails. I shuddered as the smoke cleared and Neary explained, 'That self-portrait was *executed* for rank treason!'

Hywel spoke up. 'I'm sure it was loyal.'

'The past is never that!'

There was no point arguing with him. But I was certain that the noise of the bullets would alert the Mongorgon, which was doubtless sniffing around the tracks, not to mention the authorities, to our location. Best to keep heading out of Srinagar.

I mentioned this fact to Hywel but it was Neary who answered, 'I am leaving town myself, heading south. There's room on my boilerplate for a skeleton. Come along with me.'

The offer was too good to reject. I jumped aboard.

He whistled, began moving.

Slowly at first, he trundled along the rails; but as the pressure inside him increased, he built up speed. Soon he was travelling faster than even the fittest Mongorgon might run.

'Choo choo!' he chortled. He was in his element.

I asked him, 'Did it hurt?'

'Did what hurt?'

'The modifications you made to yourself ...'

He said, 'The first was an accident. That was my arm, in fact, the one I replaced with a metal trunk.'

'What happened?'

'When I was a boy I was told by a fortune-teller that I had no fate line. So I decided to carve one into the palm of my hand in order to control my destiny! What do you think about that?'

'A reasonable thing to attempt. What happened?'

'I used a chainsaw and missed.'

Brigands!

We chugged all night through an amazing landscape. Hywel dozed inside me, but Neary remained awake, and so did I. We discussed many subjects to pass the time. Philosophy, history, elephant hygiene, literature, music, geology, politics. Then he became more personal and told me the strange tale of his life, his childhood in Gascony with Scipio and Distanto. It was a curious household, like every other.

Unlike his brothers, Neary had been unsuccessful with women. Ships and balloons never appealed to him; but he fell in love with locomotives and it was only a matter of time before he decided to convert himself into one. Since his transformation, women had ironically displayed an interest in his contours and performance statistics. Typical female fickleness! But I disapproved of such generalisations.

Perhaps the strangest things about Neary Faraway were his eyes. One was an endlessly rotating wheel, a grey circle that span rapidly. I think it was powered independently of the wheels on his feet; but I can't be sure of that. His other eye resembled a Venetian blind, and rarely did it cease fluttering. You know the boards in train stations that specify the times of departures and arrivals? It was like that.

We finally left the region of mountains and entered a rather smoother territory. This was the famous Punjab. We picked up speed and I enjoyed the wind in my sutures. I asked Neary where he was travelling to. He said his destination was the southernmost large city in India, Trivandrum. His job consisted of riding the entire rail network of the subcontinent, looking for cracked tracks and faulty signals.

Srinagar to Trivandrum was the longest stretch of all.

The sky in the east turned lighter.

Dawn came, and with it arrived a band of horsemen over a slight rise. I squinted at them and asked nervously:

'They have the manner and garb of brigands ...'

Neary nodded. 'That's what they are. They prey on the trains that pass through. I shall increase the steam pressure in my boiler; we must attempt to outdistance them, Mr Griffiths!' Again he squeezed his visage as if he suffered stomach cramps. I howled:

'They are spurring their steeds and unsheathing —'

'Curved swords. Yes, I know. And they carry spears too. Adventure is no stranger to India, my friend; it lives here all year long. Remain silent. I will do only what is right. Choo choo!'

Bitterly I snapped back, 'Is that all you can say?'

'No. I can also say "Chug chug"!'

This sarcasm withered me. I groaned. Hywel Owl woke up, yawned a modest yawn, blinked his peepers.

'*Spwng dorth!*' he cried; a normal Welsh curse.

I nodded with phoney serenity.

'Indeed so, my pocket-sized comrade. We are in trouble. Horsemen in gaudy attire desire to plunder us.' I winced as he shifted position, craning his head to peer at our grim pursuers.

'Is there nothing we can do to fight back?' he wailed.

I shrugged my bony shoulders.

Neary answered, 'I can fire my gun or turn my wheels. I can't do both. It's how the valves are arranged inside me. The same steam is channelled down one set of pipes or the other.'

'Don't stop, for the sake of all that's precious!'

It was I who shouted that ...

But Hywel frowned and took a deep breath. 'All that's precious? You mean for the sake of gold, silver, rubies, cloves, emeralds, paintings, love, sculpture, diamonds, nutmeg, theodolites, fossils, saffron, cordite, coffee, sapphires, anthracite, music, caviar, secrets, flowers, revelations, peppers, hummingbirds, thighs, bamboo, copra, jade, brandy, trampolines, globes, books, ships, bridges, cardamom, glass, aeroplanes, papyri, civets, hawks, peace, scarves, furniture, blossom, weasels, bicycles, lanterns, amethysts, bagpipes, opals, slippers, gateaux–'

His list, which promised to be interminable, was abruptly curtailed. A flung spear passed through my ribcage, penetrated his body, emerged on his other side; hung there, quivering!

'We are being assailed!' shrieked Neary. 'Choo choo!'

'Hywel is dead. Boo hoo!' I cried.

To be utterly honest, and one *should* be honest in one's own memoirs, the violent, bloody death of the midget didn't bother me too much, despite the fact he was a fellow countryman.

No, it was the location of his death that was more troubling.

Right inside me. He flopped there.

Ever had a midget expire within you? It's not edifying.

I grasped the end of the spear, yanked it out of him, flung it back at the horsemen who pounded along beside.

Of course I missed. It was my very first time.

Before you judge too severely, have *you* ever flung a midget-blooded weapon at a turbaned brigand with a harness that jangles in the still air of dawnlight? Bet you haven't. So there!

We reached a gentle downward slope. Neary picked up speed. Soon he was hurtling along at a velocity far in excess of even the swiftest horse on the mightiest hooves. The brigands fell back, vanished into specks. Neary didn't slacken his speed. Then they were gone and we were safe. I sobbed with meaty gratitude and skeletal glee.

'Shame about your reduced comrade, though,' said Neary.

Philosophically I replied, 'Ah well!'

'In this heat, he'll soon go off and stink badly.'

'Yes, I hadn't considered that.'

'India's not the place for an exposed midget cadaver.'

'I guess it isn't. But where is?'

'A land where it's always cold and damp.'

This made me pause and think.

I didn't really pause, for my average velocity on this stretch of the line was more than 80 miles per hour — but you know what I mean. I felt a sudden strong wave of empathy, or maybe sympathy, I'm still not sure of the difference, wash over me as I thought about the brigands. Surely they were only trying to earn a living; to assert their independence in a country undoubtedly oblivious to their needs?

They reminded me, in short, of the Nationalists in my own nation. The spears that are flung, the swords that jab, the bombs that explode; all spill gore ultimately in the name of freedom and justice! Don't they? And now I recalled the promise made by Neary's own brothers to aid the struggle in my homeland, to combat the English!

'*Monsieur*,' said I, choosing my words carefully, 'I have a request to make of you. Help me with the cause of Welsh nationalism! What return on such an investment can you expect? A statue of yourself in the city of Cardiff once my people are liberated.'

To my astonishment, he said, 'Sure. Why not?'

Various Other Doings

I imagine you are wondering what became of Mr Jason Rolfe, the bicycle assassin? I don't mean he assassinated bicycles; he was mounted on one of those machines. I wish you wouldn't pretend to know less than you do, just for the sake of having a laugh at my expense! Anyway, the last time we saw him, he was still in Alirgnahs.

His pulsejet-powered velocipede carried him through a narrow pass on the eastern rim of that lost land. Through Tibet and China he sped, and at last his store of fuel began to run low. He imagined that his bicycle would finally come to a halt before he reached the Pacific Ocean. He was happy about this; he couldn't ride over waves.

In the ancient city of Chengdu a girl was carrying a bowl of food from her house to the workshop of her father; she tripped and dropped the bowl and the porcelain shattered. She went to fetch a mop to clean up the mess, but it was too late for that. Jason Rolfe roared down the street, he skidded on the greasy noodles and lost control …

His bicycle veered off the highway and screeched into the entrance of a factory. It was a factory that made gunpowder; and the vibrations of his engine caused piles of the stuff to collapse. There might have been a vast explosion, but luckily that didn't happen. However, lots of the powder fell into the automatic feeder that was connected to the combustion chamber of his engine, filling it right to the brim.

He came out of a rear door and rejoined the street, but the damage had already been done. He had accidentally refuelled himself! Now there was sufficient explosive material to keep him going as far as the ocean and far beyond too. He scowled and shook a fist at nothing in particular.

'I'll get you for this, Lloyd Griffiths, I swear!'

The owner of the factory watched him depart; then he phoned his elder brother in the coastal city of Fuzhou and explained the situation.

'If he is allowed to drown in the sea, I'll never be able to claim damages from him in court. You must keep him alive ...'

The brother said he would think about the problem. The only solution that seemed practical to him in the timeframe remaining was to construct an unusual type of ship. I forgot to mention that he was a shipwright. The ship he built was more of a barge, really. It consisted of a single deck, and a wide and long treadmill occupied most of that deck. This treadmill was connected to a propeller under the hull.

When Jason Rolfe reached the docks at Fuzhou, he didn't simply zoom into the sea; he landed on the deck of the barge. The wheels of his bicycle turned the treadmill, keeping him balanced and steady, and the revolution of the treadmill turned the propeller. And thus did Mr Rolfe set off on his long maritime voyage to California.

And before you object to the implausibility of that, let me state that the factory owner and his brother had many clients and friends all over China and that it was a fairly simple matter to recruit them, using the telephone, into shepherding Mr Rolfe along the correct route. With roadblocks and false signs they were able to create the necessary detours to ensure that he arrived in Fuzhou docks on schedule.

Clever people, those Chinese! Don't you agree?

I do. Good writers too. Permit me to recommend one named Lu Xun. I have just finished reading a slim collection of his short stories called *Old Stories Retold*. In some ways this book is untypical of his work: it's much less political in tone and less realistic.

I never intended to use my memoirs to recommend writers to you, but it can't hurt just this once. Having said that, I have already praised Robert Graves, haven't I? No matter. I can't force you to read anyone's books. It's not even compulsory to read this one!

Mr Rolfe vanished over the watery horizon.

In the meantime, Sadegh Safani, the Persian alchemist responsible for guiding Jason Rolfe into Alirgnahs in the first place, was making his way back home. Over the mountains to the west of that fabled land he trudged, stopping for the occasional break in the treeless landscape. He was seated on a boulder when he noticed something.

A tiny speck was approaching him. It was another traveller, a very rare occurrence in these wild parts. Sadegh waited patiently. The speck slowly grew larger. It was a man garbed like a sailor, which made him seem even more out of place. Sadegh watched and waited. When the newcomer was within earshot, the alchemist shouted:

'Good day to you! Nice bleakness for a stroll.'

'Indeed so,' came the reply.

The stranger soon stood before Sadegh. He wore a black pea coat and his chin was unshaven; his hypnotic eyes were a match for Sadegh's own mysterious orbs. They regarded each other.

'I'm going home to get back to work. I work from home,' said Sadegh with a tinge of defiance in his voice.

The sailor without a ship smiled thinly and nodded. 'You haven't seen a journalist around here, have you?'

Sadegh frowned. 'What sort of journalist?

'He's Welsh. He works for *The Western Mail*. His first name is Lloyd and his surname is Griffiths. I promised to accompany him to Wales. We were going to overthrow the English.'

Sadegh chewed a thumbnail. 'I haven't, sorry.'

The sailor sighed. 'Pity. I lost him in Dresden. I've been searching for him ever since. My name is Scipio Faraway. He had a weird odour about him, the stench of a fungal infection, which theoretically should make his trail easy to follow; but I've lost it—'

A sudden impulsive generosity seized Sadegh Safani; this happens to alchemists. He blurted, 'Look, I'm an adept. Back at my castle in Persia, I have a magic mirror. If you stare into it and concentrate, you can find the location of anyone you seek. Why not come back with me and have a go? I have other amazing things too. Carpets that can fly, spirits in bottles and even a potion that can blend people.'

'Blend people? You mean merge individuals into a single whole? That is very interesting. I'm intrigued ...'

'So you'll come back to my castle? The battlements are slippery, but it is mostly an extremely nice edifice.'

Scipio nodded. 'Sounds great. Yes, I accept.'

A Transindianocean Tunnel, Hurrah!

Neary slackened his speed, came to a gradual halt and sent me to fetch a pail of water for his boiler. I misunderstood his instructions. 'I couldn't find any *pale* water,' I said, 'so I brought you this greenish kind instead. It came from a murky pond yonder.'

I can't honestly describe his gaze as withering, partly because it was an unusual combination of spinning grey wheel and fluttering blinds, neither of which wither much, but I felt reprimanded by it. Then said he with the most amount of sarcasm any sentence can hold without spillage, 'Did you say you were a writer, Mr Griffiths?'

'A journalist,' I corrected.

'Even so, Mr Griffiths! What newspaper?'

'*The Western Mail*,' I replied.

'Ah! That explains everything. Fill me up.'

I did. 'Enough?' I said.

He gurgled. 'Yes. All aboard. Off we go! Choo choo!'

We continued our journey, crossing the invisible border that separates North India from the much greener South. As he went, he told me a secret that made me gasp with wonderment.

Do you ever gasp with wonderment? Not much, I bet!

Be honest. With yourself and me.

Because gasping with wonderment is something human beings only do correctly when they are youthful and still optimistic about the future and their place in it. As a callow youth I gasped with wonderment every other day. The stars, the moon, the curve of girls. I gasped with wonderment at them all, to an excessive degree. Now I do it only every other plot twist, or less often than that. Sad but true.

'There is a series of railway tunnels under the oceans of the world. It's a huge engineering project that the major railway companies of the world have been collaborating on for ages.'

'My wonderment levels are dangerously high in reaction to this news! You aren't toying with me, *Monsieur*?'

'You'll see the truth for yourself if you accept my offer.'

'What offer is that, pray tell?'

'We are rapidly approaching the town of Nileswaram, which is one of the main turning-off points for the Transindianocean Tunnel. That tunnel is a shortcut back to Europe. In fact it comes out in Wales in a place with a name I've forgotten. So tell me now.'

'Tell you what?' I blinked metaphorically. All my blinks, squints and other eye muscle manipulations are merely figures of speech, but I guess you've already worked that one out.

'Do you want me to turn into that tunnel's mouth?'

'Yes, yes!' I shouted in delight.

He nodded. 'Very well. On your own head be it.'

That sounded like a threat.

I puzzled at the oddness of his tone; as if he was warning me against the very course of action he had recommended! But I shelved my doubts, for the advantages of a direct line to Wales were too significant to ignore. My luck is changing, I informed myself!

Are you quite sure about that? came my own reply.

Don't scowl at me! I retorted.

Why not? I *am* you! I snapped back.

Uppity for a bleedin' skeleton, aren't you? sneered I.

You can talk! And I'm not bleeding!

It was a cuss word, stupid!

This ridiculous argument with myself might have gone on indefinitely, with no obvious winner, but Neary distracted me with a shout, 'Here's the turning ahead. I change tracks *now.*'

Suddenly we were on a set of glittering rails that curved away from the main line that led into the station at the coastal town of Nileswaram. Very close to the sea we were. I smelt the brine, felt the spray of the waves. It's an interesting part of India, a region of waterways and islands; but I didn't get a chance to appreciate it fully.

The line dipped down, entered the mouth of a tunnel. We were in pitch darkness; and in other kinds of darkness too, surely? Neary activated the lamp that doubled as his third mystic forehead eye. The clattering of rails was louder down here, as the echo reverberated off the bricks of the walls and ceiling. It was claustrophobic, yes; but I couldn't deny the talents and vision of the people who had built it.

Neary gave me a brief lecture on its history.

'A railway genius by the name of Kingdom Noisette was responsible. He drew up the plans, did all the calculations, managed the whole thing. I told you it was a collaborative effort. And so it was in terms of labour and finance! But Noisette was the main force behind it. He is my hero, in fact. Funnily enough, he also turned himself into a train when he was young. I didn't slavishly follow his example in that regard; it is coincidence. I am a train, he is a train. No causation at all.'

'Great minds chuff alike?' I ventured.

He was pleased with that maxim and giggled. Then he increased speed and said, 'It's a long way to Wales.'

'I'm prepared for the hardships of the journey.'

'It'll be boring. Terribly so.'

'*Monsieur*! I have read the novels of Jane Austen!'

'You consider yourself immune?'

'To tedium? Heavens no! But I am tough enough.'

And I truly believed I was!

Beneath his steamy breath he hissed, 'We'll see.' And that was the end of the conversation. Nothing can daunt me now, I decided; but I failed to convince myself of that truth. The sombre walls flashed past without any kind of variation in their appearance.

The pressure kept increasing. We were far beneath the seabed. I guess my ears would pop if I had them.

With no sky above, and no sun, moon or stars to fill it, I was quite at a loss to tell night from day. The hours crept past; or were those 'hours' just minutes? Neary wasn't much company. He had lapsed into a reverie and it was utterly impossible to extract meaningful talk from him. Occasionally a snatch of melody would issue from his pig-iron lips, but it was always a melody I didn't recognise and I was unable to accompany him or even tap the correct rhythm with my knuckles.

I slept standing up. My dreams were pointless.

For some bizarre reason, I dreamed of Jason Rolfe, the man who kept trying to kill me. He was still mounted on his bicycle; but his bicycle was mounted on a treadmill that was turning so fast it was smoking. On every side around him was the ocean. Somehow he had got hold of the tusk of a narwhale and was cradling it like a lance. He muttered to himself: 'I'll get you for this. Lloyd Griffiths! I will!'

I snapped awake. Nothing in the tunnel had changed.

But then I squinted. What was that?

Far ahead the tunnel came to an end. A brick wall!

I screeched, 'Stop the train!'

Neary ignored my shout. In fact he went faster.

'Choo choo!' he chortled.

We were about to smash into the wall! Then I noticed the mouth of a second tunnel, a narrower passage that curved down and to the left. With a shout of pure fear, I gripped Neary's shoulders and jerked them with all my strength, steering him manually!

He choked back a curse and struggled against me.

But it was too late. I had won.

We had switched lines!

'You idiot. What the hell are you doing?' he roared.

'Saving our lives,' I responded.

'What do you mean?'

'We were about to crash into a solid wall.'

'No we weren't, you oaf! That was just a curtain painted to look like a solid wall! Such curtains are hung at specific points throughout the tunnel to make it easier for train drivers to know where they are in relation to the geography of the planet's surface.'

I reluctantly acknowledged my error. 'Oops!'

'You have diverted me down one of the abandoned tunnels. This is a very bad outcome. I can't reverse.'

I was flabbergasted. 'You have no reverse gear?'

'Why should I? It's not normal for skeletons with dead midgets inside them to travel with me and twist my shoulders without an invitation to do so! I have never needed a reverse gear!'

'What shall we do?' I asked.

'We have no choice but to keep going.'

'Where does this tunnel go?'

'Africa, Mr Griffiths. It comes out in the jungles of Guinea. But there is something else I need to tell you.'

'What's that?' I trembled.

'The reason *why* this tunnel was abandoned ...'

And he told me. I blanched.

Next Stop: The Future

No I didn't. How can a skeleton covered in brown fungus blanch? It was another figure of speech. At that particular moment, I felt like a figure of derision, which is even browner.

The tunnel to Africa was abandoned because of a curious anomaly in the magnetic field directly below it. Thanks to all the latest bunkum, hoo-ha and other pseudoscientific flapdoodle, I am able to reveal that the anomaly influenced the chronoflow, the flow of time itself! There was a time dilation effect.

Anything moving along that tunnel would exist in a time-stream faster than the one on the Earth's surface.

Days would pass below; but weeks above.

In other words, the tunnel was an accidental time machine!

And we were stuck inside it …

The year when we entered the tunnel was 1915.

It would be later when we emerged. Later than it ought, I mean. It was our fate to be cast into the future.

I badgered Neary to give me an estimate. He finally stated that perhaps our journey to Africa would 'take' two decades. When we surfaced in the forests of Guinea it could be 1935.

We would end up in a science fiction world!

I couldn't imagine what enormous changes might have taken place in a span of 20 years. It was inconceivable. All sorts of weird marvels and miracles of science and engineering would be commonplace. Helicopters would exist for real; those female men called ladies might have the vote; I was even willing to speculate that the nations of Europe would gather into a federation with a single currency!

I did share some of these ideas with Neary.

'Don't be an ugly, stupid, moronic, worthless fool!' he growled. Clearly he was devoid of sufficient vision.

Abruptly I realised I would miss having any wartime adventures. The conflict between Britain and Germany would surely be over by then? I'm against war in principle, but I had been looking forward to witnessing the astounding campaign of Spicer-Simson against Von Lettow-Vorbeck on Lake Tanganyika. If you don't know who either of those gentlemen were, I recommend finding out in books.

Anyway, I digress … And during this digression, things on the surface of the world are moving much faster than beneath it. Jason Rolfe crosses the Pacific Ocean and reaches the shore of California; then he zooms off across the United States of America. And as for Scipio and Sadegh, not to mention Distanto, they will soon —

But everything in its proper place. Patience!

It dawned on me that Hywel Owl, the deceased midget inside me, was bound to go rotten in the heat of Africa. Eventually, of course, his corpse would turn completely to slime and drop out of me in foetid gloopings of stinky miniature man mush; but before that stage, he would be maggoty. I would be ashamed to be seen in public like that. The only alternative was to pay a surgeon to cut him out of me.

But I had no money. And I was scared of doctors.

'There *is* another option …'

It was Neary who said that. I suppose I must have been articulating my thoughts aloud. 'Truly, *Monsieur*?'

'Yes. We're headed to Africa, Mr Griffiths. West Africa. The original home of voodoo! I'm sure we can ask some sorcerer to turn Hywel into a zombie. That way, he won't go off.'

It was an intriguing notion.

To pass the time, I asked Neary to tell me any stories he might know. I didn't want anything harsh and factual; something light and escapist was a better option, I insisted. He took a deep, shrill breath and began reciting a short novel from memory, some nonsense about a miser, a brace of ghosts and a disabled boy. When it was done, he asked me to return the favour; I attempted to tell him the story of *The Shaving of Shagpat*, but the order of events was hopelessly jumbled.

'You're not a very entertaining passenger, Mr Griffiths.'

'I apologise,' I said sincerely.

'Who was the author of that fantasy you messed up?'

'George Meredith,' I replied.

'Very well. I shall seek out the original book.'

'Do they have bookshops in —'

'Africa? Of course! It's not a landmass of savages!'

I chewed my bony lower lip.

This tunnel was much thinner than the one that stretched to Wales and I was compelled to duck several times in order to keep my poor skull intact at the apex of my spinal column. And the rails were warped; Neary almost overturned on several bends.

It was impossible to estimate when we reached the coast of Africa, for the tunnel passed under the majority of the continent in order to surface in Guinea in the far west. In my mind I felt the weight of hippopotami, lions and giraffes far above my cranium.

After what seemed an eternity, a point of light appeared at the furthest limit of my vision. 'The exit!' cried Neary. 'Be sure to protect your vision, Mr Griffiths, from the bright daytime sun. Ready?'

I nodded. I was more than ready. But I didn't take his advice. As soon as we burst out of the ground, I allowed the rays of our parent star to fill the craters of my sockets with gold.

'Fresh air again!' I gasped. 'Freedom and life!'

Neary applied his brakes.

And came to a halt with a squeal.

Here was the end of the line. A pair of buffers jutted from a rock, and a rotting wooden platform served as a station. But there was nobody there and the entire facility was overgrown.

'It *was* abandoned,' Neary reminded me.

I gazed at our surroundings. To be truthful, there was little to see. Just vast trees, dangling vines, impenetrable undergrowth. Monstrous blooms puffed their decadent scent at me.

'Do you know your way around these parts?'

'No, Mr Griffiths. Do you?'

'I don't. Do you suppose we are near civilisation?'

'Nowhere close, is my guess.'

'Surely there must be ports and embassies?'

Neary offered me a leer.

'We are as far away from those as it's possible to be in West Africa. In Guinea all the main cities lie on the coast. We are high in the mountains. I daresay there are some settlements within walking distance, but they will hardly be equipped for visitors.'

'Maybe it's better this way?' I ventured.

He nodded. 'As I said earlier, we're in the future now, so I doubt it's a good idea to plunge immediately into the deep end. Urban environments, full of futuristic appliances and customs and who knows what else, might unsettle our minds. Imagine a citizen of ancient Atlantis suddenly finding himself stranded in modern Paris!'

I frowned. 'I think he would cope quite well.'

Neary huffed and glowered.

I wandered a little distance away from the makeshift platform. A pale object gleamed among the tangle of greenery. I parted some vines to take a closer look at it. A pillar of some sort! A stone column erected by a lost race to prop up a long-collapsed roof? Then I reached out and felt it. No, it wasn't stone. It was made of bone!

'Some sort of tusk!' I cried.

Neary examined it by extending his metal arm, which I'll admit I still think of as 'truncated', and caressed it lightly. 'The horn of a Catoblepas, Mr Griffiths; a mythical creature.'

'It has been carved into the shape of a —'

'Yes, a banana. Strange.'

Neary extended a pair of artificial legs, tucked in his wheels, stepped off the rails and lurched over to my side. He said, 'Maybe it's dedicated to the supreme monkey god, Zumboo?'

'Oh no, not to him!' came a rich and powerful voice.

We span around and squinted …

An enormously impressive figure strolled out from behind a tree. Was it a man or an ape? Somehow it combined the best qualities of both, with none of the defects. It threw back its head and laughed. This laughter was warm and life-affirming, not sardonic or malign at all. We waited for his laughter to subside to a mere chuckle.

'To me! It's dedicated to me! A little extravagant, I thought. But I can't complain about such a touching gesture. The people who carved it for me elected me as their chieftain and willingly became members of my tribe. I bid you welcome; for ordinary humans are just as precious to community life as any humanzee. Come!'

I stuttered, 'Humanzee. You mean to say —'

The figure bowed deeply.

'My name is Fabalo. You are my honoured guests.'

I didn't know what to say.

But Neary did. He blared, 'Choo choo!'

'This way,' smiled Fabalo.

Humanzeeville

The tribe that Fabalo ruled was several hundred strong. The ordinary men and women tended to dwell in huts; the humanzees generally lived in the trees. But there was considerable overlap in domestic arrangements. Most members were neither pure human nor pure humanzee but an incalculable hybrid of the two extremes. The laws of Humanzeeville were liberal, wise and highly evolved, or else extremely perverted, depending on your point of view. Myself, I rather liked them.

Fabalo lived in modest splendour in a large treehouse.

He had everything he wanted. 'So *this* is utopia?' I breathed, as I lay on a mat woven from leaves and accepted a drink of strongly fermented banana sap from a saucy huchimpess.

'That's not a real word, is it?' wondered Neary.

'Is what not a real word?' I asked.

'Huchimpess,' he replied.

'Probably not; but it'll do for now.'

He shrugged and I redirected my attention to my host.

Fabalo sat on his haunches.

'I believe in the light touch. There are enough bellicose dictators in this world of ours. I rule as gently as I dare. If I had to, I would trample all my enemies, both domestic and foreign, like grapes in a winepress; until juice that is actually blood spatters my legs right up to my inner thighs. Only as a

269

last resort, though! My fondest hope is never to kill anyone. I want to be known as the most benign of all tyrants. I'm already the hairiest; that can't be disputed! Peace is my motto.'

'This world of ours?' I prompted.

It turned out that Neary's chronological estimate hadn't been too bad. It was now the year 1938. The First World War, barely begun when I was in Alirgnahs, had been over for two decades; but the nations of Europe were getting ready for another attempt.

'The bloody fools!' swore Fabalo quietly.

I finished my brew. 'Tell me, sir. Do helicopters really exist? Do they ply the skies like sycamore seeds?'

'Not yet, young fellow. You must be patient.'

'What about universal suffrage?'

'You mean, do females have the vote in your homeland? Yes, they do. In real terms, though, they are still treated as inferiors. In Humanzeeville, everybody has equal pay and rights.'

'And tell me furthermore, sir, are the states of Europe all joined into a single enormous federation yet?'

'No, no! How would a Second World War be feasible if that was the situation? It would be called the Big Civil Continental War or something like that. Pay more attention, please.'

This reprimand was delivered in kindly tones.

'You are happy here, sir?'

He waved a strong and hairy hand. 'Almost. My main regret is that I once lost a son. He wandered away and we never found him. I still think about him from time to time.'

'Did he have a name, sir?'

'Yes. Fabalo Junior.'

'Do you suppose he might still be alive?'

'Unlikely, but possible.'

Neary cleared his metallic throat with a steamy cough.

'I note that your settlement is defended with pits and stakes. Are you expecting trouble from outside?'

Fabalo grinned. 'You are perceptive, *Monsieur*!'

Neary nodded. 'I'm a locomotive.'

'And I'm a skeleton,' I said, not wishing to be left out.

Fabalo sighed and explained:

'The dictator Stalin is interested in this part of Guinea. He knows that humanzees are loose in the jungle. He has spies everywhere! Ultimately, he plans to seek us out and convert us to communism. He thinks we can be used to spread revolution throughout Africa. Some of his ideological enemies, refugees from the days of the Tsar, believe we can be used to spread counter-revolution! It's absurd.'

I nodded; but then I had an idea.

'You have no wish to become pawns in a political game? Maybe I can write a piece on this. I'm a journalist.'

Fabalo was enthusiastic. He cried:

'Certainly, certainly! Provided it's not for *The Western Mail*. An issue happened to fall into my hands once.'

I lapsed into an embarrassed silence. Neary said:

'Imagine the superb irony of a re-enactment of the Russian Civil War in the heart of the African jungle! Fought between rival humanzees! Such a superb scenario would make an excellent script for a film or pitch for a work of fiction, don't you concur?'

Fabalo raised a bushy eyebrow. 'I do not.'

'Tell me, sir,' I began nervously, 'I don't suppose you know if Wales, the land of my birth, is free from English domination? I'm aware that it's an obscure struggle, but perhaps—'

'Not free at this present date,' said Fabalo.

'Ah. I suspected as much.'

'Cheer up, Mr Griffiths!' he roared. 'You wouldn't want to go back in your condition anyway, would you?'

I rankled at his presumption.

'But it's high time skeletons were accepted in society; so as a matter of fact I *would* like to return, sir.'

He grinned sympathetically or maybe empathically. 'I wasn't referring to the skeletal part of your appearance, but to the dead midget inside you. A vector for disease when he goes off.'

'Oh him!' I had forgotten about Hywel Owl.

'I can help you, Mr Griffiths ...'

'Really, sir? How, sir? Please do, sir!' I babbled.

Fabalo explained, 'I'm a voodoo sorcerer of considerable skill. It won't be too hard to turn that little chap inside you into a zombie; that will stop him putrefying. What do you say?'

'Yes please!' I winked at Neary, who nodded.

'I'll conduct the ritual tonight.'

'Why, that's perfect, sir! May I write a piece about it?'

'Of course. But not for—'

'I know, I know. *The Western Mail*. I won't!'

Fabalo pursed his lips.

'Has anyone ever told you, Mr Griffiths, that you look a lot like David Livingstone, the famous explorer?'

'But he died in 1873! I'm tired of these jokes!'

Fabalo frowned. 'Dead, is he?'

It was plain he hadn't known. He shrugged.

'Rest now. Later I will summon you. The entire tribe will gather in the clearing for the voodoo ceremony. If you wish, in the meantime, you may enjoy any erotic dalliance with any huchimpess that takes your fancy; but only if they are equally willing.'

My grin, which had spread wider than a giant spider's legs in response to the first part of his speech, collapsed into a pucker. What female would possibly care for amorous adventures with a skeleton? Almost none. With a sigh, I resigned myself to celibacy.

I stretched flat on the mat and fell into a light doze.

My dreams were vivid but calm.

I felt myself shaken awake. Hours had passed already. Fabalo squatted next to me and hissed, 'Ready?'

Stifling a yawn, I nodded and followed him out of the treehouse, down the rickety ladder to the ground.

Humanzees had gathered in a circle.

It was dusk. Torches illuminated the clearing. The entire

population of Humanzeeville was present to observe the voodoo ceremony. Inside me, a dead midget slumped and slowly decayed, blissfully unaware of what was about to occur to him. I looked at Fabalo and appreciated how much finer a lifeform he was than my old boss, Ben Gordon. He had painted his body and wore a frightful wooden mask.

Just beyond the firelight, Neary was making friends with an elephant; I recognised his silhouette. They were exchanging buns with their trunks. Elephants aren't typical in that corner of Africa, but several dozen beasts had wandered by accident into the lush mountains of Guinea from distant parts and settled comfortably there.

Drums started playing. The rhythm was intoxicating!

The crowd began swaying.

The rhythm divided into two separate pulses, then four, then six. The complexity of these polyrhythms didn't prevent the resultant music from being wholly organic and funky.

I slipped into a trance, my bones vibrating.

It was an intricate set of resonant frequencies that gripped me; but the effect was invigorating, ecstatic.

Fabalo danced around me, shaking a stick that was carved to resemble a banana; or perhaps it was a banana that looked like a stick. He muttered and shrieked in a language I didn't recognise. Periodically, he cast fistfuls of strange herbs into the fire; they erupted in a wash of green, blue, purple and amber flames. Then he screamed:

'Come back to life, little fellow! I command you!'

Hywel's eyes snapped open …

He gripped the bars of my ribcage, rattled them.

I felt sick, appalled, terrified!

The ceremony had worked. Voodoo magic was real!

I had a zombie inside me.

'Mwwwuagghuagh!' groaned Hywel Owl.

'What's he trying to say?' I whispered, as the midget shook me again. Fabalo answered in a tranquil voice:

'Nothing intelligible. Ignore him. He's a zombie. His body is alive but he doesn't possess a soul. He won't go off, but he's incapable of intelligent conversation. Don't tempt him into a debate, whatever you do; it's one of the most frustrating things imaginable. Anyway, the ritual is done. I have saved you from stinking very badly.'

Then he widened his nostrils and added, 'Having said that, you smell just as pungent as before. Did I fail?'

I put his mind to rest. 'That's my own odour. I have a fungal infection that's sucking my marrow out of me.'

'Your marrow? Do you grow vegetables then?'

'Not that kind. My bone pulp.'

'Ah yes, I see ... And yet ...' He waved a hairy hand.

I thanked him again for his kindness.

'Think nothing of it, Mr Griffiths,' he replied, and then he said, 'Visit me at midnight for a cup of banana tea and a chat. There's something you need to know. It's quite important.'

I promised that I would. Then he turned his attention to the members of his tribe. He was a chieftain and it was his duty to solve all their domestic disputes and financial problems. Absolute power isn't necessarily fun and games all the time. Ask any dictator.

The Finnish But Not The End

I did as Fabalo wanted and went to visit him. He seemed concerned. The banana tea was tasty enough, but his tone was anxious. He said, 'Are you possessed by a spirit, Mr Griffiths?'

'No, I don't think so,' I answered truthfully.

'Well, I'm certain that you *are*.'

I greeted this news with mild shock. 'A good spirit, I hope?'

His expression was serious.

'Afraid not. It's a grotesquely evil ghost. I detected it during the ritual to turn the midget inside you into a zombie. It tried to jump into my mind while I was communicating with the voodoo gods. But I blocked it with a firewall, which is a magical barrier.'

I frowned at this and said:

'I'm a skeleton. I wonder if it is my own ghost that has possessed me? Most people have their ghosts inside them, between their flesh and their bones. Lacking flesh, I wear my phantom on the outside, logically. Is that what you detected? My own soul?'

He shook his hairy head emphatically. 'Does your soul speak Finnish, Mr Griffiths? Is it a vicious killer?'

I shook my head. My brown bones tingled.

Then I jumped up in horror.

'Jukka-Petteri Halme!'

Fabalo leaned forward, squinting. 'Oh yes?'

'He was a genius of unconventional warfare, a mercenary with cold eyes that belied his jovial smile, and a former associate of the notorious arms-dealer Basil Zaharoff. Wanted as a criminal in a dozen countries! I saw him die in an aeroplane crash.'

'You were near him when the accident happened?'

'No, but I watched it through a spyglass. It wasn't really an accident, but an act of deliberate sabotage.'

Fabalo stroked his chin, nodding sagely.

'This is my hypothesis, Mr Griffiths. I believe that at the moment of his death, Jukka's ghost entered the spyglass, rushed down it and jumped into your eye. He 'lived' on the surface of your eyeball, revolving around it endlessly, thanks to a scientific principle known as the Coandă Effect. But when your eye was plucked out, he took refuge in your fungus. Now he is spread all over you like—'

'Marmite?' I ventured, and when Fabalo frowned deeply I said, 'It's a type of brown butter popular in Britain. A product made from the leftovers of the beer fermentation process.'

'Ah, I see. Well, in that case, yes, like that.'

I clapped my bony palms.

'A ghost like Marmite! Who could have imagined that?'

'We must get rid of it,' said Fabalo.

'What? Marmite? Never!'

'No, no, you dolt. The ghost of Jukka Halme!'

'Why? Is he dangerous?'

'If he succeeds in controlling the fungus fully and the fungus succeeds in controlling you equally fully …'

The urgency of the matter finally hit me.

'What can we do, sir?'

'There *is* an answer, don't worry. Another voodoo ritual, but one more complex than the previous ceremony. Basically, it entails the transference of your mind and soul into another body. Then the bones of your skeleton can be burned and the infection and ghost destroyed. But you can only be ethically transferred into a body without a mind and soul of its own;

such bodies are generally in short supply. In fact, there's only one available in this locality at the present time.'

And he glanced meaningfully at the midget.

'Hywel, you mean?' I cried.

To which the midget answered, 'Mwwwuagghuagh!'

Fabalo nodded sadly. 'Yes.'

'You want to transfer my identity, the identity of the journalist Lloyd Griffiths, out of the skull of the skeleton in which he currently resides and into the mindless brain of the zombie midget that currently resides inside the aforementioned skeleton's ribcage?'

'If you want to put it that way, yes,' Fabalo said.

'Is there no alternative?'

He sighed and stroked his chin, because characters always stroke their chins at moments of crisis, at least in *my* adventures, and said, 'Yes, there is an alternative. You can allow the phantom of Jukka Halme to take over your nervous system, to control you like a man driving a sleigh. In short, to usurp the very essence of yourself.'

And deep inside me, in some hidden recess of my soul, there surged a mocking laugh, very faint but insistent, and a voice that whispered, 'Far above the Arctic Circle, in the land of the night that lingers, on the banks of the River Ounasjoki, I dallied with an owl. It was an unearthly owl and it should have scared me, black with bright red eyes it was! I knew that it planned treachery and so I gobbled it up for supper at last; I swallowed it whole and for months it flapped inside my stomach, hooting prophecies. I heeded them not; nor will I ever do so!'

The anecdote turned into a snorting chuckle that died into silence. Yet there was something feathery in that silence; a beaked quality, an essence of talons that I couldn't properly define.

I said to Fabalo with a shiver, 'I'm ready for anything.'

'Truly, Mr Griffiths?' He reached out to clamp a massive hand on my knobbly shoulder. 'Are you certain?'

'I would much rather be a Welsh midget than the puppet

of a Finnish spook! Jukka Halme is pure evil. Or if that's overstating the case, then he's at least five-sixths evil and one-sixth indifferent. I want to make my mark on history as a writer, not as a fiend!'

Fabalo looked uncomfortable. 'Ambitious, eh?'

I shrugged. True, I hadn't yet written anything that had made much of an impression in the wider world. I wasn't as accomplished a journalist as Jack London or Henry Morton Stanley, but I lived, and still live, in hope. Living in hope is easier than living almost anywhere else. For one thing, it can be taken along with you, like a tent.

A trumpeting sound sundered the jungle silence outside.

Neary was cavorting with new friends!

The flapping of giant ears sent a breeze through the foliage, a breeze that smelled of groundnuts, frogspawn, fermented snake venom, cassava and the fresh ichor of squashed bugs.

'Elephants,' I announced unnecessarily.

'They have accepted him as one of their own,' Fabalo remarked, half in admiration, half in disapproval. 'It might end in tears, it might not; do you have an opinion on your friend's behaviour? It is unorthodox for any man. Even weirder for a locomotive.'

'I believe he is lonely. Indeed, I suspect that all the Faraway Brothers are lonely. This thesis hasn't occurred to me before, but it seems obvious now, despite Scipio's chasing of women, despite Distanto's self-reliance, despite Neary's transhumanism ... Perhaps they belong together, a happy family once again? Triplets reunited!'

Fabalo expressed scepticism. 'You're not a qualified psychologist, are you? Better to avoid the subject of families, in my view. The interactions are too intricate, complex, prone to misinterpretation. I wonder where my lost son can be! Poor Fabalo Junior!'

I shared his pain; not very strongly, I admit, but with all the goodwill I could muster. We sat in quiet contemplation for a further ten minutes and the trumpeting started up again, then died down. I thought I heard Neary shout the word 'buns!' in an imploring voice; but it was extremely faint and my imagination wasn't reliable at that time.

Fabalo gestured at the sky through the open doorway.

I gazed at the tropical stars. They burned with almost no twinkle. And a thin crescent moved amid them like a sickle. 'A full moon is needed for the transference ritual,' he explained.

'Another ten days or so. I'll be ready,' I said.

'What if Jukka Halme gains control of you before then?' Fabalo was genuinely worried about this prospect.

'Then you must disable me somehow. Stop me from moving,' I said in a little voice. 'Remove my legs ...'

He nodded. 'That is essential for the ritual anyway.'

I didn't ask him to elaborate on this.

The awkward silence returned.

'Music,' he said absently. Then he hummed a melody with his noble lips. I frowned. I had absolutely no inkling that my fate was to be bound up with that tune so fundamentally!

More about that later. After the following digression.

The Promised Digression

Mr Jason Rolfe had indeed crossed the Pacific Ocean all those years ago. I ought to explain what happened when he eventually reached the coast of California. The owner of the gunpowder factory in Chengdu had plenty of cousins living and working in the United States and had already contacted them by telephone to warn them of the jet-assisted cyclist's arrival, for he required their assistance to facilitate his plan, which involved shepherding Mr Rolfe right across the continent to New York, where another treadmill barge was waiting to convey him over the Atlantic Ocean to Europe. The factory owner wanted Mr Rolfe to circumnavigate the globe and return to China, right into his vengeful arms!

That's how indolent some villains are. They can't be bothered to pursue their victims, but arrange for the victims to come to them. However, if too many variables are involved, even the most cunning plan designed by the greatest genius is likely to fail. That's what happened in this instance. One of the cousins was drunk and didn't shepherd Mr Rolfe properly; his false signs and roadblocks were positioned badly. That was in Utah. Mr Rolfe took a right turn, instead of a left, and kept going. Before too long he was in Mexico, heading south toward the narrow isthmus that connects North and South America. Over the desert he roared, hurling up clouds of sand, dust and grit and obscuring himself.

Like a thunderbolt hitched to a storm, he dragged these

clouds behind him. When the factory owner learned the news, he wailed and jumped up and down in anguish; he had no cousins in Mexico. Thus did Jason Rolfe escape the designs of an evil oriental! But let's stress this point: most evil oriental characters in most adventure tales are stereotypes, lazy products of torpid and prejudicial imaginations; but this factory owner was actually the direct descendant of aberrant white missionaries who settled in China ages ago. And so if he was a stereotype, it's a different one from the one you had in mind before reading this sentence. His up and down jumps had so much force that he broke his ankles.

Now back to Mr Rolfe in Mexico …

Alarmed by his sudden appearance, people threw food at him, tortillas shaped like discs that could have sliced off the head of a feebler man; but he caught them and munched. The rains were infrequent, but thirst wasn't a problem for him; he had removed his helmet and now used it as a vessel to store the precious liquid. Southwards he went, through Guatemala and Honduras, Nicaragua and Costa Rica; and then into Panama and over the canal via a bridge. From there he somehow managed to cross the perilous Darien Gap into Colombia. In that land of melancholy songs, he rumbled through the forest, over mountains speckled with poisonous frogs, across the border into the vastness of Brazil.

Deep in the immense jungle lived a man known as Dom Daniel. Some who knew him called him a charlatan; others, a visionary genius. He was acutely troubled by the impact of mankind's doings on the environment; it was many decades before such concerns became fashionable. It was Dom Daniel who had commissioned Distanto Faraway, the airship pilot, to take his collections of seeds to Hippolytomia, that anomalous isle with a tropical climate located above the Arctic Circle. It was Dom Daniel who was now engaged with the breeding of plants so tough they would be impervious to the axes and saws of illegal loggers. That was his latest project to protect the forest against human encroachment.

A wealthy man thanks to an inheritance, Dom Daniel had

purchased a large tract of the Amazon in a very isolated region. Here, in the solitude and obscurity he desired, he was free to conduct his research without any kind of government or commercial interference. Somewhere between the Juruá and Tapauá Rivers, his plantation thrived. He had raised a mansion in the middle of it; he had abandoned his original house after loggers had cut down all the trees surrounding it. That was far to the east in Tocantins and he regarded his own experiences there as akin to the persecutions of a prophet; one day the last tree in the world would fall. The worry was with him constantly. He alone seemed to care.

In the study of his mansion he experimented with genetic codes. More by chance than design he created some outstanding hybrids with unusual properties. Among the clutter of his possessions, the cabinets of samples, the books and charts, the microscopes, thermometers, clocks, barometers and other scientific devices, he produced a new subspecies of rubber tree that couldn't be chopped down. An axe or machete would simply bounce off. Even dynamite was ineffective against it. The sap it oozed was much thicker and stronger than the sap of the standard rubber tree. Dom Daniel decided they were worth growing. He filled his plantation with them and waited patiently to observe developments.

The splutter of a distant engine intruded on his peace.

He gritted his teeth. A motorboat?

No, it wasn't coming up the river; it was in the jungle itself.

It was, of course, Mr Jason Rolfe ...

Weaving between the trees at high speed, the intrepid cyclist clenched his handlebars extremely tightly and licked away the perspiration pouring down his face onto his upper lip. He still blamed a particular journalist for his tribulations. 'Lloyd Griffiths! When I get my hands on you ...' But at that moment in time, it appeared very unlikely he would ever be given the opportunity to wring the neck of yours truly.

Meanwhile, Dom Daniel was reaching for the blunderbuss hanging by its trigger guard on a hook on his study wall. He intended to repulse with grapeshot this noisy trespasser. When the gun was loaded, he threw open his windows and leaned out, jutting the flared barrel into dense greenery, waiting for the appearance of the invader. Then he had a better idea. With a chuckle, he retracted and emptied the gun.

Why shoot grapeshot when you can fire dynamite sticks instead? After all, the blunderbuss was a large example of the type. Many hissing sticks could fit into the barrel. The explosions wouldn't damage the rubber trees, but the intruder would be concussed to death.

And that's what he did, turning the rather old-fashioned weapon into an analogue of a grenade launcher. Jason Rolfe had no inkling of this. All his concentration was utilised in avoiding collisions with trees. Suddenly he entered a region of vegetation even denser than those he had already negotiated. Rubber trees trailing vines, dripping sap everywhere. With an expression of mortification, Mr Rolfe lifted his hands from steering duties and brushed the vines aside. Sap fell onto him. His arms were now at full stretch, clearing a path for himself between the trailing creepers. The sap continued to drip, setting his arms firm.

He discovered that he was unable to move them at all.

More sap fell; he noticed something.

A glint of light on glass. The window of a mansion!

Then he heard a bellowed curse.

A gun erupted; numerous spitting projectiles span toward him. Unable to take any kind of evasive action, he watched helplessly as they tumbled into the automatic feeder of his engine.

'Dynamite? You've refuelled me, you fool!' he cried.

The sap still fell, thickening …

Thickening, setting, flattening out.

His arms were slowly being turned into wings.

Rubber wings, resilient and reliable.

But not much use in jungles.

Fortunately for him, he broke out of the zone of

experimental rubber trees into a narrow clearing. This was the landing strip that Dom Daniel used to fly in supplies when he needed them; for although his ecological consciousness was enormous, he wasn't entirely against the products of a modern world if they suited his purpose.

An aeroplane stood at the far end of the runway.

Mr Rolfe raced toward it …

He shut his eyes, imagining the collision with such exactitude that he actually felt not only the pain of the inevitable crash but the blissful peace of its aftermath, when death came to soothe everything and make him just as he was before he was born.

But that's not what happened. His wings worked.

Up into the air he went; his bicycle clutched tightly between his knees, his outstretched arms coated in rubber performing superbly to create lift. I guess his angle of climb was very steep. Otherwise he might have bashed himself on the treetops and become stuck in the canopy permanently, like a frustrated fruit of failed vengeance.

He soared above the jungle. The winds pushed him.

Toward the northeast he flew.

He began laughing with the sheer joy of flight!

Down below, having observed all this through a spyglass, Dom Daniel hurled his blunderbuss on the floor and began jumping up and down on it, just like the factory owner in Chengdu.

Do all foiled schemers do that? I guess they do.

But what do I know about it?

I'm just a journalist, a living skeleton.

Soon to be a zombie midget!

Anyway … Mr Jason Rolfe continued flying. He soared through clouds full of rain and slaked his thirst, but food was more of a problem. He was able to peck at grains of pollen that swirled past his head, but they weren't very filling. No matter! His velocity was such that he would cross the sea in a matter of days and be above land again; and yet, when he checked his fuel levels, he was dismayed to learn there were enough explosives in his feeder to carry him on his present course entirely across Europe, dumping him at last in the freezing Barents Sea.

'Many thanks, Lloyd Griffiths!' he snarled bitterly.

In fact, that wasn't his destiny …

No sooner did he reach the continent of Europe, passing above a small fishing village called Buarcos, than his pitilessly long journey came to an end. Sand dunes undulated below. There was the crack of a rifle shot. The pulsejet engine was disabled by a lucky bullet. Mr Rolfe went into a dive. He had lost all power; and most of his speed and lift. He doesn't recall too much of the immediate aftermath. He does remember striking the top of a particularly soft dune and tumbling over and over. Then a woman seated on a unicorn was smiling down at him.

Her long, wavy black hair streamed in the breeze and her eyes glittered in the moonlight. He didn't miss the fact that she held a gun in one hand, an anachronistic flintlock model. She rescued him, took him back to her camp, tended to his injuries and fed him.

She was Luísa Ferreira, the Bandit Queen; and when he was better, he was invited to join her band of outlaws.

He accepted at once; he'd always wanted to be a rascal.

She asked him one day, 'What weapon?'

He replied, 'May I choose any?'

She nodded. 'Yes, we have a wide selection of carbines, swords, axes, daggers, morningstars and halberds.'

'Morningstars? What are those?'

'A kind of mace with a spiked ball on the end. I'm sure you have read about them in historical novels.'

'Are the spiked balls on the end of a chain that can be swung around? If so, I do know what you mean.'

'No, that's a flail. We don't have those. A morningstar's spiked head is attached firmly to a rigid handle.'

He sighed. 'That's all very well, but my favoured weapon is a lance. I know how to use a lance properly.'

'Really? What's the secret, Dom Jason?'

'To *cradle* it, that's what! And to jab like this, one, two! There's sweet delicacy in the art of lance work.'

'Very well. I'll tell my craftsmen to manufacture a lance especially for you. How long would you like it?'

Impulsively, Mr Rolfe cried, 'The longest ever!'

Luísa nodded. 'No problem.'

And it wasn't either.

The Xylophone

The full moon rose over the dense canopy of trees and, even though I fully understood the necessity of the coming ceremony, I listened with an anguished heart to the pounding of the drums.

The ghost of the Finnish mercenary who lived in the fungus spread on my bones was growing stronger, constantly wrestling with my own mind for control of my movements, trying to take over my body. Often I found myself speaking with his grim voice.

For instance, he might force me to talk thus:

'Did I ever tell you about the time I saw a sea monster near the Åland Islands? It was swimming only a few kilometres offshore. It looked like a small island itself, but I wasn't deceived. Many predators on this world of ours have learned the arts of camouflage to enable them to sneak unheard and unseen to within striking distance of their victims! So it was with this beast. I licked my lips and selected a saw from a shed of tools. Then into the waves I dived, swimming toward it. Foolish monster! It would never trouble the foam of my country again!'

'Stop it! Shut up!' I groaned in my own voice.

But the ghost of Jukka Halme was persistent. 'I dived beneath it; with my saw I cut a neat circle out of its centre. It screamed and thrashed! But there was nothing it could do, for I had removed its horizontal face from the remainder of its bulk. Onto this face I climbed, while the rest sank to a watery doom. Then I tormented the thing for weeks, sailing it along the coast, slaking my thirst for horror on its helpless but sentient visage. The responses my blade's teeth were able to elicit from the being! You would scarcely credit such spectra of agony —'

'You are the true monster, not it,' I roared.

Neary was standing beside me. He rested his prehensile steel trunk on my shoulder and said, 'Come with me, Mr Griffiths. Everything is ready for the ritual. Don't be frightened ...'

He led me considerately toward the clearing.

Fabalo stood there with his sleeves rolled up. Normally he didn't wear a shirt; so the enormous importance of the occasion wasn't in doubt. The other citizens of Humanzeeville stood in a wide circle. It was a situation similar to the zombification ceremony that I had already endured, but the atmosphere was even more intense. As if aware of the momentous events about to unfold, even Hywel stirred.

'Mwwwuagghuagh!' he groaned

Fabalo regarded me and said:

'You are in the process of being fully possessed by an evil spirit, Mr Griffiths, and there's only one way of preventing Jukka Halme taking you over completely. Cleansing fire must consume the bones that form your skeleton. It would kill you forever if we did that, of course; but a method exists for transferring your soul, mind and personality into the midget you keep inside you. Do you agree to it?'

I nodded mutely. My voice was a shrivelled nothing.

'In that case,' he continued, 'as I have secured your consent: let's get the ritual going! To work, my friends!'

This command was directed at the members of his tribe.

With howls of glee, they rushed at me.

I stepped back, stumbled, fell.

Jukka Halme was roaring in my ears, stamping around

in my soul. He finally realised that his supernatural existence was in jeopardy; but there was little he could do to protect himself. The humanzees were strong and determined. They pulled me apart.

'That's right!' cried Fabalo, 'Dismantle the simpleton!'

'Neary!' I screeched. 'Help me!'

But he refused to answer my plea. 'Sorry, no. It's for your own good, Mr Griffiths, truly it is. Be brave.'

'But it hurts! It bloody does!'

'I understand. I turned myself into a train, you know; but I didn't make a fuss. I clenched my jaw and endured.'

Fabalo said, 'This is the worst part and it's almost over.'

'Well, in that case—' I gasped.

'That's the spirit, Mr Griffiths. Choo choo!'

I felt my legs wrenched from my pelvis; then my arms were tugged off and my skull detached from my spine. Each rib was peeled back, freeing Hywel Owl for the first time in decades. He tumbled onto the ground and righted himself with a slack expression.

'Mwwwuagghuagh!' was his comment on this.

I regarded my deconstruction with a mixture of fascinated terror, wild curiosity and gullible disbelief. Have you ever regarded anything in quite that way? Every separate vertebra was knocked loose, and within minutes not one my bones was connected to any other. My clavicles and scapulae lay mixed on the ground with assorted fibulas, tibias, femurs, ulnas and a pair of unfunny brown humerus bones.

'Well done!' shouted Fabalo. 'And now for stage two!'

'What's that?' my jawbone clacked.

'Turn him into a xylophone!' ordered Fabalo.

This operation was performed with a careful eye for detail. There must have been highly skilled craftsmen among the citizens of Humanzeeville. My bones were used to construct a marimba, a fancy jungle xylophone; a beautiful if slightly morbid instrument tuned to the pentatonic scale. From a distance it seemed I was made of some expensive hardwood rather than bones, because of my shiny brown fungus.

Fabalo leaped in front of Hywel and fixed the dead gaze of the zombie with his own eyes. 'To hypnotise a walking cadaver isn't easy, but I think I can do it. I must persuade him to play.'

'Games, you mean?' I chimed.

'Not those, Mr Griffiths! Never games.'

And then I realised, in the dim sort of way that xylophones think, that a melody was going to be played on me by the midget. A voodoo melody that would complete the act of transmigration of souls. Music is magic; I had always known that. Here was proof.

Fabalo completed the hypnotism, snapped his fingers.

Hywel Owl lurched towards me.

'Give him some mallets,' ordered Fabalo.

A pair of small mallets was placed into the white hands of the zombie midget, and he grasped them with perfect undead confidence. He raised them, brought them down on my notes.

I yelped. But my bones responded with harmonious chords.

Fabalo clapped his hands.

Rattles started up to accompany the tune.

Which rapidly grew frantic.

I have never seen a zombie midget so ecstatic!

Hywel Owl almost levitated as he hopped from one foot to the other, banging fearsome arpeggios and lunatic syncopation on what had once been the scaffolding of my anatomy. Something in those played bones responded to his vibrato, to his dynamics and grace notes, began to shift, to come loose. It was the separate parts of my soul, I realised; out of my bones they rose, like the vapours that come off evaporating minims when the tune simply gets too hot for them.

Out of my bones and into the midget's head!

Suddenly Hywel's vision cleared.

I blinked and staggered.

The melody came to an abrupt end.

I was holding two mallets.

I dropped them, steadied myself on the xylophone.

Then I heard Fabalo shouting.

'Success! Welcome to a flesh body again, Mr Griffiths! But now there is only one soul left in the xylophone; the spirit of Jukka Halme. Burn the bones quickly, comrades. Burn them!'

Humanzees ran forward with flaming brands.

But Jukka wasn't defeated yet.

He began trundling on his little castors.

I don't know why xylophones are generally mounted on castors; that's simply how it is. The castors in this instance were kneecaps. Yes, I know that means there were only two castors on the instrument instead of four. Sue me if it bothers you. Off fled the xylophone into the jungle, with the humanzees in pursuit. Fabalo shouted:

'Don't let him get away! He's pure musical evil.'

But Jukka managed to elude them.

They returned crestfallen, the brands spluttering.

'Ah well!' sighed Fabalo.

I didn't care that Jukka Halme had escaped; for, although reduced in size, I was a real man again. Yes, technically I was just a walking corpse, but I've learned to be grateful for small mercies; and they don't come smaller or more hideous than Hywel Owl.

That's too self-absorbed of me. Let's consider the bigger picture. Could the xylophone survive in the jungle?

Probably not. There were far too many dangers. Chimps, for example, would ambush it and pull it to pieces; rhinos would charge it, even though there are no rhinos in Guinea; quicksands would suck it down, not giving it the chance to play a final dirge ...

But Jukka Halme was the ultimate survivor.

Maybe he did thrive in that green labyrinth. Perhaps he even reached outer civilisation and influenced it.

Somewhere in the world, maybe next door to you right now, a brown bone xylophone that is also the ghost of a wicked Finnish mercenary still lurks and throbs. I don't know for sure; I have no proof. All I'm willing to say is that the vilely possessed xylophone escaped into the jungle in 1938 and less than 20 years later a new kind of music called rock and roll appeared from nowhere. Coincidence?

Coincidence

I was a midget. I was happy. Neary and Fabalo congratulated me on my new dimensions and substance, and they both admitted that they'd found my former incarnation as a skeleton rather distasteful. I don't know if that was good politeness or bad sincerity.

The days passed in the utopian peace of Humanzeeville.

There wasn't much for me to do.

So that's what I did: very little. Neary spent his time with his elephant friends. Fabalo was mostly busy with the administration of the commune. To be honest, I began to grow bored.

One morning I went to the bone banana and prayed.

I probably had a touch of fever.

Whatever the explanation for this extraordinary behaviour, I knelt in the shadow of the giant fake fruit and clenched my little hands together. I had grown accustomed to the body of the midget; it was no less flexible than my previous avatar and the posture I struck on that occasion was one that perfectly symbolised supplication.

I said, 'I know you were raised, O mighty banana, in honour of Fabalo the Humanzee; but so impressive a structure must surely be sacred to the primal jungle deities too! Therefore I call on Zumboo, Spanko and Basha, the three biggest monkey gods, to hear my plea! I'm bored here,

295

twiddling my tiny thumbs. Send me adventure!'

The old truism is true — be careful what you pray for.

I guess that's why it's a truism ...

Later that day, I was taking a communal flute lesson on a platform in a tree when a hellish shadow blotted out the sun. We raised our eyes to the sky, and what I saw there liquefied my clotted zombie blood with terror. A gigantic man with two heads was descending into the clearing! That's bad enough, but even worse was the fact I recognised the double-headed monstrosity. I dropped my spittle-flecked flute and shrieked for help as the visitor gently touched the ground.

'Hubengo Gordbloaton!'

Yes, it really was he; but vastly bigger than he'd been at the time of his death in the mysterious land of Alirgnahs. A bizarre amalgam of wicked collector and newspaper editor, the nightmare of his arrival made me feel intense regret that I had prayed at the banana for an end to boredom. This creature was devoid of compassion.

I called a dire warning: 'Mercy has he none ...'

My calls were heeded.

Neary appeared on the scene with Fabalo. They both approached the intruder. In Neary's metal trunk was a club. Best to take no chances! I thought the giant with two heads would jump forward and crush them, but he bobbed harmlessly enough.

Fabalo prodded the figure with his spear.

Then he relaxed and laughed.

'It's not a living being! It's just a balloon! A balloon in the shape of a gross mutant!' he cried as it deflated.

His weapon had punctured the fabric of the thing.

The abomination sagged.

But something moved inside it.

Hands appeared in the rent that Fabalo had made; they widened the rip and turned it into a thin doorway. Other forms pressed against the creased skin from the inside and I wondered if the real Hubengo Gordbloaton was about to emerge, despite his death, out of the pretend one; like a kangaroo hopping from the pocket of destiny.

When I edit these memoirs, I'll replace that simile with a better one, if I remember. Be sure to alert me if I forget. Thanks in advance! But in the meantime, the tearing intensified.

'The balloon is giving birth!' marvelled Fabalo.

'Choo choo!' chortled Neary.

'Not so, but there are passengers within,' I said.

'I was joking,' sighed Fabalo.

Two figures emerged from the hole, blinking. My jaw went slack and I began dancing on my stubby legs.

'Scipio and Distanto Faraway!' I giggled.

That's who it really was!

The brothers looked no different from the way I recalled them, despite the passing of many years. Neary was overjoyed; he rushed forward and they all embraced with more slaps on backs than any previous reunion in any historical period at any latitude.

I was no less happy. 'This is more extraordinary than anything!' No-one accused me of exaggeration.

The group hug ended …

Neary introduced Scipio and Distanto to me; they accepted the news that the journalist Lloyd Griffiths was a zombie midget without a flicker of surprise or dismay. Scipio winked. 'I knew it was you as soon as I saw you,' he declared. 'I recognised you despite the fact you look completely different and have an entirely different voice. You even smell better than before. But you're still the *same*.'

I was touched by that observation. What a hero!

We welcomed the arrivals into Humanzeeville, gave them food, drink and other attention. I was burning with curiosity about their exploits since I had last seen them and begged them to tell me everything. They seemed willing to do this. Distanto went first. 'Many things have happened since we were in India together,' he began.

'Please go on,' I urged.

He smiled and said, 'I left you while holding onto a fickle balloon that I'd stitched together from drying laundry. The winds were capricious too and I was carried all the way back to Alirgnahs! That was the last place I wanted to be. I decided to make another balloon, an improved version. I looked around for suitable materials, but there wasn't enough fabric in the entire land for such a project. The yeti helped me as best they could; but they had little knowledge of airship manufacture. Only one object existed that might be used for a canopy.'

I waited for him to reveal what it was.

He did so. Like this:

'The corpse of Hubengo Gordbloaton, eviscerated and with the bones removed, so that only the empty shell of the cynical fiend remained. The yeti had a secret gas that might be used as a helium substitute; I won't go into details about how they synthesised it. A diet of beans was involved. I had already cured the skin of the cadaver over a slow fire. Now it inflated to enormous proportions. The nether regions were sealed with a hatch and the interior of the airship was fitted with a small cabin. I floated out of the secret valley and over the mountains.'

'In which direction?' I asked.

'The winds carried me westward; eventually I crossed the border into Persia. Running low on supplies, I decided to land and obtain food. There was a castle directly beneath. I landed on the battlements and secured the balloon to a crenellation. Then I went to look for the owner of the castle. I bet you can imagine my astonishment when I chanced on Scipio! He was in the company of an alchemist ...'

Scipio took over the story. 'That was Sadegh Safani, the owner of the castle. I had met him while looking for you, Mr Lloyd. He had a magic mirror that he promised would show me your location; and so it did, but the information was useless to me. For the mirror revealed that you were travelling through time and thus unavailable; and that you wouldn't return to the present until 1938. When you did return, you would appear here, in Guinea. It told me that too. So I had plenty of time to catch up with you. I teamed up with my brother properly.'

'We drifted around the world several times in my balloon,' confirmed Distanto. 'Getting into scrapes and whatnot. It was fun. Then it was time for us to come here and meet you ...'

I clapped my hands and chuckled. 'It's so good to see the pair of you again, especially Scipio! No offence, Distanto; it's just the way things are. But why haven't you aged in all that time? It has been more than 20 years since we were last together; yet you look no older than you did back then. Or is that a trick of my memory?'

Scipio said, 'During our travels we went to Russia and met a surgeon by the name of Filip Filippovich Preobrazhensky. He inserted the glands of monkeys into us; he assured us it was an effective rejuvenation remedy and so it was! Convenient, huh?'

'So you are part ape too?' I marvelled. 'In that case you have come to the right place. Humanzeeville!'

'Monkey,' corrected Scipio.

Fabalo leaned over and whispered in my ear, 'Monkeys and apes are different. Like stools and sofas.'

I said to Scipio, 'Well, now you're here, what are your plans? Are you still willing to help my people, the Welsh, overthrow the English? I won't hold you to your promise, of course.'

He smiled. 'I always keep my word, Mr Griffiths.'

'Much obliged, *Monsieur*,' I said.

His eyes twinkled like stars that guide mariners into port, where they meet ladies with twinkles of their own.

Then he added a proviso:

'But there is something rather more important to do first. An evil force has appeared in the world; its name is Hitler. The English are fated, in all probability, to oppose that force. It wouldn't be right to weaken them yet. I think we ought to destroy Hitler first and *then* proceed to fulfil the vow I made to you. Is that acceptable?'

I was in full agreement. 'Of course! Naturally!'

Fabalo squinted and said, 'How do you intend to combat this Hitler? I can see that you are both fine figures of men, but you're still only human. I fear he will be too strong for you.'

Scipio replied, 'We don't imagine we'll be able to annihilate him just by our own efforts; we simply intend to help as much as possible. But we hope our other brother, Neary, will join us in this quest. Indeed, we have a plan to increase our own potency.'

Neary rumbled up. 'Oh yes? What is it? Choo choo!'

Scipio held up a glass vial.

'The powder in this vessel was given to me by Sadegh Safani. It can fuse people together. Why don't we triplets take it and become one being? We will be akin to a demigod ...'

Neary didn't hesitate in nodding his approval.

I watched in amazement as the three brothers each swallowed a pinch of the alchemical powder. Then they held each other in another group hug and squeezed as tight as possible.

There was an enormous *bang* and a flash!

When the vapours cleared ...

A bizarre creature stood before us. It had two legs with three feet on the end of each, one enormously wide torso, three heads, five flesh arms, one metal arm, 24 fingers and maybe 90 teeth. The metallic arm hissed steam. The mighty thighs, each as thick as a tree trunk cliché, quivered with force and manliness.

This being radiated serenity and justice.

For a moment, it paused and filled its vast lungs with jungle air. Then it waved a fond and fateful farewell and sprang away in a sequence of huge leaps; the crashing of trees in the distance grew fainter, like the thunder of a passing storm. I trembled all over.

I never saw the Faraway Brothers again.

I am an old man now; who knows if they are still alive? I doubt it. But I feel sure they kept their promise. Hitler *was* defeated. As for that other promise, about the Welsh and the English ... All I'm willing to say is that the blended brothers bounded off into the jungle in 1938 and exactly 60 years later, in 1998, the Government of Wales Act was passed; the Welsh Assembly was set up in Cardiff and given freedom to make its own laws. I went there once and loitered outside the debating chamber. Xylophone music came from inside. Enigmatic.

Apedog At Last

There was a rustling in the undergrowth. A figure of noble demeanour broke through and stood in the clearing.

'I'm ready for my incident.'

I was dumbfounded. 'What incident?'

'An apedog incident. I'm an apedog, you see …'

It was Fabalo Junior!

The original Fabalo was overjoyed. 'My son!'

'Hello Dad. Sorry I'm late.'

'It's never too late, dear boy. Where have you been?'

'Far away. I went to Russia and was given the pituitary gland of a dog. I was already half ape, half human; so the outcome wasn't what the doctor who operated on me expected.'

'And you have been searching for me ever since?'

'Sort of. I dallied a lot too.'

'Welcome home, anyway! Are you hungry?'

'Famished. My nature means I have very precise dietary requirements. You wouldn't have a bone banana spare, would you? Afterwards, can we play a game of fetch? Do you mind?'

'No problem. But what incident were you referring to?'

'Aren't I supposed to have one?'

'Not necessarily. No.'

'Fair enough. It was just an assumption. On the way here, I did spend some time in Germany. I learned that the Nazis were experimenting with a toxic gas that would make their enemies infertile; but they hadn't got it quite right yet. Had it been used, it would have rendered the entire human race incapable of breeding. Then there was some kind of accident and the gas escaped and spread everywhere.'

'What! Does this mean the end of the human race?'

'I suppose so. The gas makes *all* primates infertile; so it's the end for all chimps, gorillas and baboons too.'

'And the end for humanzees!' wailed Fabalo.

His son sighed. 'I don't know what can be done about it. Luckily, I'm an apedog, so not affected by the gas. And I have been sleeping around a lot since I reached puberty, impregnating women. Hey, maybe my task is to be the biological father of the coming race? Maybe everyone born after 1938, including anyone out there reading these memoirs of the journalist Lloyd Griffiths, is part apedog?'

'Indeed. There's your incident for you!'

'Oh yes, so it is. Right under my very nose! Typical.'

The Final Chapter

This is the final chapter of the book I'm writing. Don't be deceived by any that come after; they aren't official. Are you enjoying my memoirs so far? I appreciate your company, you know. Don't doubt that for a minute. You are exactly the kind of reader that an author dreams about; attractive and elegant, as well as tolerant and wise. Take a look at yourself in the mirror right now. Outstanding, don't you think?

There was *another* rustle in the abused undergrowth …

Bandits on horseback appeared!

The leader was a girl with fictional qualities that happen to be real too. Very rare it happens that way round …

Her long, wavy black hair streamed in the breeze and her eyes glittered in the moonlight, even though the moon hadn't risen yet; I didn't miss the fact that she held a musket in one hand, a primitive matchlock model. She was Luísa Ferreira, the Bandit Queen.

'I remember you. You haven't aged a day! Have you gone for monkey gland treatment also?' I gasped.

'No,' she said, 'I'm just naturally youthful.'

'Welcome to Humanzeeville!'

'Thank you. But my followers are here on business, not pleasure. Take a look at them. Recognise anyone?'

I peered intently at the rogues and rascals in their silks, leathers, brass armour and embroidered shirts. 'Yes, I do,' I said. 'For that is your cook, João Seixas, the former lawyer; and over there is Pedro Marques, a fellow with wavy hair that's the colour of the moon. Maybe his hair is the source of the moonlight that makes your eyes glitter. See how good my memory is after more than two decades?'

'I wasn't referring to them,' she said.

'Who then, Dona Luísa?'

'This person here, Mr Jason Rolfe. We have been looking for you on his behalf for a long time. He has some unfinished killing to do with you. We made a lance for him, following his specifications exactly: it happens to be the longest lance in the world.'

I blinked and regarded it.

'Yes, it's so long that it actually goes right round the world. Might that not be something of a hindrance rather than an advantage?' I wondered, but Mr Rolfe scowled and snapped:

'Leave details like that to me. You've had this coming for ages, Lloyd Griffiths! Prepare to be perforated!'

And he jabbed forwards with his weapon.

But the lance was so long that it truly did circle the planet; the point of it was directly behind his buttocks.

And when he thrust with it, he jabbed his own posterior.

He yelped and ran forward …

As he ran, he swung his arms, as runners tend to do.

So the arm that cradled the lance swung forward and the point jabbed him again. He ran another step. Ouch!

Once started, the cycle was self-propagating.

Prompted by the jabs, he accelerated his pace. The jabs, therefore, poked him harder, stimulating him to even greater speed. Off into the jungle he went, shouting with rage and pain.

He had just invented the pulsejab engine!

And so began his second circumnavigation of the globe, this time on foot. A remarkable achievement …

We watched him depart into the annals of history; or if not into those annals, then some alternative annals.

I said to Luísa Ferreira, 'Why not settle down here? The

opportunities are probably just as good as back in Portugal. And why not marry me? I can see you are every man's dream girl. I know I'm a zombie midget; but you won't find a finer journalist anywhere. And even if you do, that's not the point. I'm fully domesticated.'

'Thanks for the offer; but no thanks,' she said.

She rode away on her unicorn.

I went back to Wales.

The Book Group

The tale was done. The members of the book group mostly sat in a circle on the floor, propped up by cushions, and sipped their red wine languidly. One of the more forceful members stood and paced the room. He held a copy of this book in a white fist. His beard bristled. His spectacles caught the light of the tasteful lamp.

'I'm just not convinced at all,' he muttered.

One of the other members said, 'Certainly it's an unconventional kind of novel. It begins in a fairly sober, serious tone, then it quickly gets more absurd. The three parts have different flavours. I can't decide if they make a sum greater than each section.'

'But is it actually a novel? Or does Lloyd Griffiths truly exist? Maybe these really are his memoirs?' interrupted a man who wore a thick turban; but the man with the beard sneered.

'That's just a conceit; and a bad one at that!'

Someone else said, 'It contains too many errors for it to be factual; for example, the character called "Hubengo Gordbloaton" was originally two men in a large suit, but when Distanto turns him into a balloon, Hubengo is treated like a single entity with one communal nether region that can be used as an access hatch. If the tale were genuine, such an error could never occur. To my mind, it's lazy fiction—'

'Not so! Not so!' objected a man with a Czech accent. 'If

this book is a work of imagination, an editor would have ensured such discrepancies were removed. The discrepancies remain. As far as I'm concerned, that is evidence that the story is authentic.'

'Nonsense! The Faraway Brothers never existed, I'm sure of that. Do any photographs exist of the triple-headed creature they became? Apart from this account, is there a *single* reliable eyewitness report of such an anomaly roaming the world; and we're expected to believe it helped out in the war effort! It's a paltry joke!'

'Yes, the whole thing is so farfetched I'm amazed anyone here could take it seriously for an instant ...'

'Why did we choose this title for our book group?'

'Good question! I loathed it.'

'Gentlemen, gentlemen!' pleaded a man who resembled a sailor, his earring flashing in the glow of the soft lamps. 'We selected it at random from a box of books we found dumped outside a charity shop. Fate made the choice; don't berate yourselves.'

'I hope the next book on our list is something better,' snapped a man who seemed to be a priest; perspiration stood out on his forehead. He had contracted malaria and never entirely got over it. 'Does anybody have the list? I haven't seen it yet myself.'

'I have a copy here,' came an obliging reply.

'Well, what is it?'

'Jane Austen, I'm afraid ...'

'Oh no! That really is the final straw. Surely there are better ways of creating a social life than this?'

'You're not planning on leaving the group?'

'Yes, frankly I am. If an utterly ridiculous fake memoir by some failed journalist named Lloyd Griffiths is followed by a boring domestic idiocy of that mannered hag, then really —'

'You know something? I am inclined to take seriously the notion that the book we have just read, *Captains Stupendous*, is true. The first part is a reasonably orthodox adventure story; midway through the second part, the tone changes somewhat; the third part is eccentric in the extreme. But consider *when* the change begins.'

'Soon after the narrator is turned into a skeleton?'

'Exactly! And wouldn't a skeleton be a much less sober narrator than a flesh and blood man? It makes sense.'

'No, it doesn't. It's still a mound of festering —'

'I'm not saying you must like it, but it *is* more consistent than you give it credit for. It's not just random —'

'Wait! What's that noise?'

'What noise? Oh, that weird hissing ...'

'And look at that shadow on the wall! What on earth —'

'I don't believe it. A Mongorgon!'

'Impossible. That's just a creature inside this book. We are *outside* the story, where such things don't exist ...'

But the Mongorgon chuckled as its snakes reared up higher. Its teeth chattered. 'You're mistaken about that.'

The man with the spectacles demanded, 'Mistaken? You don't belong out here. How dare you suggest we are wrong about anything? Get back inside the text before I telephone the pest control department of the local city council and get you removed by —'

The Mongorgon spoke over him:

'You aren't outside the book, but inside. You have always been inside, for you are the minor background characters that appeared in the sundry chapters of the three sections. Take a close look at yourselves. Don't you recognise your own identities? You are Stepan Rehorek, the Czech sailor; and you are Captain Marlow Nullity; and you are Dumitru Banuş; and so on. The book hasn't ended, you fools!'

'Liar! The final chapter has already been and gone. It was called "The Final Chapter", and the last sentence in it was "I went back to Wales". See for yourself if you don't believe me.'

The Mongorgon sneered. 'You are Mihaila Adrian, also a character in the book; and you are Victoriano Huerta; and you are Dom Daniel; and you, with the large turban, are Sadegh Safani; and you are Nikola Tesla; and over there is the factory owner from Chengdu, who doesn't seem to have a name at all; and Mr Higgs, the dissolute railway manager based in Srinagar, is pouring himself more wine ...'

'And who the hell am I?' demanded the fevered priest.

'Father Phigga,' said the Mongorgon.

The priest trembled when he heard this; whether from his disease or from existential shock is debatable.

'Even if what you say is true, it doesn't excuse you from breaking and entering this property. So get out!'

The Mongorgon's serpents shook their heads.

'Not before I have slaughtered you,' the beast said nonchalantly. And before anyone could react to this threat, it jumped forward; the snakes on its back darted out right and left, delivering fatal bites. 'I like to see loose ends tied up,' the Mongorgon added.

Wine glasses tinkled; their contents splashed.

Men collapsed to the floor.

Twitched and expired.

There was silence. The Mongorgon turned very slowly to look out of the page; to look directly at you, the reader, and lisped, 'Do *you* have any issues with this book? Yes you. No good just sitting there with that smug expression, as if I can't see you.'

There was a pause; a pause you created.

It licked its lips. 'If you *do* have any issues, I'll be more than willing to discuss them with you.' Then it smiled horribly. 'Live inside these pages, I do. I can come out any time I please. So remember ... Don't glance over your shoulder at night when you hear a strange noise. Look between *these* covers instead. But I don't want to alarm you unnecessarily. I know you'll do the right thing and never criticise —'

It would have said a lot more things that would have been deeply unpleasant, and probably you would have been troubled by them. But a metallic elephant's trunk pushed itself in through the open window and began spouting steam.

The steam filled the room, obscuring the Mongorgon and muffling its words to the point of inaudibility.

You can't see a thing now. Neither can I.

Which leaves us no choice.

It's all over. Goodbye.

And take care.

F I N I S

ABOUT THE AUTHOR

RHYS HUGHES was born in 1966 and began writing from an early age. His first short story was published in 1991 and his first book followed four years later. Since then he has published more than thirty books and his work has been translated into ten languages. His main ambition is to complete a grand sequence of exactly one thousand linked short stories, a project he has been working on for more than two decades. He is now three-quarters of the way through this opus.

CAPTAINS STUPENDOUS is his attempt to write in a genre called 'Steamprog' that he has invented just now.

MORE TELOS TITLES

HORROR/FANTASY

GRAHAM MASTERTON
THE DJINN
RULES OF DUEL(WITH WILLIAM S BURROUGHS)

SIMON CLARK
HUMPTY'S BONES
THE FALL

SAM STONE
ZOMBIES IN NEW YORK AND OTHER BLOODY JOTTINGS
A horror collection of 13 stories and 6 mythological poems

KAT LIGHTFOOT MYSTERIES (Steampunk/Horror Series)
ZOMBIES AT TIFFANY'S
KAT ON A HOT TIN AIRSHIP (
WHAT'S DEAD PUSSY KAT?

THE DARKNESS WITHIN
A thrilling sci-fi/horror novel

JINX CHRONICLES
Sci-Fi Post-Apocalyptic Trilogy
JINX TOWN - Book 1
JINX MAGIC - Book 2 (Coming in 2015)
JINX BOUND - Book 3 (Coming in 2016)

DAVID J HOWE
TALESPINNING (Horror Collection encompassing stories,
screenplays and gruesome extracts)

URBAN GOTHIC: LACUNA AND OTHER TRIPS edited by
DAVID J HOWE
Tales of horror from and inspired by the *Urban Gothic*
television series. Contributors: Graham Masterton,
Christopher Fowler, Simon Clark, Steve Lockley & Paul Lewis,
Paul Finch and Debbie Bennett.

RAVEN DANE
ABSINTHE & ARSENIC
16 tales of Victorian horror, Steampunk adventures and dark,
deadly, obsession

PRINCE OF RAVENS (Coming in 2015)
Exciting alternative history with a supernatural twist

KIT COX
DOCTOR TRIPPS SERIES:
A Neo-Victorian world where steam is pitted against diesel,
but which side will win?
KAIJU COCKTAIL
MOON MONSTER (coming in 2015)

SPECTRE by STEPHEN LAWS
Something is stalking the Chapter, picking them off one by
one, something connected with their past, and with the girl
they used to know.

KING OF ALL THE DEAD by STEVE LOCKLEY & PAUL
LEWIS
The king of all the dead will have what is his.

THE HUMAN ABSTRACT by GEORGE MANN
A future tale of private detectives, AIs, Nanobots, love and
death.

BREATHE by CHRISTOPHER FOWLER
The Office meets *Night of the Living Dead.*

HOUDINI'S LAST ILLUSION by STEVE SAVILE
Can the master illusionist Harry Houdini outwit the dead
shades of his past?

ALICE'S JOURNEY BEYOND THE MOON by R J CARTER
A sequel to the classic Lewis Carroll tales.

APPROACHING OMEGA by ERIC BROWN
A colonisation mission to Earth runs into problems.

VALLEY OF LIGHTS by STEPHEN GALLAGHER
A cop comes up against a body-hopping murderer.

PRETTY YOUNG THINGS by DOMINIC MCDONAGH
A nest of lesbian rave bunny vampires is at large in
Manchester.

A MANHATTAN GHOST STORY by T M WRIGHT
Do you see ghosts? A classic tale of love and the supernatural.

SHROUDED BY DARKNESS: TALES OF TERROR edited by
ALISON L R DAVIES
An anthology of tales guaranteed to bring a chill to the spine.
This collection has been published to raise money for DebRA,
Featuring stories by: Debbie Bennett, Poppy Z Brite, Simon
Clark, Storm Constantine, Peter Crowther, Alison L R Davies,
Paul Finch, Christopher Fowler, Neil Gaiman, Gary
Greenwood, David J Howe, Dawn Knox, Tim Lebbon, Charles
de Lint, Steven Lockley & Paul Lewis, James Lovegrove,
Graham Masterton, Richard Christian Matheson, Justina
Robson, Mark Samuels, Darren Shan and Michael Marshall
Smith. With a frontispiece by Clive Barker and a foreword by
Stephen Jones. Deluxe hardback cover by Simon Marsden.

BLACK TIDE by DEL STONE JR
A college professor and his students find themselves trapped
by an encroaching horde of zombies following a waste
spillage.

FORCE MAJEURE by DANIEL O'MAHONY
An incredible fantasy novel..

CRIME

THE LONG, BIG KISS GOODBYE by SCOTT MONTGOMERY
Hardboiled thrills as Jack Sharp gets involved with a dame
called Kitty.

ANDREW HOOK
A series of exciting crime novels putting a neo-noir twist on
the genre conventions of bums and dames
THE IMMORTALISTS
CHURCH OF WIRE

MIKE RIPLEY
Titles in Mike Ripley's acclaimed 'Angel' series of comic crime
novels.
JUST ANOTHER ANGEL
ANGEL TOUCH
ANGEL HUNT
ANGEL ON THE INSIDE
ANGEL CONFIDENTIAL
ANGEL CITY
ANGELS IN ARMS
FAMILY OF ANGELS
BOOTLEGGED ANGEL
THAT ANGEL LOOK
ANGEL UNDERGROUND
LIGHTS, CAMERA, ANGEL

Made in the USA
Charleston, SC
25 August 2014